Lizzie Borden, Girl Detective

Lizzie Borden, Girl Detective

Richard Behrens

NINE MUSES BOOKS

Some of these stories first appeared in *The Hatchet: A Journal of Lizzie Borden &*
Victorian Studies and *The Literary Hatchet.*

Stories from *The Hatchet* and *The Literary Hatchet* are reprinted by permission of
PearTree Press, © 2006, 2007, 2008 by Richard Behrens.

Nine Muses Books

New England, USA

LizzieBordenGirlDetective.com
NineMusesBooks.com

© 2020 Nine Muses Books
© 2020 Anna Brindisi Behrens

ISBN-13: 978-0-9912784-5-9

Cover design: Stefani Koorey © 2010, All Rights Reserved.
                 Lizzie Cameo by Marc Reed. © 2010, All Rights Reserved.
Illustrations: Stefani Koorey, Marc Reed, istockphoto.com

To Anna
For showing me the Miracles of Air

Also by Richard Behrens

Lizzie Borden, Girl Detective (2010, Pear Tree Press)

The Minuscule Monk: A Lizzie Borden, Girl Detective Mystery
(2015, Nine Muses Books)

The Audible Amnesiac and Other Lizzie Borden, Girl Detective Mysteries
(2018, Nine Muses Books)

Garden Bay Stories (2018, Nine Muses Books)

Of Moons and Monoliths (2018, Nine Muses Books)

Lizzie Borden, Girl Detective (2020, Nine Muses Books)

$\mathcal{A}$CKNOWLEDGMENTS

Great thanks is due to Shelley Dziedzic, my very own Victorian Historian and Lifestyle Consultant who has helped to dress up the imaginary Fall River of these tales and lend to its inhabitants a loving attention to detail that can only come from such a wonderful time traveler as Ms. Dziedzic.

And many thanks to Stefani Koorey, my editor and publisher, for believing in the character and helping me find a readership; and to Kat Koorey for all the hard work in editing, researching, fact checking, and otherwise supporting this project, as well as being the first person to ever say to me, "I read your story seven times!"

Gracious debt is also due to Jill Dalton, Jack McCullough, Len Rebello, Mark Walter, Marc Reed, all the Mutton Eaters, Pear Essential Players, members of the Lizzie Borden Society, the Fall River Historical Society, Ted and Lorraine Gregoire for being the first fans, to all who helped film the Lizzie Minis for Garden Bay Films, Donald Woods and Lee-ann Wilber of the Lizzie Borden Bed & Breakfast for giving me the opportunity to write portions of this novel at 92 Second Street, and the many Bordenites around the globe to whom I offer these tales hoping to make them laugh and wonder if this fabulist dream could really have happened.

Although these stories are imaginative works of fiction, the most seemingly implausible element, the Fuzzle Talk of the Sporting Boys in "The Melancholy Scion" does oddly enough have an historical basis. Many of the whimsical phrases and portmanteau words come from the diligent research of my most excellent skenchback Jeffrey Kacirk whose fascinating book *The Word Museum* (Barnes and Noble Books, 2004) is a great source of what Mr. Kacirk calls "abandoned expressions and philological relics."

A special acknowledgement must also go to Lizzie, her family, and all the people who were caught up in the tragic events of 1892. I hope I have served them respectfully.

Richard Behrens
2010

FOREWORD

My great friend, Richard Behrens, the author of this book, passed away in 2017. Lucky for us, his creative genius has not disappeared with his earthly form. His works live on for all of us to enjoy.

As the original publisher of the *Lizzie Borden, Girl Detective* stories, first in my journal devoted to Lizzie Borden studies (*The Hatchet: A Journal of Lizzie Borden and Victorian Studies*) and, later, in *The Literary Hatchet*, a journal of provocative fiction, poetry, and art, I always considered my work with Richard to be a labor of love. His words needed to be published because they are so great!

Now that he is gone from us, it is only fitting that this book go to his new publishing home, Nine Muses Books, owned by his widow, Anna Brindisi Behrens. I send this book to Anna as a token of my gratitude and friendship.

Stefani Koorey
Westport, MA
March 2020

CONTENTS

To our dearest and most dedicated readers,

Since we began presenting the cases of Lizzie Borden, the Girl Detective of Fall River, documenting the daring adventures of this most fascinating young woman of our Commonwealth, we have often been asked to reveal the details of her very first case. Lizzie was extremely reluctant to talk about the affair, since it involved a detective yet green, one who had not yet harkened fully to the call of her profession, and who, thus, perforce, had experimented with a less than elegant methodology. In fact, Lizzie's first case was one in which she nearly led herself into oblivion through a lack of observational rigor. But after much negotiation with Miss Borden, we have convinced her that our readership should know of the Adventure of the Forlorn Maggie. For this is a tale in which a daring fourteen-year-old girl unexpectedly found within herself much courage, sharp reasoning powers, and a moral fiber of which she previously was unaware.

For your consideration and most delightful amusement,
The Editors

THE
FORLORN
MAGGIE

1874. FALL RIVER, MASSACHUSETTS.

HIDDEN WATERS

The water-falls of the Quequechan once sparkled over their time-worn rocks, lording over a landscape in which the hornpout darted away their life-span in the dark recesses of the watery depths. That river is no longer visible to us: it flows beneath the churning wheels of the mighty mills. It is a cruel exercise to walk the perimeter walls of the dusky buildings, under the shadow of the smoke stacks and the grimy rows of windows, and imagine the Mother river beneath our feet. All we shall see is the modern factory bent across nature like a triumphant predatory beast over its fresh kill. The river, its soulful waters from so long ago, its cascades and the meditation of its flow, is now a buried corpse; lost, seemingly irretrievably, beneath the burnt red brick and the underground engines thus fueling the infernal machines. Indeed, men and women have been bound to these machines, ever to toil like submissive servants of some vast cavernous spirit.

This loss of nature was the price paid for the rise of commerce and a leisure class that need not waste their days away at the spindles and looms of industry, for on this bright and slightly-chilled September morning, not a few short blocks away from the mills, the downstreet area is awash with activity. Those with time enough on their hands (and more than a few dollars in their pockets) stroll the sidewalks, gazing through the shop windows, pausing briefly to discuss with each other the time of day and the conditions of the weather, not to mention the latest fashion of dress and much gossip about their neighbors.

Fall River, the City, unlike the stream that had surrendered its appellation even before being buried in the darkness of the mighty mills, is very much alive—Fall River is now the urban phoenix, vibrantly visible to all who walk freely under the sun.

TAKING HER FANCY

Amidst a sidewalk sea of bowler hats and frilled bonnets, frock coats and flounced bustles, two women walked from opposite directions along the main street. One came from the north, City Hall rising behind her, where the center of Fall River banking and government sustained itself with its imposing granite tower. This woman was quite young, full in the face, with light hair and a cheery little smile that curled at the edges as she soaked in the life about her. She walked with an upright and dignified posture, a lofty attitude of certainty.

The other woman was considerably older and came from the south-west. She was gaunt and sallow, covered in a threadbare print dress and a worn bonnet; her gait was clearly more rushed and less-directed, as if she had been seized with some nervous energy that had driven her compulsively into the streets. At each step, she seemed in danger of pitching forward upon the ground. No one around her seemed to notice her condition.

The two women, complete strangers, came together in the doorway of Hodges & Son, a fabric store near the corner of South Main and Columbia. The young girl was paying more attention to her surroundings, and so had time to avoid the imminent collision. The elderly woman stared wildly at her more youthful counterpart as if she were looking down upon a disobedient domestic. Then a stark change swept over her face, her features rapidly composing themselves, and said in a whispery Irish voice, "I am sorry for this, Miss. Please take your way and I shall follow." She raised a shaking hand, bidding the young girl to pass.

The woman's sunken eyes looked filled with sorrow and danger, the young girl thought, but she refrained from showing any overt concern. With a deft lifting of her skirt, she pranced into the store and went about her business.

As she picked through bolts of fabric looking for some choice material to bring to her dressmaker, the young girl kept an eye on the strange figure that had followed her in. The elderly woman was fidgeting about, her fingers quivering over fabric sample, but her eyes remained unfocused. The store owner, old man Hodges himself, a beefy man with large hands and an even larger set of muttonchops that expanded his head liberally in both directions, carefully walked near her, unobtrusively keeping a close eye upon his merchandise.

Feeling that the store was now safe in the competent hands of Mr. Hodges, Lizzie Andrew Borden, the young girl in question, gave up her surveillance of this most suspicious woman and went about examining a few choice samples. She poked about on a table where some bolts and sewing materials were laid out, then sidled alongside the notions counter to admire some cards of mother

of pearl buttons, when her eye rested upon a resplendent silver plate pin tray. A few common pins rested within, which must have been a convenience for the shop girl who was wearily winding up fabric on bolts at the other end of the counter. Lizzie's appraising eye noted the little repousee pansies, the unfurling ribbon bowknot, and the quality quadruple plating. Gorham—Yes, surely it was Gorham silver plate—and quality too!

Lizzie sniffed the air appreciatively and nonchalantly turned her back to the counter while holding up a card of buttons to the light for inspection. With one deft movement of her right hand, the silver tray found a snug home inside the back waistband of her skirt. The oval contours of the tray rested undetected over the accommodating shelf of her bustle.

As if the fates were conspiring to stroke Lizzie's guilty conscience, she spotted the elderly woman not two tables away at the cutting implements. Mr. Hodges, distracted by a flurry of activity at the front counter, had ceased to monitor her; and lo, she was also passing something small into the folds of her dress. There was just a brief flash of something metallic; the woman stood motionless with her arms by her sides.

"Oh, my," Lizzie thought. "If it is true that this woman has taken her Fancy as I have, I dare not raise an alarm for fear that they shall suspect me as well." She mused briefly upon her predicament. "This fabric sale will last all day," she concluded. "I shall simply come back when she is gone from the premises."

Then, as Lizzie strolled towards the front, preparing to escape into the streets, the elderly woman darted forward, running noisily to the front register behind which a young Mr. Hodges, a thin and weedy version of his father in appearance, the same beady-eyed face, but lacking the hairly establishments, stared straight at her. The woman reached over and, without any attempt to conceal her action, grabbed the cash box, removing it from the counter and headed rapidly for the door. At that moment, both Hodges the Father and Hodges the Son raised a general alarm by shouting: "Stop that woman! Oh, do not let her get away!"

The assembled customers, mostly women holding samples of cloth and bolts of fabric, looked up with startled cries. There was a scuffling and the elderly woman dropped the cashbox to the wood-slatted floor as if she were coming out of a trance. She raised a hand to her forehead and swooned downwards, landing with a pronounced crackling of her stiff bustle, directly at the feet of an increasingly nervous Lizzie Borden.

Lizzie raised her hands instinctively above her head, as if proclaiming her innocent to all about, thus proving somehow she had nothing to do with the attempted robbery. Many a time in the past when she had taken her Fancy, whether it was in fabric stores, apothecaries, or flower boutiques, being at the center of everyone's attention while the Fancy was concealed in her clothing had caused great anxiety; and often at night her dreams were turned to dread nightmares in which a thousand eyeballs stared unblinking at her while silverware, pearl mirrors, and hat pins tumbled to the ground from beneath her skirts.

As Hodges & Son ran for the street to call a policeman, Lizzie glanced around, trying to perceive where, in the confused midst of the disturbance and the large number of customers surrounding her, she could dump her silver tray. Divesting herself of any incriminating evidence was, at that moment, her chief concern. She abandoned the thought of getting rid of the item only when a young police officer entered the store and ran to the collapsed woman.

"What is this?" the officer asked, bemusedly. Hodges & Son, with arms flailing, hastily gave their perspective on the preceding events. The elder Mr. Hodges pointed at Lizzie, which caused her heart to skip a beat. "This girl can verify what I have said. She was not three feet from the crime when it happened!"

"Here, this is young Miss Borden," the young officer grinned. "Hello, Lizzie. How's the family?"

"Fine," she replied, hoping to be as monosyllabic as possible. She recognized Peter Gaskell Bence, not her favorite policeman, but a happy enough fellow.

"What did you see?" he asked. "Are Hodges & Son telling it straight?"

"Why," Lizzie said, tossing explanations about in her head, "I did see this woman up close, but from my vantage she seemed very nervous, almost starved. I would say if you examine her, you'll find evidence that she is positively malnourished. Perhaps she hasn't eaten in quite some time, two days perhaps, or an interval that you and I would find intolerable. I would say from her vestments that she is a cloth doffer at one of the mills, or even possibly a domestic on the Hill, perhaps removed from her job and failing to find a situation that would sustain her life in the meanwhile. I would say she came in here hoping to find a soul who would take pity on her, and, sensing only the indifference of commerce, she gambled away her liberties by plunging for the till, hoping beyond hope that she could steal the money and save her life."

There was a thundering silence. All eyes in the store glared at Lizzie Borden. Mr. Hodges broke the calm: "You seem too clever for your own good, young Miss. While you are seeing suffering and starvation, I'm just seeing hard earned dollars being filched from under my nose! 'Tis not my business that she was sacked from the mill!"

"Well," Officer Bence said with a broad smile, "let's arouse this lady and get her side of the story. Then we'll take her down to the station house and see if justice can be distributed one way or the other."

They made an attempt to awaken the woman. As they pinched her cheeks and slapped her chin and pulled at her shoulders, Lizzie saw a few twitches and eye movements suggesting that the woman was feigning unconsciousness. But she kept quiet about it, being mindful of the silver tray in her dress, hoping that it would not slide out over her bustle pouf and reveal her perfidy.

A few customers from the store stepped forward and offered to help haul the woman to her feet and carry her down the street to the police station. However, without warning, the fainted woman's eyes fluttered and, for the first time since her outrage, they opened.

"Oh, have pity," she said in a whispery voice. "Have pity on poor Fiona Conway. Ah! Have pity on the hungry!"

"There, there," Officer Bence said. "Justice shall pitch her scales and we shall balance the weight of the matter."

For a moment, the woman gazed perplexedly at the policeman's smiling face as if trying to untangle his curious metaphors, then she quickly fell back into a deep slumber. It took two men to support her weight and they moved her towards the door and into the street beyond.

"And you, Miss Lizzie," Officer Bence said, crooking a finger at her. "I'd like you to come along to make a statement and identify this woman before the Marshal."

Lizzie's heart sank again. With a helpless shrug, she followed the men out of the store and up the street—towards the last place on earth where she wanted to be with a pinched Fancy in her bustle.

MUTINY ON THE DURFEE

The Central Police Station on Purchase Street was not a building that Lizzie Borden had ever wished to visit. In her childhood imagination it had always been a place inhabited by all the monsters of society that she wanted banished from her world. Its tall tower rose over the surrounding buildings like an ominous fortress of torture and the stench from the nearby horse yard was quite wretched. As her official escort led her to the tall iron doors, she froze, pressing her feet tighter against the ground. The silver tray in her bustle suddenly felt heavier.

"Forgive me," she muttered to Officer Bence. "I have not a sense of where I am going or for what reason."

"Don't fear," he said gently. "We're only going to book Miss Fiona Conway, if that is indeed her name. We need you here as a material witness."

Summoning her strength, she advanced and entered the main hallway. All about her were policemen in their shell helmets, many of them conversing with each other, paying no attention to her presence. However, in her mind's eye, they were all staring suspiciously at her weighted bustle, looking for traces of her Fancy. Lizzie nervously paced down towards the squad room between a gauntlet of officers, and was relieved when Officer Bence offered her a seat on a bench near the Marshal's office, leaving her quite alone. Here she was able to retreat into the role of spectator, where she could simply observe people and not be compelled to take part in any action. She felt safer that way: being unseen but all-seeing.

The squad room was crowded, buzzing with activity. A sporting boy and his fancy girl were seated behind an untidy desk, being shouted at by an irate detective. A few Portuguese laborers were trying to make sense to a stupefied policeman who did not speak their language. Several other citizens of Fall River were present, apparently there to make complaints, or having been summoned to address matters of urgent police business. And a tall, long-haired man in a black frock coat sat near the filing cabinets in a gloomy solitary meditation.

Lizzie was about to turn her attention toward the open doorway of the Marshal's office, through which she had heard some muttering, but quickly snapped her gaze back at the tall man in the black frock. At that very instant, he stared back at her, and both of them bolted upright in their seats.

"Father!" Lizzie shouted, then slouched downward, pressing her lips together as if trying to prevent her blurted word from advancing too far towards anyone's ears.

Andrew Jackson Borden rose to his full height and advanced stealthily across the room. His daughter bravely stepped up to meet him, her chin rising to just below his bristly beard.

"Yes, Daughter," he said grimly. "I must confess that I have police business this afternoon. But I am shocked to see you in these premises. I don't suppose you are here because you have been taking a bit of … uh … your Fancy."

She waggled her slack face. "No, Father. You need not fear; there shall be no visits to the shops today. I have cleaned my hands of that habit."

"I am glad to hear of it."

As he spoke, Andrew was reaching towards his face as if to scratch it. He did this several times before Lizzie realized that he merely did not know what to do with his hands. "So," he said, "what exactly is your business here today?"

Lizzie fluttered her lids. "I can honestly say, Father, it is of the most perplexing nature. I am an innocent observer this time, purely a victim of circumstance. For upon my visit to Hodges & Son, a Maggie lost her reason and tried to pilfer the till. She was seized by the younger Hodges and brought here to this very station where no doubt she is being interrogated in the back rooms as we speak. They claim that I saw the offense, that it happened right before me, and are asking me to make a statement as to her guilt."

"And what would be the girl's reason to do such a rash act?" he asked. "Does she not get paid well by her employer?"

"I believe she has lost her situation. Hunger, despondency, and despair have driven her to such a gesture."

Andrew grunted. "Well, if there is justice in this town, she shall hang!" He turned from her to retreat to the bench; Lizzie followed behind, anxiously.

"Father!" Lizzie shouted, pulling at his arm. "What a brutal thing to say."

"She robbed a concern," he said casually. "There are laws for that. I pay enough tax money to put our peace-keepers into office. I'd like to see them stick to the letter of the law for once."

"But hanging! She is certainly not innocent, but I can honestly say the circumstances were quite understandable."

"How much was in the till?" Andrew asked.

"I do not know, but Hodges was doing a brisk business on a bolt sale."

Andrew snorted. "Enough for a scaffold, sounds like it."

"Father, I will not continue this debate with you. You know nothing about this crime and can't pass judgment on broad facts. I shall see that her offense be put into perspective."

"To each his own," Andrew said resolvedly. "The whole affair means nothing to me. I am here on matters that shall deserve the gallows."

"What may that be?" Lizzie asked, holding her breath.

"I am hesitant to tell you since I do not want to alarm you, Mrs. Borden, or your sister Emma." He glanced both ways to ascertain their privacy, then lowered her onto the bench, seating himself next to her. "I do not think that you know about the brigantine, the *B.M.C. Durfee*, that sailed from New Bedford upon two Aprils past?"

"I know a little, Father. The ship fell into evil times. The crew mutinied and murdered the Captain before tossing him overboard. They were captured off Barbados and brought back to New England in irons."

"Yes, they were evil men who did evil things. They did it all for money, imagine that. Captain Coffin is now resting in his watery bed, and his wife is despondent because of the nefarious deeds of Joseph Shove, Samuel Howe, and Oliver Fleet."

Lizzie screwed up her eyes. "But Father, were not Shove and Howe the two men who were hanged in New Bedford this past summer for their role in the affair?"

"Why, yes, Daughter."

"But you mentioned a third man."

"Fleet, yes. He was the third man, and, of the three, he was the most seething with devilish fire. He escaped from custody, killing two officers, and was last heard from in a taunting letter to the New Bedford police department, saying that they would sooner catch the Devil himself than catch Fleet-Footed Fleet. This angered the Governor to no end, and the entire Commonwealth of Massachusetts has been keeping a harsh vigilance for him."

Lizzie lowered her face, bewildered. "I have heard of the sorrows of Sarah Coffin. I did not know that her solitude was the result of her husband being murdered."

Andrew's already bitter stare grew darker. "It is said that in the mutiny, Fleet picked Captain Coffin up over his head and snapped his limbs like twigs, and when the Captain's cries were so pitiful that the Great Adversary himself would have wept to hear it, Oliver Fleet fiendishly laughed through his teeth."

"So they believe that he will return to Fall River?"

"Daughter, now we get to the heart of my business here. Fleet-Footed Fleet yearns for nothing but to be reunited with a fallen woman of this city who has taken up with him. Not only has he returned to Fall River, but he is in this very building!"

Lizzie felt a deep shudder and drew her arms tight about her shoulders. "Dear Lord," was all she could say. "Are we safe?"

"As safe as the City Marshal and his gallant lawmen can make us," he said assuredly. "For the man is in shackles in the lock-up. I have not seen him yet, but I shall within the hour."

"You?" Lizzie asked. "Why you?"

Once more he glanced about to certify that no one could hear. "Here is where I am most ashamed, Daughter. I must confess that four years ago I invested heavily in the *B.M.C. Durfee*. I own a hearty portion of its stock. Its success would have meant a valuable expansion of my capital. The dividends from its sugar and molasses run would have been quite handsome for me. The mutiny was a savage blow, from which, financially, a part of me has not since recovered."

"So are you here to give Mr. Fleet a part of your mind?"

"My Daughter," Andrew said sternly. "The officials merely want me to look him in the face and say Yea or Nay that it is positively him. I may be one of the few men in Fall River capable of fingering him. While others have seen his likeness, he has changed it through alteration of his whiskers. But I have heard his voice, a deep tone, which can rattle your bones when you hear it. The police believe my testimony will be binding, and they will be assured that they have their man. It is a heavy burden."

"Yes, Father. A heavy burden, indeed, which I share. For I am also here to identify a prisoner, although I am determined to prevent Fiona Conway from hanging as long as I can testify to her sorrow! Just because she is a Maggie, that doesn't mean..."

Andrew stiffened and his eyes turned to marble. "Did you say, Fiona... Conway?"

"Why, yes. We heard her name from her very lips as she swooned on the floor of the fabric store."

His face brightened. "Why, she is our woman!" He threw back his head and cackled.

"Father, is your reason unhinged? What do you find amusing?"

He got to his feet and fingered his lapels. "Why, I have found a way to lighten my burden. Fiona Conway is not a Maggie, as you put it, but Fleet-Footed Fleet's lady of the night, his fallen woman of Fall River!"

A shaft of light descended inside Lizzie's mind. "I have been such a fool," she announced. "Father, you have handed me the missing piece of the puzzle! Fiona Conway did not attempt to lift the till because she wanted to steal the money. It was an act of desperation, yes, but not one of passion. She knew that her long-lost lover, one whom she despaired of ever seeing again, was within police custody, and she deliberately broke the law in order to join him in the cells!"

"You are sure of this?" Andrew said hastily, "Perhaps it is not her but ..."

"There is only one way of finding out," Lizzie shouted, and then darted across the room to a desk where Officer Bence was taking statements from Hodges & Son.

"Violate my peaceful business, she did!" the elder Hodges was shouting. "On the day of the bolt sale, no less! Now I have a half-witted tide-waiter tending till and a bumbling Bristol man walking the floor while we waste our time here! The store will be in chaos by the time we get back!"

"Officer Bence!" Lizzie shouted in a loud and startling voice, causing Mr. Hodges to bury his rambling words inside the waggling of his side chops. "I know this is a strong cause to advance," Lizzie explained, "but the Maggie known as Fiona Conway can exonerate herself if only the truth will out."

"Are you mad?" Hodges the Son said. "You saw what she did, you were right there!"

"Yes, but I have information that you must consider." She turned and motioned for her father to advance.

Andrew crossed over nervously and stammered, "She is right, Lizzie is right. We do not believe that she intended to steal the money. We believe she intended to be caught before she left the store."

Mr. Hodges pulled at his chin. "What? Of all the preposterous monkey-dash!"

With a quivering voice, Andrew explained his story to the astonished assemblage. He paused a few times, blushing at his own public admittance that his own money had once sunk like rocks to the bottom of the ocean instead of providing him with healthy dividends. While he related his tale, Officer Bence's face grew lighter and less ponderous, while the faces of Hodges & Son grew more gloomy and despondent.

When her father had finished, Lizzie completed the picture with her interpretation of the events in the fabric store. "The Maggie's plan was to get inside the cell with her lost lover. What she plans to do, whether she plans to help him escape, or she merely wants to lay one more look upon him before she next sees him dangling from a rope, I cannot say. But it is certain that she is not what she claims to be."

The Officer was hurriedly on his feet and headed for the City Marshal's office. "He must hear this," he said bemusedly. The tall, ponderous Marshal had soon joined them, stroking his beard, while Officer Bence repeated Andrew's story.

"By Jupiter, this is fire indeed," the Marshal nodded. "The girl is a crucial part of our prosecution, we must see to this immediately. Officer Bence, please advance an invitation to all our guests here to join me in five minutes in the interrogation cell. Both Fleet-Footed Fleet and our Irish scullery maid are in for a momentous surprise."

"Aye, Marshal," Bence said, and then turned to Lizzie, Andrew, and Hodges & Son with a chuckle. "You're all coming with me to the Tower," he announced.

"Now, Daughter," Andrew said, patting the back of her hand. "We shall witness the sinking of Fleet-Footed Fleet."

"May God have Mercy on the Maggie," Lizzie intoned.

A HEART UNVEILED

They climbed the wooden stairs into the station tower where sunlight flooded the hallway, coming in over the rooftops of the smaller surrounding buildings. A short ten minutes previous, Lizzie would have been horrified beyond sensibility to walk this far into the station, no matter how secure the locks. From the street, she had always glanced up at this tower as if it were Fall River's dark castle, deeper and more haunted than the currents of the hidden river below the mills.

But now, as she entered flanked by her father and the City Marshal, accompanied by Officer Bence and Hodges & Son, she swaggered with a sense of excitement, experiencing a desire not only to be a spectator, but also a direct participant in the drama that was unfolding about her. Her mind no longer lingered on her bustled Fancy.

Entering the lock-up, Lizzie immediately was overpowered by a harsh odor. To the far right was a barred cell, inhabited by a few drunken vagrants. Their strange aromas, mixtures of various scents typically absent from Lizzie's comfortable and reasonably clean surroundings, mingled with those wafting from the horse-yard below, and filled the whole interior of the tower with an almost palpable wave of unbearable air.

To the left was a solitary lock-up inside of which an indistinct form was silhouetted against the light flooding through the back window. An officer was already on guard nearby, and he stood to attention as the Marshal gave a barked command. Lizzie's eyes were adjusting to the contrasting shadows and now she could make out, within the confines of the cell, an imprisoned man perched on a cot like a braced animal; she could discern two angry eyes and a savage mouth surrounded by thick black hair.

"Stand to attention," the officer-on-duty said harshly. "The Marshal will address you."

"You can tell the Marshal," a deep voice sounded from the darkness, "that he can kiss my bottom's beard!"

"Do you see?" Andrew asked excitedly. "How brutal! For that alone he must hang!"

"Hang?" barked the man. "And who are you that you shall judge me?"

"Andrew Jackson Borden," said Lizzie's father. As he puffed up his chest and thrust out his whiskers in a mild attempt at confidence, his voice crackled and his trousers trembled.

"Never heard of you," the man said with a dismissive sneer. "How can I be judged by a complete stranger?"

"I am not a complete stranger. I personally recruited you from the Iron Works to be first mate on the schooner. Do you not remember? I came to your apartment…"

"Nope," the man said lightly.

"I brought you round to the shipping office. I was there when you signed your lay commission."

"I am not the man! But wait, I have heard of you, Andrew Borden. You're a furniture maker. You made my cabinet. Perhaps I recognize you from the day you carried it up my back stairs like the servant you are!"

"God's wounds!" Andrew shouted, and curled his fists.

The Marshal stepped forward. "Fleet, be still. We shall corroborate with one more witness. If two people positively identify you, then we shall ignore your claims that you are Horatio Phelps of Boston."

"Then you shall be a poor policeman, for I am Horatio Phelps. My business is real estate. I have witnesses!"

"A drunken card sharp and two prostitutes," shouted the Marshal. "And the only real estate you own is currently being used as a brothel."

"Stuff your witnesses," Officer Bence added. "We have your girlfriend."

The man, full of swagger and boisterousness, went strangely silent. Then his voice returned with a disoriented scatter in its rhythm. "What are you talking about?" he asked. "I don't have a girlfriend. Perhaps you are mistaken…"

The metal door to the prison opened with an ominous squeak, and two officers entered guiding Fiona Conway between them. She was dull in her senses, her eyes barely open, her face slack and pale. She moved forward like a senseless thing, stepping where the two officers urged her to step. They stood her before the lock-up.

"Fiona Conway of County Galway," the Marshall explained. "I believe that you know this man?"

Fleet muttered the name, "Fiona...", then choked and broke out into a coughing fit. "You had me over for a bit! I know not this woman."

The woman calmly lifted her face and peered into the dimness of the cell. "But I may know this man," she said in a bitter voice. "Let me a little closer..."

Lizzie came forward and took the woman's hand in hers. She held it gingerly and stroked it with her other, while saying gently into the woman's ear, "I know what you did in the store, Miss Conway, and I know why. I beseech you, help us to bring a bad man to justice today. If anything, for the sake of Captain Coffin's widow."

The Maggie turned her head and looked at Lizzie with a strange light in her eyes.

"Let go of this man," Lizzie continued, "and live the rest of your life in peace. He shall be sent to the gallows by a jury of his peers."

"He shall go to the gallows?" The light sparkling in her gaze seemed almost like hope.

"Yes," said Lizzie still holding her hand. "You need not lie and let him free. For then he would forever rule tyrannically over your life, and you shall always be his slave. Do what is best for yourself. My father shall take care of you."

"I shall?" Andrew asked.

"Yes, and I shall make sure you are housed and fed and the rest of your days shall be lived in peaceful happiness. Why, you can even come and work for us! We are looking for a Maggie!"

"We are?" Andrew asked.

The woman smiled with a curious twist in her lips, and then said to Lizzie, "Have no fear. All shall be as it shall be. My love lies deep." Then she turned to the Marshal and said with a renewed sense of vigor, "Let me in to examine him at a closer range. I shall tell you if this is your man or nay."

The Marshal nodded to the police guard, who produced the key to the cell and opened the iron gate. Conway's hand slipped from Lizzie's fingers, and as they did, Lizzie sensed something odd. There was something about her hands. Something...

My love lies deep, Lizzie repeated in the privacy of her head.

As the door swung open, the river of reason that flew through Lizzie's buried mind burst free and in a split second she understood what was happening. With a hair's breadth of time as the interval, Lizzie and the Maggie leapt forward, both women flying as if they had been hurled off their feet by some demonic energy. Someone was yelling, and Lizzie was certain it was herself. Perhaps she was raising an alarm, making an inhuman inarticulate noise, because to explain in rational words would have taken too much time. One split second delay and Fleet-Footed Fleet would be dead.

What Lizzie had seen, or rather felt, all in a flash, were the smooth, white, soft hands of the Maggie, hands that were accustomed to no heavy housework, but instead had enjoyed a lifetime of silk gloves and rose water and glycerin cream. She did not feel the chapped, work-worn calluses of a Maggie, or see the red splotches that would have been impossible to disguise. These were the hands of a lady, not of a servant. These were the hands of a Captain's wife.

My love lies deep.

Before anyone else in the jail cell could move or breathe, Lizzie Borden was tossing her body through the dark air towards the disoriented Fleet, closing the distance between them. As she fell across his body, she saw a flash of light glisten on a pair of scissors: the same scissors that Lizzie had seen disappear that very morning off a cutting table at Hodges & Son and into the bustle of Sarah Coffin when she was disguised as an Irish scullery maid. It was only as the teeth of the scissors plunged with deadly accuracy towards Lizzie's back, when they were about to penetrate into her body with a speed and ferocity that nothing but Providence seemed capable of aborting, that she did recall that Coffin had been standing at the sewing table. In that brief flicker of memory, Lizzie recalled the flash of light off the hard steel disappearing into Sarah Coffin's clothing for concealment.

"For my Captain!" screamed the forlorn widow.

Then the scissors struck home and Lizzie felt as if she had been punched hard in her kidney. For a brief moment, she screamed, hearing loudly the cries of a dying woman, perhaps herself acting as observer to her own murder.

Within the briefest of intervals, Fleet-Footed Fleet had sprung to his feet and tossed Lizzie to the ground like he was dumping his slops onto a midden heap. He roared with a voice filled with fire and savagely grabbed Sarah Coffin about the throat with a massive, knuckled hand. The scissors scattered to the floor and the couple stood silhouetted against the dark light. No one could move, such was the paralysis of fear within the cell. The only sound that could be heard was Sarah Coffin choking as she struggled for her life.

Andrew Jackson Borden broke the tension by stepping forward into the cell. He walked up to Fleet, who barely paid attention to him; such was his intensity upon strangling the Captain's widow. With a strangely casual gesture, Andrew lifted his index finger and pointed it towards Fleet's head.

"Sink my investment, you will!" he shouted, and then, as Fleet's face turned to face Andrew, the finger shot forward and jabbed full force into his eye.

"Gee-yah!" the man screamed, letting go instantly of Coffin's throat. The girl slid down senseless to join Lizzie on the ground.

Fleet danced about with both his hands to his eye, his feet tapping along the stone floor, his movement much like the convulsions of a dying chicken. Then Andrew kicked him in the shins and sent him crashing back down on the prison cot.

Police officers darted forward and all became a chaotic blur. Hodges & Son ran about screaming, raising an alarm. The vagrants in the common lock-up were laughing and hooting, shaking their toothless faces. Somewhere in the middle of a dimly lit dust, the blue pewter-buttoned coats of the officers and the heavy boots of the City Marshal were rolling upon the ground, clashing with the dark patched jacket and wild black hair of the screaming maniac.

"A pestilence upon you all!" he was shouting.

In the midst of the melee, Andrew slid to the floor and found Lizzie. She was shaking her head as if trying to remove cobwebs that blurred her vision.

"Father," she said.

"Lizzie," he said gently, and pressed a palm against her face. "You are unharmed."

"No, Father," she said, amidst the tumult of the police officers, frenzied mutineer, and fabric store owners, "I feel a pain, as if the moments of my life are numbered. Ah! The darkness descends!"

She paused and glanced down at her torso, and then furrowed her brow. Reaching back behind her bustle, she pulled out the silver pin tray that she had completely forgotten since she had entered the police station. There was a hefty ding in its surface as if something hard and metallic had attempted to penetrate it.

"Lizzie!" Andrew said, pointing at the tray. "You have been taking your Fancy, I knew it!"

She held the item up to the light where it shone with an almost-spiritual air.

Then Mr. Hodges, snatching it from her hand, turned it over and examined it with a distended eye. "Young lady," he said, his face reddening. "You'll have to pay for this!"

Lizzie reached up and snatched it back. "Monkey-dash!" she spat. "Just put it on my Father's account!"

New Dawn for the Maggie

Lizzie Borden woke the next morning in her own bed in her tiny room on Second Street. The northern light came down on her, drawing her up towards a new day. As she dressed, she felt the bruise on her backside, a cold reminder of the events of the previous afternoon.

She left her room, alighting directly into the spacious bedroom of her sister Emma. The older sister was standing by the bed staring at Lizzie, her long face betraying no inner thoughts.

"Why, Emma," Lizzie said with a flutter of her lids. "Out and about so early?"

"There are visitors," her sister said, plainly.

Lizzie looked about the comfortable room with its quaint rose wallpaper, generous sunlight and fainting sofa. *Perhaps one day*, Lizzie thought to herself. "I shall have it," she completed the thought out loud.

Emma stared puzzled, opened her mouth as if about to speak, then glided out into the hallway, retreating down the stairs without another word.

Lizzie went down to the sitting room, where, to her surprise, she found Mr. Hodges & Son sitting with her father and smoking cigars. There was an affable and cheery disposition to all, and Lizzie was warmed to see her father so jovial. When he spotted her, he slapped the empty side of the couch on which he sat.

"Come Lizzie! Come sit!" he bellowed, and she slid into place beside him.

"The girl of the hour," Mr. Hodges said and his on nodded, almost reluctantly. "Why, if it wasn't for your fast action we would have been in quite a barrel of spindles, eh, Andrew? Yes, it was fortunate indeed that you are such a keen observer. I never would have guessed that Sarah Coffin was attempting to enact her higher purpose."

"If you mean murdering a man in cold blood," Lizzie said, "then I would consider another phrase besides 'higher purpose.'"

The younger Hodges waved a finger. "The man was a devil. He deserves death regardless of how it comes. I say it would have been best to let him be killed by someone who held a passion for it."

"Her hands are clean of blood," Lizzie said. "If I…if we…had not stopped her, she would have been as tainted as the man she hunted."

"Now, Lizzie," Andrew said, blowing a healthy cloud of smoke into the air. "We need not engage in any philosophical niggling. We are all alive and healthy and happy. Are we not?"

The room was exploding with a round of head nodding and hearty calls of "Yes, 'tis true," when there was a knock upon the front door. As the men conversed, Lizzie went to answer it, and, to her surprise, she saw two women standing on her front stoop. One was Sarah Coffin, now dressed in her blue satin finery and her Lady's cap, and the other, to Lizzie's even greater astonishment, was a young woman dressed in the plain dress of an Irish scullery maid with threadbare bonnet.

"Miss Borden," Sarah said gracefully, holding up a gloved hand for Lizzie to touch. "Forgive me any trespassing on your privacy, but I thought it best to come to your home and thank you personally for the great good you have done for me."

"I am honored," Lizzie said, her lips touching upon a smile.

"I have talked at great length with the City Marshal and I am pleased to say that he is satisfied with my disposition. Yesterday, I was not in my right mind. I was driven by an inner madness that I can barely identify as having come from myself. In my rage and clouded passion, I fear I could have committed murder."

"I am glad that I was instrumental in stopping you," Lizzie said.

"I don't believe anyone can understand a loss such as mine, and what an unhealthy state of mind into which it can put one. I am truly sorry if I have caused any inconvenience in your health, either physical or mental."

"I am doing alright," Lizzie said, with a slight nod.

There was a moment of awkward silence while Sarah Coffin struggled to maintain eye contact with Lizzie, then she stepped back a pace and raised a hand towards the girl behind her. Her small mouth was pressed tight, her eyes cast downwards, her hands thrust into her side pockets.

"May I introduce Fiona Conway, late of County Galway."

The Maggie dipped her knees in a slight bow. "M'am," she said.

"I have sought her out," Sarah Coffin said, "to explain to her my role in the affair, and to beg her forgiveness."

"There is nothing you need to apologize for," the Maggie said in an explosive, unexpected burst. "I have told you that in my youth I was glamorized by the man, but now in my clear sight I see him as much the devil as you do. I am glad to see him hang."

"That makes things easier," Sarah Coffin said with a weak smile, then turned back to Lizzie. "I have taken Miss Conway on as my domestic. I will provide for her a bed and a job. She shall not be wanting."

"That is very kind of you," Lizzie said. She reached over and pulled the Maggie's hand and looked her in the eyes. "The very best of luck to you!" she said.

"Thank you, Ma'am," the Maggie said, blushing a faint red, and pulled her hand back.

"Well," Sarah Coffin said, staring up at the sky. "It is a beautiful day, and I do believe I have some fabric shopping to do!"

"Good day to you both," Lizzie said smiling. "And if there is anything I can ever do for either of you, please let me know."

"I shall," Sarah said, and turned to leave. At the bottom of the steps, she paused and turned and looked up at Lizzie. "Miss Lizzie," she said. "If I had done the deed, and become a murderer, would you have judged me?"

Lizzie thought for a moment, a bit distracted by the open-eyed stare of the Maggie, then said carefully, "We all do what we must do…at the exact time that we do it."

Sarah nodded and stared into space as if digesting the words. "Yes," she said finally. "That is a good philosophy of life. I must remember that. Good day to you, Miss Lizzie."

They turned and headed upstreet. Lizzie watched them as they receded into the crowd, crossing through the bustle of the horse-drawn carts and vegetable peddlers. In the distance, a factory yard bell was tolling and the sky overhead was clear blue without any clouds.

All is well in the world, thought Lizzie Borden. *And I have made that happen. All I needed to do was to pay attention to the details. How easy it was to stop evil from happening. Perhaps if I apply these powers to other situations, other people in trouble, I shall stop more bad things from occurring.*

All was indeed well, for due to the mental and physical actions of Lizzie Borden, two tormented women of Fall River have just found their peace. Perhaps three, she added.

"I must think further upon this," she concluded, then closed the door and walked back towards the smoke-filled room of loud, laughing men.

THE
PURLOINED
CURIO

1875. FRENCH STREET, FALL RIVER, MASSACHUSETTS.

VOICES FROM THE SUMMERLANDS

Sarah Durfee Borden was growing weary of the pretense of mystery, of her mother's face glowing in the kerosene light, of the twins' cries of astonishment as each new trumpet blast sounded beyond the shadows in the far corner of the parlor. But what she was tired of the most was Elizabeth Wingate's flabby jowls nodding and chortling in some pathetic act of spirit possession. All in all, Sarah was sick of the endless séances and dancing flames, of loud snapping table raps and candle light, of cold wisps blasted from over her shoulder to make her believe that her dead father was somehow in the room.

Young Sarah, not quite fifteen years of age, born and bred in the Fall River parlors that were more suited for salons than spirit rooms, knew a charlatan when she saw one, and Elizabeth Wingate, despite her aristocratic airs and altruistic demeanor, was a fraud of the first order, a hoax mistress, a traveling snake oil peddler. How much money had the Widow Borden, her mother, spent on these endless rituals of hocus-pocus and supposed spirit visitations? How many textile dividends had been liquidated in sacrifice to Wingate's bank account? How many superstitions and weaknesses in her mother's character had been exploited by this fraud—this silly woman who had claimed that by using spirit visitation not only would she reunite Mrs. Borden with her dear departed husband, but would also locate his missing will?

"Jonathan Borden is but a mere whisper, a glimmering cloud passing through the Summerlands," the corpulent Englishwoman said in a low rumbling voice. "Mrs. Borden, you are the flame that is attracting him to our sphere of matter. He yearns only to be close again to your material manifestation."

"Where is my Jon?" Mrs. Borden cried, her face wet with her own burning sadness. "I want to hear his voice once more!"

The young twins cowered in their high chairs, small beings terrified by flickering lights and dark shadows that they could not understand. "Papa!" said the one on the left. They still could not comprehend his absence, and this farcical charade was only confusing them.

Sarah rolled her eyes and pressed her hands against the gilt tablecloth. "Don't forget to ask him to empty his slops. There's an awful smell."

The mother slapped an open hand down hard. "Sarah! Be still!"

Another trumpet blast came through the brocaded wall. The Widow Borden jumped at its sudden eruption. "What's the point, Mother?" asked Sarah impatiently. "This is all theater! There are no trumpets of the dead! I bet if you search the backyard you'll find an associate of this faker hunched behind your crunch berry bush with a small horn to deliver his blasts on cue." She poked an evil eye at Wingate who flustered in her seat, attempting to preserve an aura of solemn trance. "I would prefer you to attach your leech-like tentacles to some other poor widow and not my mother."

Wingate opened one eye and let it periscope towards Sarah. "Hush!" the Englishwoman said, raising a chubby finger to her lips. "Your father is just passing through the veil."

The Widow Borden said exhaustedly, "Stop insulting our guest, Sarah. She is not a fake. She studied with the Fox Sisters."

Sarah yelled out, "Fiddlesticks!" and fled from the table, pulling at the drapery and upsetting the candle that fell to the side and sputtered out. Within moments, she was in her bedroom, reclined on her lounge and sobbing liberally.

Now she was in a fine imbroglio. She had wanted to give Elizabeth Wingate a piece of her mind for several months now but remained silent while her mother's dwindling wealth had financed these greedy charades. If only her father had properly filed his will with the probate office. Surely he had anticipated his death by creating the document, so why had he hid it in a place where no could find it? Why did he take that secret with him to his grave?

Sarah knew that for her to expose this spiritual fraud, she would need help from an expert. But who could prove Wingate's deceptions? Or find her father's will?

As Sarah pondered these questions, she happened to glance at her writing table, and saw a framed photograph of her associates at the Women's Temperance Society. In the center, beaming with pride and decked in her Sunday tulle finest, was Sarah Borden, her eyes glowing with the optimism of youth. She remembered the day of the photograph with fondness and nostalgia, for, at that time, her father had been alive to witness his daughter's accomplishments.

Right next to her in the picture was a plump distant cousin of hers, one of the less prosperous Bordens, with her smooth round cheeks and protruding blue-gray eyes. Here was a girl whom Sarah had shared a high school classroom with, had sat next to at temperance lectures, and to whom she had confided some secrets that only girls could share.

Yes, thought Sarah. How absurd. I should have thought of it from the beginning.

I shall consult with Lizzie Andrew Borden, the Girl Detective.

A PRIVATE CONSULTATION

The Borden house on Second Street was a quaint example of the Greek revival architecture that populated the downstreet area. Each time Sarah came down from the hill, engaged on business, a social visit, or to help with her mother's banking errands, she was struck by how crowded and small everything seemed, and the Borden house was no exception. It was pressed against the bustling sidewalk where peddlers and pedestrians challenged each other for space.

Sometimes, in the downstreet area, Sarah would catch a glimpse of Andrew Borden, Lizzie's father, who was tall, thin and a bit spectral with his unkempt locks and grim straight-lined mouth that always seemed clenched. He radiated some intense and unsympathetic aloofness. It was known that this self-made man had sold coffins, and it was rumored that he was a penny pincher, that he kept his wife and two daughters on a tight leash, that he negotiated each and every coin in any business transaction and prided himself on never having spent a foolish dollar. Outside his house on Second Street, about to knock and call upon his daughter, Lizzie Borden, the Girl Detective, Sarah had to muster all her courage.

Fortunately, it was the mother, Abby, who opened the door. She seemed humorless, but pleasant enough. "Are you here to see Lizzie?" she inquired and Sarah nodded slightly. "She's upstairs reading her Plutarch, but I'm sure she is receiving."

Sarah was ushered up a high narrow and bending staircase to a second floor landing. Abby Borden, who was physically drained from the demanding climb up the stairs, pointed to what was presumably Lizzie's bedroom door. "Just knock and she'll answer. Now if you'll forgive me, I must lie down. I've been dusting all morning and I'm fairly exhausted." And then she disappeared into the guest room, a feather duster flicking about her like a tiny bird.

After knocking on Lizzie's door, it was opened a crack and Sarah saw those wonderful eyes peering outwards. "My word," came an exclamation from within. "Sarah Durfee Borden! My favorite cousin!" The door flew open and Sarah was confronted by a cheerful Lizzie. "What brings you here to brighten my day that is otherwise occupied with dreary Roman classics? Come on in, please, and sit with me."

The door widened and Sarah was ushered into the bedroom. A single bed was angled in the corner, covered with a blue embroidered bedspread. Behind it was what seemed to be a communicating door to another part of the house. To Sarah's right was a fainting couch in front of the right-hand window and a chest of drawers. To the left was a desk and chair with bookcase above. Another bookcase was against the far wall, liberally sprinkled with book spines, and draped over with a velvet portière. There were elegant prints of cathedrals and European edifices hanging from the walls. It was the bedroom of a cultured, intelligent but cloistered young woman.

"What a lovely room you have here," Sarah said pleasingly. "What wonderful southern exposure."

"Actually," Lizzie said with a sly smile, "this room belongs to Emma. The poor girl is visiting in Newport and I've temporarily taken over. If she ever suspects I'm using it as an office for my consulting agency she'll have a fit, she will!" Lizzie pointed to a room off to the side that looked small enough to comfortably stable a horse. "That's my room over there. But this is just our secret, now, isn't it?"

Lizzie motioned Sarah to the fainting couch. "Please," she said, and gracefully sank with her into the cushioned seat. "What can I do for you today?"

"Lizzie Borden," Sarah said, leaping forward with her clenched hands, "I am told you are a solver of mysteries."

"Why yes," Lizzie said with a wry smile. "I have been quite successful at solving some other puzzles that local consulting detectives have been baffled by. I helped the constabulary solve the case of the Portuguese Reprobate, and I was quite useful during the Affair of Mrs. Wilmarth's Immovables."

"And," Sarah interjected, "I did hear gossip about your role in the Riddle of the Forlorn Maggie."

Lizzie chuckled as if she were recalling an amusing anecdote. "I did not even think that one made it into the record. Well, all of these affairs earned me commendations directly from the town judiciary." She pointed to a framed certificate hanging above her writing table. "I am considering a full blown career in criminal detection if my father will provide capital for my tuition."

"Your credentials are indeed impeccable, and that is why I am coming to you today. For you see, I have a mystery unfolding within my very house. As you may know, my mother, Victoria Borden of the Anawan Street Bordens is the poor widow of Jonathan Borden, of the French Street Bordens. Six months ago, almost to this very day, my father died under mysterious circumstances while managing one of the Livermore mills. We do believe it to be foul play. He was found in an apoplectic state and quite dead. The cause of the death was never confirmed."

"My word," Lizzie said, holding two fingertips to her ovaled mouth. "That would be foul play indeed. Is there anyone that you think would harbor such hateful feelings towards your father?"

"Yes. He is Thisbalt Livermore, of the Taunton Livermores, the owner of the mill my father died in. A fouler man I cannot suspect, with his odious cigars and his corpulent belly. As a little girl I felt my skin crawl when he entered the room. For years I endured his sly flirtations, and now we suspect that he hired the agent who terminated my father's life. To make matters worse, we cannot find my father's will. That document would have provided for my surviving family, but alas we are left with a legal morass that threatens to have all my father's property turned over to Livermore. Unfortunately, my mother seeks to solve this problem through supernatural agencies."

"Supernatural?" Lizzie said. "Give me more details."

"A British spiritualist, Elizabeth Wingate. Perhaps you have seen her lecture in town about the seven-fold rays of man's spiritual origins. She is a fraud, I believe, and possibly an agent of Livermore, attempting to infiltrate my intimate family circle and obtain information about the hiding place of my father's will. I cannot prove that Livermore is behind Wingate's fraud, but if I could, it would go a long way to proving that Livermore was behind my father's demise."

"This Elizabeth Wingate, has she come recommended?"

"No, she approached us after hearing of our plight. We inquired about town and found out that she has worked with the Fox Sisters in upstate New York, but it is doubtful that anything said about her has veracity."

"Has your mother shown any previous interest in the spiritual arts to warrant such gullibility?"

"Not quite," Sarah said, and then paused, pressing her lips together.

"Well," said Lizzie. "It seems you are remembering something of importance."

"Quite right, Lizzie. You see my mother has a Spirit Box."

Lizzie's eyes widened. "A Spirit Box?"

"Yes, a small curiosity Father picked up in a dusty antique store downstreet. Father was particularly afraid of it after he brought it home and was loath to touch it."

"Afraid?"

"Yes, it was said that it was haunted by evil spirits. Particularly an angry ghost of a savage Indian who wants revenge for the atrocities committed by the white colonists some 100 years ago when Fall River was not yet even a town. Some say the ghost is that of Awashuncks, Squaw Sachem of the Sakonnet. They say she was condemned to dwell within the box by King Philip himself!"

Lizzie shuddered. King Philip, a Wampanoag Sachem, had been killed almost two hundred years before during a very bloody war with the English. Many a time in her childhood, her father had told her, "Be a good little girl or King Philip will be waiting for you in your bedroom." The thought had always haunted her deepest dreams.

Drawing herself together, Lizzie uttered, "But one cannot truly believe the box to be haunted?"

"My father did, and he went to great lengths to train us from an early age not to touch it. It sits there, alas, in Mother's Cabinet of Curiosities in the parlor, collecting dust. No one, especially Mother, dares to touch it."

Lizzie's eyebrows furrowed. "Does this Elizabeth Wingate know about this Spirit Box?"

"Well, yes, Mother was particularly interested in getting Wingate's opinion as to its supposed possession. Wingate wanted to take it with her to examine it, perhaps to perform a spiritual rite that would clear it of any possession, but Mother became hysterical and told her that no human on earth should touch it or else it would unleash King Philip himself and we shall all be brought to woe. Wingate told her to leave it be for now and when they have contacted my dear father's spirit in the Beyond, they will ask his counsel on the nature of the Spirit Box's inhabitant."

"So Wingate is interested in this curio?"

"Very much so. We certainly hope the old woman has some truth in her claims for supernatural powers. We would certainly love to have that old Spirit Box cleared of spirits. I have had many nightmares about that damned box."

Lizzie Borden, the Girl Detective, glowered in the dusty afternoon light. She scratched her chin and then pressed her hands against her bengaline dress. "Sarah, in a few scant moments you have provided me with a complex mystery that will indeed be a challenge. I shall take this case, and I ask for nothing more in return than a most excellent and hearty meal and an evening's delightful banter with your wonderful family when the affair is finished."

"Why certainly, Lizzie Borden," Sarah said happily. "You are indeed a gem of a girl. When do we begin?"

"Right this very moment! I shall inform my father's wife that I am going downstreet. I believe he can help gain information about this Livermore character. I wish to assess him myself."

The two girls left the room and entered the guest bedroom which they were surprised to find empty. "Mrs. Borden must have finished her chores," Lizzie announced.

They were startled to hear Abby's dour voice come from behind the bed where she lay on the bare floor, invisible to their eyes. "Over here Lizzie! I seem to have fallen off the bed while napping. Can you take a moment to help me to my feet?"

"Lizzie," Sarah said with alarm. "Your mother is in peril!"

Lizzie took a deep breath, her eyes twisting upwards with a forceful annoyance, and muttered, "She is not my mother! She is my stepmother!"

AN INVESTMENT PITCH

Andrew Borden, a tall dark figure, grim like a provincial undertaker who had just come into some inheritance, ambled down the street on his way home for dinner. His thin emotionless mouth and cold marble eyes greeted his fellow citizens who bothered to tip their hats and say a kind word of greeting.

"Good day, Mr. Borden," said one corpulent gentleman.

"Good day, Borden," Andrew muttered back, nodding his head. He vaguely remembered the man: J.F. Borden. Or was it T.E. Borden? Or perhaps that was another Borden. He couldn't keep them all calculated in his head and it sufficed to just call them Borden. No one would question him since he was a man of means and could walk downstreet with dignity and respect.

He reached his home and climbed the steps, retrieving his key from his pocket. In the front hallway, he was met by his youngest daughter, who came up on him from behind and tapped his shoulder. He seemed more than a little perturbed as he placed his hat on a standing rack.

"Nay, daughter," the poker-faced patriarch muttered. "Coming at me in such a manner is not fitting. What is your business?" He stepped into the sitting room to get his newspapers and Lizzie followed.

She smiled devilishly and slid onto the low sofa against the far wall. "Nothing, Father. I am merely curious how your day went."

"Twenty seven dollars in revenue for the Maple Street property," he bemoaned, as he flipped through the papers. "Plus a plundering of my daily tills from Mr. Carpentiere who seems to have forgotten that his talents lay more in the peddling of feather beds than in the creative fiddling of my audits."

"I'm sorry to hear that Father. But I'm wondering if you are better off putting your energies towards the associations within the textile community, than building furniture that you sell at most excellent prices befitting our Commonwealth."

Andrew peered up from his news stories, his eyes twitching. "What the devil do you mean, daughter? Borden and Almy is doing well by me."

"Yes, but there is great money in banking and textiles. I hear that Mr. Livermore is without a partner these days. His former co-president is simply late of this world, having died at the mill a few months back."

"I have heard of such things. J.A. Borden was a far cousin of mine, and I believe he left his widow with sufficient funds. Livermore is not someone I ever had a fondness for. His reputation recently has been a bit scandalous."

"How so?" Lizzie asked.

"Many say it is a mistress. His poor wife does suffer. I say that these times are not befitting for a man of industry."

"I suppose there is no harm in offering him your financial services,

Father. I'm sure he could be quite reasonable when presented with a flow of money. After all, he is one of the most important textile merchants in town."

Borden brooded by the fireplace, his fingers tapping on his watch fob. "I suppose you are correct. I shall pay him a visit anon."

"What better time than the present," Lizzie said. "I hear he takes his dinner in his mansion between eleven and noon. And it is within a short walk from here."

"Up the damned hill!" Andrew scowled. "I swear an oath, daughter, you are going to be the death of me!"

Lizzie smiled and patted the horsehair sofa that was so comfortable beneath her on this quaint summer afternoon. "Why Father, such a horrible thing to say," she coyly whispered.

THE DRAGON'S DEN

On the street, a bowler-hatted gentleman lifted his palm to his brim. "Good day, Borden."

"Good day, Borden," Lizzie's father replied, and then gave a polite nod to a passing woman. "Good day, Mrs. Borden."

"God's graces on you, Mr. Borden," she said with a solemn nod of her own.

"And how is Mr. Borden this fine forenoon?" asked Andrew.

"None too well. He is currently consulting for his health with Dr. Borden."

"Would that be the Dr. Borden of Borden Street?"

"No," said Mrs. Borden. "That would be the other Dr. Borden."

"My word, you are correct. Forgive me, Mrs. Borden."

"Think not upon it, Mr. Borden." And they were past.

"How many Bordens are there in Fall River, Father?" Lizzie asked, clutching his big knuckled hand.

"Not enough for confusion," Andrew said loftily, then tipped his hat to another passing gentleman. "Good day, Borden," he announced.

Eventually, Lizzie and her father stood before the stately Livermore mansion. Overhead clouds passed behind its gables with gaseous indifference. "If only," Lizzie mused, "you had bought us such a fine dwelling on this hill instead of that midget cheese box on Second Street."

"Hush," her father said, raising a single finger to his thin lips. "Be quiet daughter, do not stress my patience."

A harried butler answered the door and took Andrew's card, peering up at him as if he were his better. Andrew huffed his way into the house and Lizzie followed. After a time sequestered in a drawing room, father and daughter staring at a billiard table that was so large it wouldn't even fit into their parlor, the teakwood doors flew open and in strolled Thisbalt Ajax Livermore, holding a wide beer flagon, his mouth stuffed with a generously rolled cigar.

The textile tycoon was more corpulent than Lizzie had imagined. His face was a fiery splotching of skin disorders as if some fierce mold had hatched on his lower chin and spread across his muttonchops, ear and forehead. There was also the glistening of medicinal gel that gave his head the appearance of wet rotting fruit. Lizzie fought back the urge to turn away her disgusted eyes.

"Borden," he said, dipping his chin in Andrew's direction.

"Mr. Livermore," Andrew said with reverence and a bit of awe. Lizzie had never seen her Father humbled so. "How are you doing on this fair day?"

Livermore puckered his lips. "Pash and twaddle! Have you not heard of the unfortunate Mr. Tweed of New York? He has been apprehended and is now wallowing in a common prison cell." Livermore puffed on his cigar like it was an extension of his face. An inky cloud wafted about his speckled head. "Borden, that is alarming news. I do not believe men of industry are respected in this day and age. No good can come of that."

Lizzie took a breath and interjected. "I do believe Mr. Tweed to be of a criminal disposition unbefitting an elected political official. I do not think a cell can be low or dank enough for his kind."

Pin-pointed eyes emerged from the darkening smoke. "Borden, you must have a sit-down with this young lady and correct her misdirected thinking."

"I endeavor to acculturate," Andrew sighed. "Lizzie, however, directs her thoughts elsewhere."

"There is nothing misdirected about my thought," Lizzie said, pulling at her ruffles. "I merely suggest that no man, no matter how wealthy or industrious, should be above the law. If Mr. Tweed has robbed New York City of millions, he must be called to justice."

"The courts shall decide," Livermore said, choking on the dusty air. "Meanwhile, Tweed is indisposed to a chamber not befitting a man of his industrious character." He paused to sip from his flagon. After lifting his dripping face from the brew, he sputtered, "But such talk merely takes us from our purpose. What can I do for you today, Mr. Borden?"

"Lizzie here has advised me to hitch my wagon to your train, so to speak. She suggests that I invest my money in your textile interests."

Livermore took two puffs of his cigar and said with a grunt, "How much and how soon?"

Andrew fell back on his heels. "Well, I suppose we can set up a meeting at the Bank to discuss the particulars."

There was silence in the room for a space.

"No particulars," Livermore shrugged. "Just sign a check at the front office."

"For what amount?" her father stuttered. His legs were visibly trembling.

Livermore's eyebrows extended to the top of his pasty scalp. "How the blazes should I know; you're the one who made the offer. What's your game? I've seen you, Borden. You make feather beds and coffins don't you? You grew up on Ferry Street. You raised yourself from the shame of nothing to where you are today, just like myself! Give me all you can spare, and in return I'll give you a cut of the great expansion that is about to occur. Are you not a man of vision? Do you not have financial instincts?" He paused and savored his tobacco, then stared back at Andrew. "Is that all? What are you gawking at?"

Andrew's fingers clutched at his side. He seemed to be trembling from the top of his pate to the bottom of his congress boots. "Uh…yes, I suppose that is all."

"Hmmm…yes. Well, I do believe you have turned out to be a fine ally, Borden. I look forward to seeing your money."

"I suppose that would be advantageous to both of us. Good day, Mr. Livermore, and I thank you for your time."

"Yes, my time." Livermore turned towards the massive fireplace that dominated one wall of the room and stared up at the array of framed Daguerreotypes that fringed the mantle. "I have nothing but time, Mr. Borden."

Lizzie and her father interpreted the sight of his back and the smoke curling from his head that it was time to leave.

Back on the front porch, Andrew stared down at his daughter and pressed his lips together. "My fortune at a clap," he groaned.

"Nonsense, Father. Livermore will take good care of you. He'll treasure your contribution."

"What is this really about, Lizzie? My word, girl, you are never what you seem."

"Not what I seem, Father," Lizzie said, beaming. "But what I have seen."

The framed Daguerreotype of Elizabeth Wingate, nestled on Livermore's mantelpiece, sitting in the prized position dead center between images of illustrious colleagues and family members, had told her all she needed to know about the connection between the fake spiritualist and the textile tycoon.

A WIDOW'S PREDICAMENT

Sarah Borden met Lizzie Borden downstreet at the apothecary as she was leaving with a string-tied bag of rat poison. Her most excellent cousin was beaming with rosy cheeks. "Did you discover something, Miss Lizzie?"

"I prefer to remain reserved on the subject, Sarah. For now, I wish to accompany you on a social visit to your mother. I have much to discuss with her."

An hour later, they were seated in the very parlor room where Wingate's ceremonies were enacted. Lizzie sat with the Borden family, the twins bouncing around the room with urgent energy, and the Widow Borden, grim and sallow looking, seated in her chair of mourning, her eyes begging for respite.

"It has been a trying ordeal," the Widow Borden was saying. "Elizabeth is doing the best that she can but these things take time. Once you have become a shade in the Summerlands, it is very difficult to maintain contact with the material world. But I'm hoping that Jonathan's resolve to fulfill his love for me is stronger than those incorporeal bonds that are tying him to the afterlife."

"Or perhaps," Sarah quipped, "we aren't paying Wingate enough money! I'm sure if we doubled her salary, suddenly Father would start yapping."

"Sarah!" came the maternal rebuttal. "Please be reverent towards Mrs. Wingate, especially in the presence of our guest!"

"You must consider, Mrs. Borden," Lizzie said boldly, "the possibility that the spiritualist is not quite as effective in her conjurations as she may have advertised."

"Nonsense, she comes with the highest recommendations. She..."

And Sarah joined her mother in unison, "...studied with the Fox Sisters!" and then added "What a load of horse droppings."

The Widow Borden's eyes went milky as she thought back into the past. "I went to a performance of the Fox Sisters in New York a few years back. They were performing at the Academy of Music and drew quite a large crowd. They brought back a young boy who had been crushed under a mule at a Nyack farm. He wandered across the stage with these large accusing eyes. It was the most frightful thing I had ever seen. But it filled me with the strength I needed to endure Jonathan's death. I felt for the first time that there is hope, that he is not forever lost."

Sarah said grimly, "Mother, this has gone too far. Lizzie Borden is here to help you find the will, not to contact the dead."

Lizzie's eyes strayed towards the Cabinet of Curiosities that flanked the far wall. It was large and heavy with bronze claw feet and decorative flanged framings. Inside lay various items, many of them primitive artifacts that the Bordens had picked up from Jonathan Borden's sea voyages when he was a textile merchant abroad: African idol heads, JuJu sticks, and other implements of superstitious value.

"Perhaps the will is hidden somewhere on the premises...perhaps in one of the curiosities in your cabinet. Stuffed perhaps into a voodoo doll?"

"Alas," the Widow Borden said, resignedly. "I have examined all those items."

"All of them?"

"With the exception of that..." she pointed with a trembling finger.

Prominently, in the center cube of the cabinet, sitting alone with plenty of breathing space on both sides, was a large rectangular box, noticeably Western in style, with shellacked sea shells delicately placed in a rim along the joint lines.

"The Spirit Box," Sarah said. She got to her feet and started towards the cabinet, but halted, her feet glued into place. "For someone so unbelieving," she confessed, "I am afraid of that thing. Father himself told me of the evil that dwells within."

"We must leave it for now," the Widow Borden said solemnly. "It is cursed and cannot be touched or moved. When we ever depart this house, for whatever reason, we must leave it behind. Let the next resident of 9 French Street inherit our heavy burden."

"How did the Spirit Box get in the house in the first place?" Lizzie asked. "Surely it didn't just appear one night."

"No, that it didn't. It was my beloved Jonathan who brought it home from work one day. He said that it must never be opened, ever. Except on one occasion."

"And what occasion would that be?" asked Lizzie.

"In case of his death. He said it must be turned over to his lawyer at once. That only Joseph Coffin of New Bedford, his life-long solicitor, knew how to undo the curse of King Philip."

"Odd, I never heard of a lawyer practicing the spiritual arts."

"It struck me as odd indeed. But Jonathan himself filled us with such fear that we cannot even touch it to give it to Coffin. We figured we'd rather let it sit there and contain its evil rather than take the risk of Coffin exposing us all to woe."

Sarah said quietly, "There may be a connection with Thisbalt Livermore and that box."

"Hush!" said her mother.

"There's no point in withholding information from the only person who can help us, Mother." She turned to Lizzie. "Livermore was over for dinner with his dreary wife, this raggedy thing he drags behind him whenever he wants to make a splash on the social register. And in the middle of cigars and brandy in the billiards room, Livermore excused himself and went to find the water closet. When he didn't return, Father set out to fetch him and discovered him in the parlor trying to break into the Cabinet of Curiosities with a hatchet. He was snarling like a dog, in fact. Father said it was the most frightful thing. A week later...he..." Sarah fell forward with a sudden sob.

Lizzie put her hand gently on her cousin's shoulder while she regained her composure. "Why would Livermore be interested in the cabinet?" she asked.

"He may have been after the box," the Widow Borden said. "I do believe he is drawn towards evil, and wants to corrupt us all by discovering the secret of the box." Then her face became more drawn than ever and she moaned, "A week later my poor Jonathan was found dead in his office. He was slumped back in his chair with the most hideous look of horror on his face. His hand was outstretched on the table pointing towards the far bookcase. We never knew the significance of the gesture. But I believe that he may have been visited by the shade of Awashuncks, Squaw Sachem of Sakonnet."

Her hands flew to her face and tears fell copiously from her red eyes. "Oh, I am the most wretched woman who ever lived! I yearn for peace! And for Jonathan!"

"Mrs. Borden," Lizzie asked. "Is there any reason to believe that Elizabeth Wingate is also interested in the Spirit Box?"

"Nay, in fact she seems to dismiss my fear of it as trivial. She claims that when we settle the affair of my poor husband, she will address the box."

"Address it?"

"Perhaps I shall let her remove it from the premises. She knows how to handle it, more so than Solicitor Coffin would. Yes, I'm sure Mrs. Wingate will know how to contain the evil of the box and then it will no longer be in our house."

"Yes," Sarah interjected. "Let her have it. Let the curse be on her head, the old fake!"

Lizzie Borden nodded thoughtfully. "Mrs. Borden there may be more to this than meets the eye. I do believe I can help you, but I need your cooperation."

"And what would that be? Anything to remove this curse from my life!"

"I need you to schedule a séance with Elizabeth Wingate, here tonight, and invite me along. I need to be present at the conjuration of your husband."

The Widow Borden composed herself by dabbing a handkerchief to her red cheeks. "Why yes, that can be arranged. Mrs. Wingate is always pressing me to make another attempt each and every night."

Lizzie pressed her hands happily down onto her knees. "Fine then, tonight it is. And with your leave, invite along into our company any members of the legal profession you happen to know, anyone with an open mind for such supernatural matters. Just send a note round my home with the exact time of our congregation and I shall be here a half hour before to set up."

"Set up? Whatever can you mean?"

Lizzie rolled her eyes to the ceiling. "Oh, I merely meant that I will prepare myself for the proper mood. You never know what will happen. It is not every day that I get to meet shades of dead Indians!"

THE ELECTROMECHANICIAN

Homer Thesinger was called by many in Fall River the "Boy Inventor," but his preferred term for his chosen profession was Electromechanician, a word he had first seen used in *Telegrapher* magazine to describe Mr. Thomas Edison, Homer's most valued role model. He spent his days in his father's basement on Prospect Street tirelessly tinkering with his electrical and telegraphic apparatus, his endless flywheels, batteries, electromagnets, relays and receivers, determined to be one of the first to make marked improvements in multiplexed signaling. He was regarded by most as intellectually promising but lacking serious prospects when it came to a career.

In the midst of his stubborn and time-consuming work, he often joined Miss Lizzie Borden for some refreshments at the South Main Street Apothecary where he would boast about his own inventions and visions for machines not yet invented. He held a bit of a torch for Lizzie. He admired the way her mind sorted out a considerable amount of factual data, always managing to piece together a larger picture that was absurdly obvious once you divined the solution, but which had been doggedly evasive during the crime solving. He felt she accomplished, with the puzzling mysteries brought to her by her clients, what he was attempting to do when he engineered some electromagnetic device: to fit it all together into an elegant and obvious solution. For this reason, his inventive mind and mechanical competence had served her well in more than a few of her detective cases.

So it came as a pleasant surprise one afternoon when Homer received a note by messenger to meet Lizzie at the Apothecary on South Main Street and that he should bring his Sazaphone, a complicated contraption of rubber tubing and ear-shaped lozenges that were designed to project voices from one part of a room to another. Homer had invented the device for a school performance of *A Midsummer Night's Dream*, but it had never been used because it had been so effective that members of the rehearsal audience had trembled in fear of the spectral voices that emerged from its cups. The presiding theatrical director finally deemed the device infernal and had banned it from the school grounds.

Homer appeared in the Apothecary with his inventor bag slung over his shoulder, the Sazaphone protruding through the burlap like a bunched serpent coiled inside. Lizzie was up on a stool sipping her syrup water and tapping her toes on the cross bar. "Homer," she said with a sigh. "You have acted promptly. Once again I need you to aid me in my exploits."

"And what, pray tell, are those?" Homer asked. He was used to Lizzie allowing him only enough information about her proceedings that he needed to know, no more, no less. "I have a meeting of my Fluted Shaft Society at eight tonight," he explained. "We're designing a cylinder that will capture the human voice in coded format so it can later be reproduced mechanically. We're hoping to obtain a patent and make money selling it to industry. We believe it will replace the stenographer. We're calling it the VocoPhonometer."

"A machine replacing a human voice," Lizzie mused. "This century has brought nothing but technical marvels into our everyday life. But anyway, Homer, I believe I can have you at your Fluted Shaft meeting by its pre-ordained hour. Here's what I want you to do for me. How well can you climb through shrubbery?"

"I don't believe I have any practice in that area."

"No matter. The trick is to avoid getting the seat of your pants stuck on thorns. I have faith that you can accomplish that."

Homer rubbed his pants legs with a trembling hand.

"And," Lizzie continued. "I need you to rig up some sort of harmless explosion. Something with a snap and a bang to it!"

"What exactly are you proposing, Miss Lizzie Borden, Girl Detective?"

She smiled. "Well, I'll tell you. But you must follow my instrucions precisely!"

After sundown, Homer Thesinger, hauling his burlap sack over his shoulder, entered the Widow Borden's French Street garden by the side path of the house and immediately encountered the crunch berry bushes that whispered in the wind below the brightly lit parlor window. Through the glass, he could see a gathering of people, including the Widow Borden and her children, and Judge Mason and his tiny wife. They were standing around the parlor table just as Lizzie had described, and within a moment or two, a rotund woman, dolled up in a head scarf entered the room fluttering her fake eyelashes. This, no doubt, was the phony spiritualist, Wingate. Homer didn't like her one bit. Imagine taking advantage of poor widow Borden's grief, and in plain view of the young twins.

His eyes lit up a bit as Lizzie Borden and Sarah Borden entered the room, nodding their heads in quaint curtsies and allowing Judge Mason to press his walrus mustache against the backs of their hands. After a few polite pleasantries, they all settled down around the table and the kerosene lamps were lowered as Wingate sat like an erect Buddha in front of the massive Cabinet of Curiosities. Her candle flickered upwards, giving her face a ghastly glow as she threw back her head, her eyes going pearly white.

Lizzie sat to the side, peering intently, her eyes darting over every minute detail of the scene. Judge Mason and his wife held their silence, clasping each other's trembling hands. The twins hid behind their mother's chair as the Widow Borden pressed a handkerchief to her prematurely tearing eyes. Sarah looked as diffident as ever, just like she did in Latin class whenever Miss Handy gave a particularly dull lesson.

With a scowl and a silent curse, Homer stepped awkwardly across the dank undergrowth as his ankle caught on some root that arched upwards from the soil. He noticed it was a lead pipe. There was a muffled gasp in the foliage and Homer froze in his tracks. Fearing it to be a trapped animal of some sort, he trailed his fingers along it, and began patting a rounded surface that crinkled like felt. He lifted it and immediately saw he was removing a bowler hat from a figure that was hunched in the bush. With a slight yelp, the person released his breath and threw up his hands.

"By Jove!" Homer cried out. "Who the devil can you be?!"

The hunched figure trembled. "It's only I, poor Tom Crank! Don't be stern with me, Master Thesinger. I'm only doing my contracted duty!"

Tom Crank was one of the more feeble-minded students at Fall River High School. He had shared many a lunch hour with Homer Thesinger where he had proved continually how slow-witted his mind could be. Homer shook his head with disbelief and pointed at the pipe. "What's this blasted thing for?"

Tom reached up, his hands grasping a tarnished tin trumpet. "It's mere fascination, sir!" he said with alarm. "I've been paid my wages! Wingate's got her subterfuge and I'm a cursed man!"

Homer grabbed the boy by his lapels and shook him until his eyes went crossed. "You mean you're the one whose been blowing these trumpets?"

"Aye, sir. I don't mean to be insensitive to the Widow, but I've been paid a most excellent wage. And I always did want to be a musician."

Homer released the lapels and stepped back a pace. "You are nothing but a mercenary."

"Aye, that I am. And there's no shame in it when you're trying to turn a penny for your hungry family."

"Whatever Wingate is paying you, it's tainted money. If you want some redemption for your part in this subterfuge, I recommend you do exactly what I tell you to do!"

Tom's face contorted, and then his eyes sparkled with some hope. "Oh to be sure, there's nothing more sublime than to correct crooked ways. Just show me what to do and I'll do't."

Homer reached behind him for his rucksack. With a cherry glow in his eyes, he dipped his hand inside and pulled forth his Sazaphone, now a tangled mass of rubber tubing.

"What in the name of the Twelve Tribes be that?" the trumpet hustler cried in astonishment.

Homer Thesinger, the Boy Inventor, just grinned.

A Spirit Box Opened, A Demon Set Free

Lizzie had noticed from the very first that Elizabeth Wingate was keeping her back to the Cabinet of Curiosities. It seemed to be a deliberate avoiding, rather than a casual ignoring. Up close, the spiritualist's face was flabby and pasty, and her eyelashes were obvious fakes. As soon as the lights were dimmed and the candlelight filled the room, the rappings began. They seemed to be coming from the table, but it could very well have been underneath the table. Those attending seemed too terrified of them to pay much notice to particulars.

"We are gathered here tonight," Wingate said suddenly, "to draw forth the specter of Jonathan Aloysius Borden from the beyond, from the Summerlands. May his presence here be potent and puissant."

"And don't forget to bring his checkbook," Sarah whispered into Lizzie's ear, provoking a sharp giggle. Wingate's eye flashed to the side, demanding silence.

Mrs. Judge Mason twitched in her seat. "I hope he comes soon. It's awfully cold in here."

Lizzie noticed the draft as well. No doubt the window just beyond the parlor door was kept wide open. If all had gone well with Homer in the garden, there should be a lozenge shaped cup snaking along the floor at this very moment.

"Jonathan!" Wingate cried out. "Come forth from the realms beyond!"

Suddenly, without warning, there was a haunting groan. The two small twins began to cry and Mrs. Judge Mason let out with a shriek.

"Victoria!" came a spectral voice. "Victoria! I have come back to you!"

The Widow Borden leapt to her feet and held out her arms, tears pouring freely down her face. She was too choked up for words.

Wingate stared, puzzled, at the parlor door. Lizzie suspected that she was baffled as to the nature of the voice. It certainly was different from the utterances made by her accomplice in the garden. Homer was being extremely clever.

"Victoria!" it continued. "This woman, Wingate! She is not a friend!"

Wingate snuffled. "Why, Jonathan," she said purposefully. "You must be confused. I am your familiar, your material basis in the waking world."

"You are nothing but a desperate fake!" the voice shouted.

There were muffled gasps, as Wingate sat poker-faced.

Lizzie pulled out a handkerchief from her dress pocket and pushed her nose into it, letting out with a sharp sneeze. Then, just on cue, as her hands came down from her face, a terrific noise filled the room. A new voice, warbling, deep and loud careened off the walls and echoed between the doorways. Lizzie smiled subtly. Homer's Sazaphone was working its magic.

"This is Awashuncks, Squaw Sachem of the Sakonnet!" it screamed. "The fires of tribulation are coming down upon French Street ready to consume utterly the misbelieving! Oh fly! Fly while you can! King Phillip shall have his revenge!"

The assembled guests stared at each other with alarm, then turned to

Wingate who was sitting with a perplexed frown that outdid their own. "Wingate!" cried Sarah. "If ever there be a time that you confessed to fraud it must be now! You have either gone too far, or we are about to be consumed by the Tribulation!"

Wingate spoke with a choked throat. "Alas, I cannot say this is subterfuge."

The voice spoke again. "Let my words be a warning to your eternal souls!"

Mrs. Judge Mason gathered her composure enough to speak a single sentence. "Perhaps dear," she said hoarsely, her face getting paler with suppressed fear, "we'd best listen to her advice." Then she swooned into the arms of her husband whose walrus mustache bristled with rage and fury. "Wingate!" he puffed. "Stop this farrago immediately! We've tolerated your frauds because they amused us, but this..."

Wingate lifted her empty palms into the air. "I only wish I could."

The voice shouted over the din, "If you do not flee, the house will be set aflame and all within it shall satisfy the swollen appetite of fire." Then there was a small explosion that illuminated the room, followed by a smell of sulfur and charcoal. With this sudden assault on their senses, many of those present gasped and started violently for the exits. The Widow Borden gathered the twins, who were paralyzed with fear. Lizzie rose from her seat, fearing nothing of course, but curious to see what Wingate would do next.

As Mrs. Judge Mason was revived by the pudgy hands of Judge Mason, Sarah, right on cue and with a wink to Lizzie, motioned for everyone to head for the French doors leading to the main hallway. "Fly to safety!" she commanded, and everyone listened to her directive. All but one, of course.

Elizabeth Wingate ran straight for the Cabinet of Curiosities. From the folds of her blouse she produced a small claw headed hatchet which she raised with terrific violence against the Cabinet's glass front.

"Got you," Lizzie smirked.

The spiritualist deftly smashed the hatchet into the pane of glass that separated her from the prized Spirit Box. For a brief moment, the flabby woman stared through the shattered glass, then dropped the hatchet to the ground with a dull thud and with trembling fingers lifted up the shell-rimmed box in the air, muttering under her breath, "I have seized the prize!" She swooped it down to be buried within the folds of her blouse, then bolted for the door.

"The purloinment of the Spirit Box," Lizzie thought, "proves everything. This case is as good as solved."

Following Wingate out of the house, she came upon an odd scene on the front lawn. Deputy Sheriff Wixon, a tall handsome man with a generous mustache, was holding Homer Thesinger and Tom Crank by their collars with two respectful hands.

"Here's a pretty how-dee-doo!" Wixon was shouting. "What is this nonsense? Ghosts and trumpets!"

"Let my man go," Lizzie and Wingate said in perfect-pitched unison, then stared at each other as if they had both shown up at a ball dressed in the same gown.

"Deputy," Judge Mason said, holding up his wife who swooned with a near-fainting dizziness. "They are innocent. I think I know what has transpired here tonight." He pointed downward to the streamers of rubber tubing that were hanging from beneath Homer's jacket, and the bent tin trumpet that was dangling from Tom Crank's belt. "I believe the poor Widow Borden has been the victim of an elaborate fraud to obtain her money and to steal her husband's will."

"What?" Wingate sputtered. "My intentions towards the Bordens have been nothing but honorable." She lifted her hands up in the air as if to demonstrate the straightforward fact that she had nothing up her sleeve. Unfortunately, at that very moment, the Spirit Box emerged from its hiding space within her blouse and slid down her hooped skirt to the ground, hitting the lawn with an audible thwack and turning on its end twice before coming to a dust-stirring rest.

"That," Wingate said glumly, "was not quite to my advantage, now, was it?"

Mrs. Borden stared in horror at the Box, then glanced up at Wingate who was edging her way towards the garden path.

Lizzie stepped forward and pointed a stern finger at the spiritualist. "Mrs. Wingate, I'm afraid I must ask you to remove the slipper on your left foot and snap your toes."

The woman's cheeks went slack. "What a preposterous proposal," she blurted.

"No, I'm afraid that I have to ask you to do this toe-snapping right away."

Wingate peered about as if trying to discover some escape route from the garden. With a sudden grunt and a lurch she bolted from the crowd and headed straight for the path off the property. At first Deputy Wixon made some attempt to follow, but Lizzie lifted a single finger encouraging him to stay his hand.

Before Wingate could reach the safety of the street, there was a quivering sound as if a large strip of metal was being twanged, and her agitated body seemed to lift completely from the ground. For a second she hovered in space as if suspended by invisible entities, and then came crashing with a sickening crunch to the earth. She flopped for a moment and made a crude noise as air escaped from her orifices, and then lay very still and silent.

Wixon's eyes were wide with astonishment. "I don't suppose you can explain that," he said to Lizzie.

"I can," Homer Thesinger said, beating his chest with pride. "I have laced the path to the street with my Super Durable Elasto String. The sound you heard was its marvelous flexing ability, like a piano wire being plucked. I have merely set a very primitive trap to catch a sophisticated bird."

"Well done, Homer!" Lizzie clapped, while Deputy Wixon raced forward to manacle the stunned spiritualist.

"And now for the Spirit Box," Lizzie said, holding up the shell-encrusted container. The Widow Borden shrank back with an awful creep. "No, Lizzie! King Philip! Awashuncks, Squaw Sachem of the Sakonnet! We shall all be brought to woe!"

"Nonsense. This is nothing but a curio that Mr. Borden proposed to be haunted to protect its contents. I'll show you."

Lizzie lifted the lid as several present put up their arms to shield their eyes from any supernatural events. As soon as they could see that there was no spirit, no blast of light, no demonic clouds or shrieks of the damned, they lowered their arms and peered into the interior of the quite ordinary box.

Inside was a rolled piece of paper tied with a red bow tie.

"The will!" Sarah said.

The two little twins started bouncing up and down like one of Homer Thesinger's Vertical Amusement Shafts. "The will! The will!" they were shouting.

Mrs. Borden was reduced to tears seeing her little precious girls so happy. She knew that they understood little, but they knew enough to know that their mother would be made immeasurably happy by the appearance of what they knew as "the will." And here it was: the ultimate secret of the dreaded Spirit Box of the Curiosity Cabinet.

Wixon, who had been poking around the clothing on the inert Elizabeth Wingate, came back to the crowd with a wrinkled piece of paper. "Here's a nice how-dee-do," he chuckled, glancing at its contents.

The Widow Borden took the paper in hand and arched it towards the kerosene lamp that dangled from the back porch. After a moment, her eyes flickered and she looked as if she would faint. Judge Mason came forward to support her and Lizzie and Sarah hunched over the paper.

Dearest Winnie, [it read]

The Borden family is in our proverbial grasp. As long as no one peers into the Spirit Box, we are safe. Snatch it while you can and we shall be done with this dreadful business!

I deeply regret having to procure the African potion to settle the Borden Affair, but the medical investigators were too dull-witted to see past the frightened look on Jonathan Borden's face. It was, indeed, the perfect crime!

Let Livermore be your paramour forevermore. My duckling!
My fine apparel of warm enswathed womanhood! I shall be
yours until the last trumpet sounds.

Doodles

Underneath was a crude line drawing of a man in a top hat and monocle
with exaggerated lips puckered up for amorous activity. Three X's captioned
the drawing. Sarah felt a shudder go through her skeleton thinking of
Livermore being capable of such feelings. And worse, being the recipient of
them.

Lizzie rubbed her chin. "Doodles? I never would have guessed. Not a
logical extraction from either of his names."

Sarah nodded, tears forming in her eyes. "The man killed my father."

"Yes," Lizzie said, staring at her compassionately. "I can only imagine
that feeling."

The Widow Borden snatched the Spirit Box from Lizzie's hands and held
it aloft as if it were some accursed thing. "You have plagued my life lo these
last few years, haunting my nights and making my own parlor a place of fear!
Be done with you!" And she smashed it upon the ground under her foot. It
splintered into shards and the sea shells rattled off into the grass. "Contact
Joseph Coffin immediately!" she announced. "There is a will to process!"

"Lizzie Borden," Sarah said, placing a congratulatory hand on her cousin's
back. "You have done fine work here tonight. Mother, we must reward our girl
detective with a most excellent and hearty meal and an evening's delightful
banter with our wonderful family. Even Tom Crank can join us if he chooses,
despite his culpability in this affair!"

Tom snuffled nervously. "I'd be most obliged. Poor Tom's a-cold!" And
he pulled his threadbare jacket tighter around his frame.

"Consider it done," Mrs. Borden said, holding up the will in a loose fist.
The entire family, Lizzie, Homer, the Judge and Mrs. Mason and Deputy
Wixon—all except for the inert Elizabeth Wingate and poor shivering Tom—
joined in with a healthy burst of laughter and applause.

AN EVENING'S RECAP

The scene at the factory office had been chaotic. The Fall River police had
approached Livermore directly, despite their fear of his stature and influence.
When the coterie of officers and the arresting lieutenant entered his office and
announced their charge, Livermore had cried out, "God's wounds!" and tried
to spear one officer with a large fountain pen from his desk. As a result, he
had to be tumbled to the ground and his hands tied behind his back with a

shackle. As they dragged him through the lobby of the textile administration building, employees who were so used to seeing him cross the marble floors in an ermine coat and stately top hat, now saw him frog-marched like a snarling beast, his obscene curses echoing off the ornate marble ceilings.

Lizzie and Sarah went once to the county prison to see Livermore in his cell. He sat in the furthest corner, swathed in shadow. His eyes pierced the darkness to hit them directly with a cold shudder.

"The hag and the harlot!" was his only exclamation.

Lizzie shot back with, "Perhaps, Doodles, you will be joining Mr. Tweed in chambers more suited to men of your industrious disposition." From the shadows, they could hear Livermore choking with rage and vengeance.

Then Lizzie and Sarah retreated and went to the local apothecary to relax over a few mugs of medicinal syrup water, Mr. A.E. Dobbs attending.

"How did you know that the will was in the Curio?" Sarah asked excitedly.

"It was very simple," Lizzie Borden replied. "I knew from the start that Wingate was a fraud. The rapping on the table top can be achieved quite effectively by snapping one's toes, and I did notice that Mrs. Wingate had on padded foot slippers, the type you can cast off quite easily just by lifting your foot. She also walked with a pronounced slant towards the left, showing that it was her left foot that was employed in the toe snapping."

"Marvelously perceptive," said Sarah, enthralled.

Lizzie laughed. "The credit for the discovery of the source of the trumpet blasts I give to Homer Ulysses Thesinger, Boy Inventor. I was not surprised to see Thomas Crank of Rodman Street involved. That poor boy can be easily led by wolves into walking off a cliff. Fortunately, the law has overlooked his breach of conduct and he is now at home nursing his wounds. For his role in the affair, I shall honor him with a stipend that will offset his college education, advancing his status in life far beyond what a bobbin boy in a textile mill would accomplish."

"That is very generous of you," said Sarah with a broad smile. "Poor Tom is merely a follower and was exploited by Wingate as much as my mother. We bear him no ill will."

Mr. Dobbs, polishing his glasses behind the counter, joined in with fascination. "But Lizzie, you still didn't tell us how you knew about the Curio?"

Lizzie smirked knowingly. "When Homer announced that King Philip was coming to enact his revenge, Wingate ran for Widow Borden's Cabinet of Curiosities. I found it quite significant that she grabbed the Spirit Box. I couldn't see how the Box would have been of any interest to Wingate. She no doubt wanted to keep whatever was in the box from being destroyed."

"Brilliant. So at that point you knew that Wingate was only after the contents of the box, and that she had no other interest in my mother or my family's affairs."

"Yes, and that she was in the employ of Thisbalt Ajax Livermore was obvious from the picture of her that was in his drawing room, proudly displayed on his mantelpiece. I knew there was a connection between the two."

A dark look came across Sarah's face. "But my word, Lizzie. Didn't your father hand over all his money to Livermore?"

"That is the beauty of the machinery I had set into motion," Lizzie smiled. "My father invested everything he had, so much so that when Livermore was exposed as a murderer, the Livermore Mill went into the hands of the investors. My father is now the de facto owner of the Mill! His fortune has quadrupled with one investment."

Sarah lifted her mug of syrup water and saluted her newly found friend. "Lizzie Borden, you are truly a girl detective of the first order!" Sarah exclaimed.

Lizzie nodded. "Yes," she said. "And a girl detective is what this world needs most at such challenging times as these."

The two Borden girls, joined by A.E. Dobbs, Pharmacist, engaged in hearty laughter and good company, sipped their syrup water and through the smoky glass of the apothecary front, watched the sun settle down on the quiet twilight of Fall River.

THE
EXHAUSTED
AMANUENSIS

October, 1877. Fall River, Massachusetts.

A Competitive Nature

On the very morning that Lizzie Borden of Fall River first heard of the puzzling Professor Welles and embarked on one of her most baffling adventures as a Girl Detective, she was lounging about in her sister Emma's airy and sunlit bedroom. Reclining on the fainting sofa, she basked in the heat and light of the southern exposure despite the late autumn season. Holding a pearl handled mirror up to her face, she solemnly examined her pouty cheeks, her wide eyes, and short eyebrows, feeling with her fingertips the youthful texture of her skin.

"One day, Lizzie Andrew Borden," she spoke softly to her own image, "you shall be known all throughout this Commonwealth. Children shall be singing your praises in rhyme."

The bedroom door disrupted her reverie as it rattled hard against the chair that Lizzie had propped underneath the doorknob. This was followed by a low grumbling, and the sound of footsteps drifting away in the direction of the adjoining guest room. Lizzie put down the mirror and braced herself, knowing that the second door into the room, the one from the guest chamber, would soon open. When it did, it pushed aside a small dresser that groaned forward into the room, in its turn disheveling the carpet. In the dresser's wake stood Emma Borden, her older sister, who, as was apparent from the street dust in her dress hem dragging behind her, had been running errands. Emma stood fish-mouthed, her eyes lighting up as she soaked in the invasion of her private bedchamber.

"I suppose you are wondering," Lizzie said, getting to her feet and hand-ironing her skirt, "why I am not locked up in my own room." Her eyes darted towards the small closet-like space that sat just off Emma's bedroom, in which a large bed dominated the area below a dim window. "Perhaps your seminary education did not include the art of measuring walls," Lizzie scoffed, folding her hands before her. "But if you examined that little crawl space that has been designated as my own, you will find that its dimensions fall quite short of those of your own spacious quarters."

Emma's eyes ran rampant over her sister's face, as if she were looking desperately for some hint that sanity dwelt within. She then pointed a finger towards Lizzie's bedroom. The finger stood in the air like a flagpole, quite firm in its meaning.

Wisely choosing to remain silent, Lizzie nodded, lifted her skirt, and moved towards the room. She then slammed the door behind her. Just as she had seated herself on the bed, wondering how long her punishment of solitude would last, the door banged open and Emma appeared, her words flowing just as freely as they had previously been frozen.

"You pretend that you have the disadvantage!" Emma shouted, her voice passionately reaching an upper register. "You think it's easy for me, to know that at any time you feel like it, you can come charging across my room, disrupting my peace? There is no privacy in this house! I can't sit still for a moment, not a moment. And for what? So you can shirk all your errands and run around this city playing like you are some sort of crime detective? I can't even imagine why you would do anything of the sort!"

"Perhaps it's because I'm clever," Lizzie said. "I may have the tiniest room in the house, but I certainly have the largest mind."

"And what is that supposed to mean? I want to remind you that I am thoroughly educated, and I have intellectual talents of my own. Did it ever occur to you that I might be offended by your posturing and all the attention that your superior intellect has won you? I can do your job just as well."

A broad smile graced Lizzie's face. "Why Emma, that would be delightful. Fall River will be all the richer for that. There are, sadly, plenty of unsolved crimes to go around."

Emma thrust out her chin. "I have no doubt in my mind that I can do what you can do. There is no trick to it. It's all common sense."

"Common sense? Well, then let me demonstrate, dear Emma, why I am a Girl Detective and you have been making runs to the family farm to gather the eggs for Father. I have a puzzle for you, and I want you to solve it. It is a simple one, but very revealing."

Emma's eyes turned upwards as they narrowed. "Proceed," she challenged.

Lizzie cleared her throat. "I begin. You enter into a cabin in the woods that is dark except for the moonlight coming through the single window. You find on a table a single match, a candle, a kerosene lamp, and a log of wood for the fire. Now keep in mind there is only one of each item, including only one match. Which would you light first?"

Emma closed her eyes as if trying to crank the gear shafts of her mind.

"That is obvious," she finally announced, staring proudly at her sister. "I suppose I should hang out my shingle as Emma Borden, Girl Detective, for I have solved your little mystery using simple reasoning. The candle will be the one to light first."

"Why so?" asked Lizzie.

"It is simplicity itself. The candle is the easiest to ignite, it takes but an instant. And besides: you never said the kerosene lamp has any oil, and the log of wood would need a fireplace, which you have not described. Thereby, confronted by a single match, a candle, a lamp, and a log of wood, I would first light the candle. Then if the lamp has any oil, I can transfer the flame to it from the candle, and if the cabin does indeed have a fireplace, I can set ablaze the log with the generous fire from the lamp. That, dear Lizzie, is how a seminary girl thinks!"

Lizzie smiled and began walking past Emma on her way to the hallway. "You would have to light the match first," she said as she rustled across the floor. "And that is how a Girl Detective thinks."

Emma stopped breathing as her hands curled into fists and Lizzie descended the steps, softly humming to herself. Somewhere in the distance, the town hall bell was tolling the noon hour.

THE PUZZLED PROFESSOR

Later that afternoon, a small nervous woman in a blue bengaline dress paced back and forth outside the Borden residence. As her wrung her hands together, the woman's anxious eyes were glued to the sidewalk as if she were about to make a monumental decision. As the horse traffic, street vendors, and pedestrians flowed around her, she gathered up her nerve as well as her skirts and ascended the steps to the Bordens' door. With newly found determination, she knocked.

"I must speak to the Girl Detective," she announced when a middle-aged woman, wiping her hands on an apron, answered the door. "Please announce me to Elizabeth, the clever one," the visitor said boisterously, as if she had rehearsed the line.

"Lizzie is her name," Abby Borden, Lizzie's stepmother, corrected her. "And if you must insist on indulging her in her sad fantasy, then so shall it be. Come in, please."

The woman, upon being ushered into the parlor, took a sweeping look at the small modest furniture and marveled. "I like your wallpaper," she said, pointing at the violet curls of flowers that snaked along the walls. "You have developed a tasteful interior."

"Thank you," Abby said. "I'm glad someone appreciates it. I'll go fetch the...uh... clever one."

A few moments later, Lizzie Borden entered the room, standing tall and stiff, a group of books in the crook of one arm. "I beg your gracious pardon," she said, smiling. "I didn't mean to keep you waiting, but I was in the middle of my mid-afternoon tour through these fascinating books on the medical sciences. I am taking a particular interest in the life story of Dr. Benjamin Rush, a man who, despite his erudition, experience, and wisdom, was a passionate advocate of bloodletting. It is a barbaric element of our medical climate, thankfully one that is in the process of disappearing. Why only the other day our family doctor told me…"

"Dear girl!" the woman said, stepping forward, encouraging Lizzie to move back towards the piano. "I come to you on most serious business; this is not about bloodletting, but my poor, insane husband."

Lizzie set the books down on the piano top and motioned the woman to join her on the lounge. "I apologize; it often takes moments to return from my studious trances. Please be seated, and I am all yours."

The woman nodded and began in a careful voice: "I am Julia Welles, the long-suffering wife of the great Professor John Wellington Welles, late of Brown University, now living in semi-retirement on Rock Street. We have been in Fall River for a full year now, and my serious wishes were for my husband to let his brilliant career fade behind him, and for him to enjoy his twilight years in domestic simplicity. For so long now has he been immersed in the study of mathematics. He has an almost unnatural obsession with the theories of infinity, although I fall short of understanding exactly what they are. All these years, I have taken pride in his excellence, his authority, and his natural ability to discipline his mind to solve any number of complex equations. In his prime years, he was a foremost expert on the paradoxes associated with these sciences, and learned men from all over the world would seek out his judgment and advice."

"Happily, I have heard of Professor Welles since he has moved to town," Lizzie confessed. "But my path has never crossed his, except for a paper he wrote on the speed of light through the ether that I may have read at the library. I am afraid that my knowledge of mathematics is not as strong as I would wish. However, I hold Dr. Welles in very high esteem. I am a little confused, however; do you come here with a problem relating to the Professor? I sincerely hope nothing is wrong."

"Nothing is wrong," Mrs. Welles announced. "But I am afraid that something may be wrong in the future."

"I don't follow."

"I can barely follow myself. My husband has put too much of himself into his work, laboring long and hard. In his solitude, he has long occupied his mind with mathematical paradoxes. One time he attempted to explain the theory of accelerating infinities. I followed him at first, but soon got lost in the logic, or lack of logic, and I pitied him that he often has to spend long periods inside his own mind with such thought-twisting equations. Always I feared that he would lose himself and become severely muddled. Indeed, I'm afraid that time has come."

Lizzie rocked in her seat. "What has happened?"

"Recently, he has come to the conclusion that..." She glanced about, making sure that Lizzie would be the only person to hear her. "I know this sounds crazy, but you must understand that my husband has been under enormous strain. He is of the opinion, based on his own research, that time as we know it—the time that we follow like a straight arrow throughout the day, from the moment we sit up in bed to the late hour upon which we fall back asleep—is not as straight as one would think. He actually believes that time is moving in both directions, that some of us are moving in one direction in time, and that others, like himself, are moving in another direction."

"What exactly do you mean?"

"He explains it thus: what is tomorrow for me is yesterday for him, and what is yesterday for myself is tomorrow for him. He claims that he is moving in epicycles, as he calls them; and states that although he experiences each individual day in the same time flow that the rest of us are moving in, the progression of days for him is backwards. He also claims that in this manner, he can predict my future, because to him, it is his past."

Lizzie felt a surge of disappointment. Instead of a mystery, she was hearing a simple case of an overworked mathematician who needed a vacation. "He is obviously too strained from his work," Lizzie announced. "I believe this is beyond my talents. Perhaps he should see a doctor about his nerves."

"Well, it is not his mania about the flow of time that I have come to see you about, nor is it the mystery that I expect you to solve. You see, tangential to this theory about time is his insistence that he has committed a horrible crime. And to make things worse, my husband contends that crime is still in our future, although for him, he remembers it as if it were yesterday. Indeed, it may very well have been yesterday for him."

"A crime? Has he indicated the nature of this crime?"

"I know this sounds incredible, but he claims that there will be a day and an hour in which he will cross from one time flow to another, and on that particular day, he will actually meet with himself. He claims that in a fit of hysteria, he will kill himself, or has killed himself."

Lizzie nodded and flattened out her skirts. "Yes, I see. Well, Mrs. Welles, I don't know how I can help you. I have heard of lunatics in our Taunton Asylum who have received some very excellent treatment at the hands of trained professionals. But I am not of that profession."

"I know, dear girl. I am sorry to bother you with such a strange tale this early in the day, and I know it must be severely confusing. But I do believe that my poor husband is suffering such delusional mania that he actually believes that he will be killed by himself. I know that this sounds fantastical, but I would like to hire your services to solve a crime that has not yet been committed."

"How can I do that?" Lizzie sighed. "Clues usually appear after a crime, and not before. Further, when the culprit of the crime has already confessed that it will actually happen in the future, and that he himself will be both the victim and the murderer, where do I even begin? The identity of the murderer is already solved, and the victim will only be dead for a single moment since the murder will happen backwards, hence there will be no more victim after it is committed. And the only victim before it is committed is the murderer. So where is the need for a detective?"

"Nonetheless, I implore you to take the case. I want you to spy on my husband and piece together the twisted labyrinth of his failing mind."

"How can I spy on him? From what you tell me he is a recluse on Rock Street, and I cannot be occupied by creeping around the windows and peering in. I'll be picked up by the police."

"I can arrange to have you brought in as his personal amanuensis. He has already expressed the need to finish his current thesis called "Zeno's Paradox and the Arrival at the Zero Point Through Eudoxus' Method of Exhaustion" for the *Providence Journal of Mathematical Studies*. He is desperate to finish the paper and have it published before he corrects his direction in time and survives his own murder of himself."

"Am I qualified for being an amanuensis for a celebrated professor? I clearly do not know the math."

"All will be taken care of. Previous assistants hardly did any work at all. He merely wants someone to follow him around and jot down notes that he spouts at random intervals. Oh, Miss Lizzie Borden, Girl Detective, will you help me in this matter? From the stress of it all, I am going mad myself."

Lizzie stared into space, trying to imagine herself taking notes for a Brown University Professor. There was an attractive allure to it, a quality of accomplishment. Since she had never attended a university, this would be such a great opportunity for her to experience the mind of a brilliant, if not slightly insane, man.

"I do suppose I can spare the time," she said quietly.

Mrs. Welles beamed with hope, her eyes widening, and her hands reaching out for Lizzie's shoulders. "Oh dear, I know there may be not much more to this than my husband's drift into madness, which, in and of itself, is a tragic thing, but to think that I may be able to prevent, with your help, his own murder of his future self, that gives me great comfort."

Lizzie rubbed her chin. "If this will accomplish nothing more than to give you a slightly more balanced peace of mind about your husband's condition

then I shall be glad to oblige," she said. "As you may have discovered from various sources, I do not charge any fee for my services, except the satisfaction that I am providing good deeds for my own community, by helping those who truly need help. That has been my reward."

"Yes, I have heard of your generosity. But I do insist on paying you a wage for your pretended work as amanuensis. It is only fair, since you will actually be providing my husband with the assistance that he needs. At least accept that small pittance, one dollar a day. Starting tomorrow morning at nine o'clock."

"Agreed." Lizzie was about to stand and walk Mrs. Welles to the door when she froze in place, a strange smile on her lips. "I do have one request," she said.

"Anything you wish, dear girl."

"I have an assistant of my own. Like me, she has a strong mind and is currently an apprentice to my detecting profession. I wish to bring her along, perhaps disguised as a cook or a maid. Do you have a position on your domestic staff that would suit a woman of about twenty-six?"

"Why, yes; indeed I do. The maid-of-all-work has recently fled the premises, disturbed over my husband's condition. We have put a notice in the afternoon paper, but have not yet received any responses. Do you think your assistant can handle a domestic job?"

"Without question. You have my word that she will provide impeccable service, both as the new maid and as a complement to my own investigation."

"It sounds splendid. What is her name?"

Lizzie closed her eyes, feeling for the answer with her mind rather than thinking it out. "Maggie," she finally announced.

"It is done," Mrs. Welles said happily, rising to her feet. "I shall see both of you tomorrow morning at nine. I will tell my husband that you shall be arriving in the morning."

Once Mrs. Welles was safely out of the house, Lizzie turned to ascend the staircase towards her bedroom, and spied Emma standing like a sentinel at the top of the steps.

"Maggie?!" Emma asked, her eyes rolling.

Lizzie lifted up her hands. "Now, Emma! I only had your edification in mind. I assumed you would want to take part in an investigation to improve your detective abilities."

"Maggie!" Emma repeated, her voice ascending.

THE IMAGINARY MAN

Early the next morning, Lizzie and Emma walked up Rock Street, their hands on their hats to counter the high winds that stirred about all the elegant homes of the more affluent families of Fall River. Lizzie was dressed in a tightly fitting dark blue Basque with a handsome row of buttons running down from a bow brooch under her chin. She was fretting over a pocket watch, which was nestled in her left hand, minding the time, pacing herself so they would arrive at their destination punctually on the hour. She seemed ever the intellectual young lady, straight out of school.

By contrast, Emma trailed her sister in a shapeless gingham dress with a stained apron that she had fetched from the cellar dustbin. A white cap bridled her head and a set of pockets flapped about her side flanks.

"I feel as if the entire city is laughing at me," she whispered to Lizzie.

"Nonsense," Lizzie said, not looking at her sister. "We are just a secretarial assistant and a Maggie out for a stroll."

They passed the elegant homes along Rock Street, distinctive dwellings with their gilded capitals and elegant balustrades, their Mansard roofs, and their sandstone walls and granite pillars. These magnificent homes, in which dwelt the mighty owners of the mills and the influential bankers of Fall River, were quite a contrast to the relatively shabby Greek Revivals to which Lizzie and Emma were accustomed, and seemed like Temples of Apollo by comparison. The two sisters paused before an imposing home that was graced with what seemed to be a mill tower proudly erect off the center.

"Here lives Jefferson Borden," Lizzie sighed. "Now, there is a Borden indeed."

"Did you not ever feel, Lizzie," Emma asked solemnly, "that Father could have secured us our place up here on the Hill? Perhaps if he had been far more ambitious, he, too, would have prospered as regally as Mr. Jefferson, and we would then be enjoying such a castle for our own."

"Father has done very well for himself," Lizzie said, pulling at her arm. "We cannot fault him if he has not risen as high as Mr. Jefferson, so there is no need to mourn our possible futures now."

They finally arrived at the residence of Dr. John Wellington Welles, an elegant and feminine pink house rising from the street. A narrow set of stairs led up to a small porch. They rang the bell and the lady of the house arrived, looking at Lizzie with a strange dislocation. "Ah, the new amanuensis. Professor Welles is quite anxious to get started."

"The pleasure is all mine," Lizzie said with a tiny curtsy, then ascended into the house. Emma, after a slight pause in which she detected she may be left behind on the porch, followed quickly before the door shut. Mrs. Welles looked at her with a discerning eye.

"And this must be Maggie."

"Yes," Emma said, pausing awkwardly then dipping her knees faintly. "I am...uh...Maggie."

"Fine," Mrs. Welles said coldly. "Before you do one moment of work, let it be understood that you are in service to our needs. There is one hard and fast rule here at the Professor's house, and that is the servants need to be ready at all times of the day and night to perform their duties. There is no such thing as having idle moments on your hands here. Having said that, you will now follow in the direction in which I am pointing. The kitchen is that way. Mr. Humphrey is waiting. He'll explain your duties."

Emma swallowed hard, took a desperate look at Lizzie (who seemed to be ignoring her), and started toward the kitchen with an awkward gait. When she was gone, Mrs. Welles broke out into a huge smile and poked Lizzie in the arm. "If that is truly not a maid, then she must surely be applauded for her theatrical skills!" she exclaimed. "I could not tell the difference. Come, Lizzie, I'll introduce you to the Professor."

They walked down the corridor by the side of the main staircase and came to a dark oak door that opened into a musty study with northern exposure, dominated by many bookcases. The volumes were laid out in long rows, so numerous that they obscured most of the walls, darkening the room. Centered upon the wide fireplace mantel was a marble clock, flanked by two golden lions. The clock's pendulum swung back and forth to an audible, persistent metronomic pulse.

Before the windows facing the street, stood a dark mahogany desk upon which lay mountains of paper, behind which rested a small man with an egg-shaped head bearing a fringe of white hair around the side. His face was obscured by an enormous shock-white mustache growing over his lips like a strange mammal that had deposited itself on his mouth for hibernation. The man's face turned upwards. Only the uplifting of the mustache gave Lizzie the suggestion that the man had smiled.

"This must be my new assistant!" he shouted in a thin and shrill voice, quite in character with his stature. To Lizzie's surprise, the man glided out from behind his desk without gaining any height. Apparently, he had been standing; his legs were comically short.

"Come, my child!" he said, a few stout fingers motioning her across the room. He stood in a frayed dressing gown with a tasseled cord, as if he had just risen from bed. "Come this way, and prove my hypothesis as you do so."

"I don't understand, sir. How can I prove anything by walking across the room?"

"All in good time," he chuckled. "Hmmm," he paused, one eye closing and the other one darting towards the side, suggesting that his mind was awhirl with fresh thought. "In good time. Yes, well, in one time line you are already across the room and are moving back towards where you stand now. But that is not your concern. Come, come!"

Lizzie walked towards him, slowing down as she approached a foot from his position, but his fingers still beckoned her forward. "There," he said, as she came to a halt, not three inches before him. "You have empirically proven it, just as everyone else who has walked across a room towards me has proven."

"Proven what?" Lizzie asked. "That I can walk across a room? I do have feet, you know."

"No, you have proven that Zeno's Paradox is but a mad delusion. The Paradox is the ancient riddle that points out a rather peculiar impossibility in physics. Between any two points there are an infinite number of points; therefore it should be impossible for anyone to actually arrive at any destination."

"I have heard of this paradox," Lizzie said, "in my high school class work. If you halve that distance between the two points, you arrive at halfway, then if you halve this distance again, you arrive at three quarters of the way. If you halve *that* distance, you are now getting closer to your goal, but since there is an infinite number of points to cross, you will continuously be halving the remaining distance for an infinite number of times which will take forever. It is truly a paradox."

The Professor's face brightened, his cheeks flushing. "My, you have made an old man very happy. I have never had an assistant who took any sort of interest in my theories, far less knew about them before I even explained them. I think this will be a very fruitful relationship. Please sit down, and we will discuss your duties."

As Lizzie sat, she glanced around the room and began to notice its details. Over by the door was a small standing Grecian column, upon which perched a bust of Isaac Newton, his long romantic locks cascading alongside sad eyes that were, despite all the years since his death, as yet, trying to discover the secret equations that defined the universe. About the base of the column were strewn crumpled pages from notebooks alongside several scientific journals and newspapers, as if they were leaves blown across a lawn. Upon the Professor's desk, scattered amongst the countless pages of a holograph manuscript, were various objects that seemed fitting for a man of science: a broken astrolabe, a kaleidoscope, a magnifying glass, and a large leather-bound edition of Jules Verne's *Journey To The Centre of the Earth*. The Professor noticed her specific focus on the book.

"Verne is an idealist, like me," he explained. "He believes in actually arriving at your destination." He clapped his hands. "Now, we will begin."

For the rest of the afternoon Lizzie sat enraptured by the Professor's eager sharing of his theories, elucidated with a clarity that surprised her. Although much of his discussion consisted of high mathematical principles, he spoke of them metaphorically, succeeding in painting visual pictures for her that drew out the internal logic of the equations in such a way that Lizzie, in reaching an understanding of his theses, would simply imagine arrows being shot from golden bows, stars glowing in infinite darkness, or beams of light crossing the vastness of the starry sky. As he explained more and more, Lizzie took renewed interest in his charming eyes, his generous mustache, and his gnome-like body. She began to admire him.

At the end of the day, as the sun slowly sank behind the river down the Hill, and the houses on Rock Street began to glow with the warm burning of oil lamps in their windows, he professed the need for a very early retirement, a little too early in Lizzie's estimation. He rang for Mr. Humphrey and the stone-faced man servant appeared as if he had vaporized from under the door. His well-structured and harsh mutton-chopped face bespoke many decades of dedicated service to his betters.

"Help me upstairs," the Professor told his man. "We are done for the day."

Mr. Humphrey escorted his master to the door of the study, then turned and twisted his head in Lizzie's direction, clearly indicating that she should wait for him. After several minutes, Mr. Humphrey re-appeared, a strange glint in his eye that resembled a twinkle.

"I need to discuss a delicate matter with you in private," he said.

"As you wish," Lizzie nodded.

"I am slightly embarrassed about this, but I do wish you would allow me a glance at the papers that you and the Professor are working on. I am a bit of an amateur mathematician and I can surely expand my education from seeing the progress he is making with his equations."

"I can oblige," Lizzie laughed, a bit relieved that he did not reprimand her for ill behavior towards the Professor. "I shall leave the papers on the study desk each night. Please allow yourself much freedom with them."

"I thank you," the proud man said, the glint disappearing from his eye. "And I urge you to keep the Professor in the dark about my request. He does not see me as a suitable recipient of his work, being that I am of the domestic class. If you know what I mean..."

"I certainly do," Lizzie sighed. How charming it was that a man servant was serious about advancing his education. She bowed politely and Mr. Humphrey turned to vacate the study. A moment later, Emma appeared in the doorway, her face drifting underneath a head rag, her hand holding a pail that sloshed with soapy water.

"Ready to go home?" Lizzie asked, raising a winking finger.

Emma scowled and threw the pail down to the ground, where the water splashed onto her boot. "Confound you, Lizzie Andrew!" she said, painfully. "You think I can just walk out the door like I have finished a school lesson and it is time for recess? Are you mad? They have put me up in the attic and I'm to send for the rest of my clothes in the morning."

Lizzie scratched her chin and pondered. "I did not think that Mrs. Welles would insist you play the role to the hilt."

"You make me the maid, I become the maid. You spend the entire sunlit course of the day with your midget scientist and engage in varied intellectual nonsense, while I scrub the privy and run the laundry down to the cellar. Tomorrow morning, I am to empty the slops!"

"Hmm, I will put in some inquiries to my employer."

"The employer from whom you have asked no pay but the wages of an amanuensis? How do you think that ranks against the pay of a Maggie?"

"I don't suppose they come close. Well, there is much to think upon."

A low voice, startling in its immediacy, rang out from the hallway. "The only thing to think upon, Maggie," it said, causing the two women's hearts to thump, "is that there is more ironing to be done." In the low shadows stood Mrs. Welles, an eerie displeasure across her furrowed brow. Emma withdrew with a frightened yelp into the corridor, racing towards the kitchen, dragging the pail with her.

"I am sorry to disturb Maggie's duties," Lizzie said, tipping her hat slightly forward. Mrs. Welles winked, then headed towards the front door, indicating for Lizzie to follow her. "Servants are a strange lot and it is best not to become too familiar with them. They crave attention and are often distracted from their duties."

"I will no longer pay her any mind," Lizzie said assuredly. Within moments, she was heading down Rock Street towards home, pondering Emma's dilemma, but wondering even more about the delightful paradoxes of time and space that the dear old Professor had put into her mind.

THE DARK CONCLUSION

Lizzie's session with the Professor on the second day commenced on a curious note. Upon her arrival, Mrs. Welles, whose face was flushed red with frustration, met her at the front door. "He claims he's been waiting for you for an hour," she announced.

"I am very punctual," Lizzie said, pointing to the silver pocket watch, which she had held in her palm during her entire walk to work. Mrs. Welles' face remained stiff and Lizzie went immediately to the study to find the little man was already dressed and well into shuffling his notes.

"Where have you been?" he asked, twirling the left half of his mustache. "The day is nearly half over."

"I'm sorry, Professor," Lizzie announced, "but by my reckoning it has just begun. It is barely past nine o'clock."

"Poor girl," the Professor said, clicking his tongue. "I shall make a mathematician out of you yet. Remember, the arrow of time is not constant. And it shall be sundown before we know it. Let's begin!"

Lizzie sat at the desk and spread out the papers on which she was taking dictation. She took up a stylographic fountain pen of the improved variety

that Mr. Cross of Providence, Rhode Island, had personally presented to Professor Welles as a tribute to his genius, or so the Professor claimed. She unscrewed a nearby inkwell, and with the help of an eyedropper, topped off the pen's interior chamber.

"Yesterday, you were quite adamant about the method of Exhaustion," she reminded him, "to eliminate the trivial infinities that bedevil any man who tries to accurately calculate the area of a solid object or the distance between two points."

"Not quite the precise definition," the Professor said, his crinkled eyes indicating a smile had grown under his mustache. "But I shall elucidate. It was the Greek Pythagorean Hippasus and his Theory of Incommensurable Magnitudes that started the whole thing. He shook up his community by announcing that not every value in the world could be reduced to a common unit of measure. He proved it by using geometry. It was said that he made this discovery while at sea, and that his cabin mates, who were also Pythagoreans, were so disturbed by his discovery that they tossed him overboard to his doom. Admittedly, I can't help but feel a sense of empathy with Hippasus, since I was also expelled from Brown University by my community of mathematicians. Yes, that was a sad day, but it turned out to be the start of a new life for me." For a moment, the Professor stroked his mustache and stared out the window as if remembering something from a long time ago.

He turned back towards Lizzie. "The idea," he continued, "that not everything in the world can be reduced to whole numbers led to Zeno's assumption that any quantity can be halved an infinite number of times and always be in the process of approaching zero, but never quite reaching zero. This led to the split between the concept of magnitude and the concept of number, freeing numbers from their paradoxes of infinity. The reason why I am so fascinated by this proposition is that it will defeat Zeno's Paradox and show that indeed one can transfer an infinite number of points by continually halving the distance, and eventually arriving at a destination."

Lizzie tried to scribble as much as she could, then eventually gave up. "Professor, I think it would be a lot clearer to me if you demonstrate how this relates to the concept of zero. You mentioned yesterday that zero is the point to which all phenomena tends toward, but at which they never arrive."

"Yes," he said, rubbing his cheek. "Always tending towards zero, but never arriving there. It is a maddening proposition, and one that I have devoted my entire life conquering." His eyes went dim, then he looked at her with renewed interest. "Perhaps, my dear amanuensis, it is time for me to lay bare for you my master plan as put forth in my new paper "Zeno's Paradox and the Arrival at the Zero Point Through Eudoxus' Method of Exhaustion" for the *Providence Journal of Mathematical Studies*."

Lizzie smiled at such a thought: his master plan. "Oh, do you mean that you have formulated a solution to Zeno's Paradox by defeating the Theory of Incommensurable Magnitudes?"

"Even better," he said, his eyebrows flaring. "By the Method of Exhaustion, one can reduce the increasingly infinite values, the ones that never quite reach zero, and exhaust them to a state of being trivial infinitesimals. Do you understand, my girl?"

"Well, it's not quite something I do on a daily basis" Lizzie confessed, putting down her pen. "Perhaps if you explain a little more..." From the corner of her eye, through the study windows, she saw Emma walking in the yard, holding in one hand a wooden three-legged stool and a long pole on the end of which was a limp mop. Her other hand still held the watery pail from the day before as if it had never left her fingers. She came toward the study window, glancing upwards at its tall height with a sense of exhaustion possessing her face.

The Professor glanced out the window to see what it was that had caught Lizzie's gaze. "What is that girl doing? It is nearly supper time."

"Professor," Lizzie said, authoritatively. "I have only had my breakfast a scant one hour ago. I can taste it now: coffee, oat meal, and bananas."

"Nonetheless, I must get on with my tale. At Brown University, to the frustration of the students and faculty alike, I pursued this avenue of the Theory of Exhaustion to defeat the Incommensurable Magnitudes and Zeno's Paradox. In a nutshell, they thought me to be insane. I was asked to leave."

"Clearly, they could not appreciate your advanced mind."

"Precisely. But in the last few months, I have been working arduously at this theory, and I must announce that the time—and indeed when I say 'time,' I mean 'time' in the full sense of the word—is coming soon. The answer to the riddle, as obvious as it may seem, is in my future. And the future is moving towards me at an accelerated rate."

"But Professor, the future is in the future, and we are moving towards it, not the other way around."

"Ah, you have revealed to me your precious intellect once more. Charming, for you are quite right. How can we tell if the future is moving towards us, or we are moving towards the future? And if we are both moving, then are we not accelerating the inevitable moment of collision?"

"That may be all correct, Professor. But how is this proof of your theory?"

"My dear amanuensis, when the future arrives, it will be proof that it is moving towards us. And that the moment of collision is the Zero Point in the Arrow of Time. That is when the Incommensurable Magnitudes shall be exhausted and all the past, the present, and the future will actually arrive at its destination!"

The room fell silent, broken only by the clomping noises of Emma's mop against the glass panes. Lizzie felt a lump in her throat. What the Professor just said made no sense to her, but it seemed not only plausible but also inevitable. She couldn't even visualize what it meant, or how it would physically manifest in the world—the Arrow of Time moving in both directions at once, colliding at a single point in the present and coming to a conclusion, arriving at a destination. It all gave her the same feeling of awe and fear that she often felt when she meditated upon some of the Holy Scripture's spiritual propositions, like the ones where, as in the Book of Revelations, the world shall come to an end and we shall all be called to a vast reckoning. How silly it all sounded when proposed by her Reverend; now Lizzie felt an urgency that made it feel so terribly imminent.

"Do you mean to say," Lizzie asked, "that all of the future and all of the past will collide in one moment?"

He nodded, almost religiously, as if the realization were too sacred to stain with words. "A singular moment," he said. "One that shall have no past or future. Imagine that. Our frail science and incomplete mathematics can only hint at the magnitude of such a moment."

"How much longer before this happens?" she asked daringly.

"Ah," the Professor said, tilting his eyes downwards. "That is what we are here to discover through completing my work. We must answer the question: when exactly will we reach the dark conclusion?"

Lizzie glanced once more in Emma's direction and saw her older sister struggling on the wobbly stool to keep her balance while extending her arms with the long handled mop. Emma's face was seized with a colorless desperation that bespoke only the task at hand. What innocence Emma seemed to possess now, engaged as she was in the mundane daily chores that we are burdened with, not realizing that a mere few feet away, men of science like Professor Welles were probing the very shape of time and space itself, coming to some startling and disturbing conclusions, dark indeed. How much Lizzie envied Emma now, that she did not have the burden of hearing so terrible a pronouncement. Who at the moment had less responsibility, the Amanuensis or the Maggie?

The Professor walked to the statue of Isaac Newton on its pedestal and placed a calm hand on his small shoulder. "This is a man who defined an absolute space and time. He believed that it all made sense, that one can reduce it all to formula. He didn't believe that all of history was moving towards a single moment, a singular event in which a single moment is so infinitely small no human mind would ever comprehend or even experience it. Some have announced it happened at some point in the past. Others say it will occur in the future. I say that both the past and the future are hurtling in their own respective directions towards this moment. A moment that so great a mind as Isaac Newton would find strangely impossible."

"The Dark Conclusion," Lizzie said in a whisper, her fingers trembling. "Professor," she announced. "I believe we would take our supper now."

"Excellent idea!" he said, clapping his hands and gazing at the clock on the mantle. "And just in time, I may say!"

It was only half past nine in the morning.

MAGGIE'S OBSERVATION

As the weeks proceeded, Professor Welles' schedule became more erratic and unpredictable. All evidence indicated that he was losing all sense of time, that he perceived the sun going down as the sun was coming up, and that he took his meals at increasingly shorter intervals. After a weekend break, in which Emma was surprisingly exempt (Mrs. Welles had planned a thorough cleaning of the cellar and kept the maid on through the Sabbath to execute that labor), Lizzie came back, bright and early Monday morning, to find the Professor stretching and yawning. It seemed as if he had trimmed his mustache even further, and took an inch off his scraggly white hair.

"Good evening," he said cheerfully. "I don't suppose you realize that you have missed an entire day of work. I may ask you to copy some of my notes while I get a good night's sleep."

Lizzie was about to remind the Professor that it was just a short time since the sun had risen, but she figured that he had clearly lost his reason and that he would not listen to any common sense even if she tried. So she helped the Professor up the stairs, and then came back down to the study where she found his wife, silhouetted against a window, staring at her.

"Mrs. Welles," Lizzie said. "I don't suppose you failed to notice that your husband's dementia has gone far beyond a belief in time travel. He now seems to believe that the days are getting shorter."

"An obvious ploy," Mrs. Welles said angrily. "And one I shall not suffer gladly."

"Ploy?"

"Is it not obvious that he is faking? I would have hoped that you would have seen that by now."

"Mrs. Welles, it was I who told you from the beginning that it was physically impossible for your husband to be moving backwards in time. I was the one declaring to you that he was faking. Why, you merely have to notice that he recognizes me every morning, that he remembers our conversations from the day before, that I do not have to introduce myself anew with each sunrise, as would be the case if my yesterdays were his tomorrows."

"But now," the Professor's wife said smugly. "I have better proof than that. Last night I found him cutting his own hair."

Lizzie frowned. "Cutting his hair?"

"Surely you have not failed to notice that his mustache and hair are growing shorter by the day. He was in the kitchen last night with a standing mirror shearing himself with a pair of scissors. Most certainly, he is trying to give the impression that his hair is growing shorter by the day, thereby keeping up the illusion that he is aging backwards. I've never seen a man so desperate."

"Desperate for what?"

"My husband has always been furious that he was expelled from the University, so convinced that his theories are correct that he would now do anything to prove them and redeem himself in the academic community. That is why he so badly wants to show that time and space are controllable, and that one can conquer the barriers posed by infinitesimal quantities." She paused for a moment to consider her own words. "Whatever those are…"

Lizzie giggled and lifted her shoulders. "Coming from a world where the most pressing issue of the day is a dress sale down street, I would say that makes your husband most admirable."

"Yes," Mrs. Welles said sadly. "But I wish I were married to a fruit peddler. He'd live by the clock: be on Bedford Street by seven, hawk his wares, count his daily wages, and then go home. For this entire year since he was kicked out of Brown, my husband has taken refuge in his arcane equations, and he has lost my affections." She stared despondently at the sunlight that brightened the windows. "Ah, if only he had taken an interest in the arts like his brother. I can see him as a painter, sitting in the wilds of nature with his palette and his smock. Yes, that would have been quite romantic indeed."

"He has a brother, then?"

"Sydney, two years younger, and two inches shorter. The two always argued that one wasn't younger or older than the other was. The wretched fools actually believed that they were both one year away from an ideal age that hovered somewhere in time between them. Likewise with their height: one inch off from some invisible center."

"Is Sydney also a man of science?"

Mrs. Welles laughed. "Hardly. He studied as an artist in Paris. Never have there been two brothers so unlike each other in temperament. Why, there is one of his paintings on the wall. Jonathan keeps it there as a memento, but cares not a jot for it. He took it as a birthday present, but I've never heard him say a kind word about it."

Lizzie stared at the wall where a framed painting portrayed a fog-bound seaman in cloth cap and a heavy straight-bodied jacket standing at the railing of some ship, presumably a whaler, his face pointing towards the sea, clearly contemplating the infinite, as most sailors, artists, and visionaries in any art or science will do from time to time.

"Perhaps they were not too dissimilar," came a soft voice. Both Lizzie and

Mrs. Welles jumped a bit as Emma, fully garbed in her maid raiment, stood with a bucket of soapy water in the doorway. "He paints the captain with such fondness for his inner longing," she said. "You can see it in his face."

"Then my husband has never noticed," Mrs. Welles snapped. "Maggie, I was showing the painting to Miss Lizzie. You have some wood to fire on the cast iron for supper. And you must remember my peg lamp is broken and must be mended. Hop to it, girl!" She clapped her palms together, and Emma shuffled from the room, her eyes cast downward, slightly mumbling as she moved along.

"You are unnaturally harsh on her," Lizzie said, sternly. "Remember, she is only a pretend maid."

"I am paying her wages, she will do as I say," Mrs. Welles said stiffly, and walked past Lizzie towards the hallway. "I believe he is ready for bed," she concluded, and disappeared.

Lizzie stared at the painting, trying to imagine a mind unfettered by the cares of everyday drudgery, or having to make a living, or to run errands for the household. The artist-brother must be a winged soul taken alight into a realm higher than the one pursued by the Professor, a realm all the richer for its plenitude of heart and feeling. And yet the captain in the painting was staring to sea as if he were separated from some destination where he desperately needed to be, some place that, once he arrived there, would make him feel whole again.

She turned and saw the piles of paper that she had been working on with the Professor. How vain and unnecessary it all was, for the vanity of fame in the scientific community, or the God-like desire to conquer the System of the World. All men who strove for such heights were in essence divorced from their own hearts, caring little for their fellow humans and everything for abstract principles, be they university professors or simple furniture salesmen aspiring to be bank managers. They were all poor in spirit, lacking in some quality that made painters, poets, or even the lead violinist from an Academy of Music concert, more masculine, more courageous, and nobler than all the men of money and textile that populated Fall River. How petty and insignificant seemed the contributions of a Jefferson Borden now, when Lizzie stood confronted by the lonely stare of that salty whaling captain: a seafarer about to embark on his journey to bring back the precious fuel of light from the ghostly void.

There was a flutter, and a shadow appeared in the doorway. It was Emma, again, her face partly in the shadows of the room. "You have heard it from her own mouth! The man is faking. So, we are suffering here for nothing! For the petty wages she hurls at me to endure her insults and clean her show-kettles?"

"Emma, I know this is troublesome, but we are almost at a conclusion."

"The man is insane. To me, that concludes it right there." She began to remove her apron. "I am going home."

"No, stay! Emma, I need you to trust me. Something is happening that we don't understand yet. I was hired to prevent the man from killing himself, and the attempt has not yet happened."

"According to him, it has. That's good enough for me. I want to get out of here before she orders me to bang out the horse blankets."

Lizzie went to the desk and plied through the papers with unsettled hands. "No, that does not satisfy me. To him, the past is the future. At least it is the future for us. Oh, it is all so confusing. If only the man would walk and talk backwards, something irrefutable to show that he is truly time traveling. But this whole business about epicycles perplexes me."

"Epi…" Emma tried to repeat. "What? Aren't those having to do with the planets?"

"Yes, from our position upon the earth, the planets seem to move in retrograde motion, against their natural direction." Lizzie paused and saw the confused look on Emma's face as if she were trying to remember some astronomy lesson from several years before. "Perhaps it is easier to understand like this: In the old times, we would see the planets make strange patterns in the sky. They would slow down, reverse direction, and then speed up, before reversing direction again. This was all the stranger because we believed that the earth was at the center of the universe, and all the planets and the sun itself moved about us. But putting the sun at the center changed everything, and explained the motion of the planets perfectly. Now we know that epicycles are not the planets moving backwards, but merely an optical illusion as they turn within their own elliptical orbits, unlike the perfectly circular orbits that dominated in the Ptolemaic system."

Emma's eyebrows came together at the center of her forehead. "I have no idea what you just said," she sighed.

"Oh, Emma. The lesson is very simple. When we thought we were at the center of the universe, we saw the planets as moving backwards. But when we placed the sun at the center, we suddenly realized…" She came to a sudden stop and glared down savagely at the papers clutched in her hands. They were covered with numbers, formulas, equations, all sorts of non-sensible abstractions that only a man trapped in his own head would believe, a man who thought that he was at the center of the universe.

"I think I know what's happening, Emma. Perhaps in a strange way, the universe just flipped around."

"Perhaps, but I only have a few moments before Mrs. Welles screams at me for not cleaning the grease pit."

Lizzie sat down at the Professor's desk and frantically looked for blank paper. She grabbed a sheet and then steadied an inkwell before her. "Emma, how many days have we been here? Five days on duty and two days off…"

"Seven days," Emma said in a huff, "with no days off."

"Yes, but the Professor was here the first day at nine o'clock, refreshed from a good night's sleep and ready for work. Then, as the days went on his schedule began to slip and he started to have delusions that he was several hours ahead of us, which would make sense if his own future were contracting backwards."

"I did notice such strange behavior. Why, only on Thursday did he believe that it was nine at night at only three in the afternoon."

Lizzie scribbled some notes, and then thought again. Emma stood paralyzed, knowing that there was something momentous going on in her sister's head, something that couldn't be interrupted, not even for Mrs. Welles' horse blankets.

After more calculations upon the paper, Lizzie drew an X-axis and a Y-axis and began to plot some points. They seemed to follow an exponential curve up the side of the graph. She hurriedly connected them, her drawing increasing in momentum as more of the shape of the line made itself evident. Finally, she thumped the paper and hurled the pen onto the table top, sprinkling the wood with ink.

"Emma!" she shouted. "On the morning that we had arrived, the Professor had completed an epicycle and was beginning to slow down to move back into retrograde motion."

"Which he is now doing?"

"Yes, he slowed down, then began his motion backwards again. He will kill himself in three days' time."

"Yet he is a faker. He cut his own hair to give the illusion of time travel. You heard Mrs. Welles."

"Emma, it is not important that the time travel is not happening, what is important is that he believes it. We merely have to follow the strange inner logic that he thinks to be true in order to determine what he is actually doing."

"He is moving backwards to the point where he is going to kill himself."

"Not kill himself," Lizzie said smiling. "Not suicide. He is going to confront himself and murder his double. That would not be suicide; that would be merely a metaphysical conundrum."

Emma shook her head, trying to dispel the thought. "When we find Professor Welles lying on the floor with a knife sticking in his chest, I would see that as a little more than a metaphysical conundrum."

Lizzie picked up the pen again and strained to puzzle out some numbers. "If only we can determine the exact moment where he will accelerate into that Zero Point that he talks so much about. He truly believes that he is destined to arrive at the end of time and he indicates that it is three days in his past. But three days in his past is three days in his future." She glanced up at her sister as if registering a forgotten thought. "Oh, dear Emma. Forgive me, you can go about your Maggie duties, I must work at this problem."

Emma snarled and reached for her skirts and turned to go. "It is all pig squat, Lizzie! I'm going to go home right now. And I'm going to move so fast, that it would seem as if our little house on Second Street were running towards me!"

A sharp jab stung Lizzie's mind when she heard Emma's words. She bolted to her feet, darted across the room and whirled her sister about, letting her see the excitement in her eyes. "Emma! You have given me the final piece of the puzzle! The Professor is accelerating backwards in time, so a day in the future is not a single day by our reckoning, but a shorter period of time. It is indeed as if the future were hurtling towards him. Oh, Emma, thank you!"

"What have I done? I don't understand."

"You've helped to solve the riddle of when Time will end!" And with a dramatic flourish of her arms, Lizzie disappeared from the room, leaving Emma to ponder the profundity of her own accomplishment.

"Well," said the weary house maid, pulling at her gingham. "I have solved the riddle of when Time will end. Wait till the girls back at the seminary hear about this one!"

THE RECKONING

As the clock struck eleven, Emma felt more uncomfortable than usual in her small attic room. A child's rocking chair sat against the far corner, casting an eerie shadow on the wallpaper, and Emma kept glancing at it as if to make sure that it would not move. For several hours, she tossed and fretted, thinking of how abused she felt, of all the unfair labor she was forced to endure at the hands of Mrs. Welles and Mr. Humphrey. The indignities were of a kind that not even a maid-of-all-work should be experiencing, and when this ordeal was all over, it would be Lizzie who would have to answer for it. Why did her sister remain so silent? How could she let this happen when it was within her power, as Mrs. Welles' confidant, to petition to have it stopped?

After much tossing, Emma was alarmed to see the glow of a lamp underneath her door. It grew brighter, there was a small tap, and the door began to open inwards. With a startled yelp, Emma sat up in bed and drew her knees up to her chin, only to relax when she saw Lizzie, still dressed in her day uniform, standing in the doorway with a gloved finger pressing to her lips in the gesture of silence.

"Emma," she whispered, and came to the bed, sitting gently on the side. "I have finally finished my calculations."

"I thought you went home hours ago," Emma complained.

"No, I hid in the horse barn and came back in through the unlatched side door just before sundown. I have just spent the evening calculating the exact hour when Professor Welles will confront himself as he passes in two directions of time at once." She paused, and then added, "Taking into account his rate of acceleration, of course."

"I'm assuming," Emma said dryly, "that the hour is near."

"The hour is in twenty-three minutes," Lizzie announced. "Right now the Professor is in bed, ready to wake. He has completed almost two cycles since we arrived that first day, Monday last, but because of his acceleration, time is moving faster for him. To him, it is one hour in the future for us, but that hour will only take him twenty-three minutes to experience. Therefore, we should be on guard at that time."

"Lizzie, you do know how absurd this all is. The Professor is insane and that's all there is to it."

She was about to speak again, but Lizzie's hand fell like a clamp over her mouth. Someone was moving up the hallway, no doubt drawn by the light radiating from Lizzie's lamp. Within a few seconds, the two sisters were startled to see Mrs. Welles in her nightgown standing in the doorway, her eyes dark and sullen. "Has he killed himself yet?" she asked, with a strange lilt in her voice. She sounded slurred, almost drugged. Her body swayed and she steadied herself against the door frame. "I cannot wait," she added. "I want my husband back."

"Mrs. Welles," Lizzie said, getting to her feet. "Are you all right? You seem intoxicated."

"Something in my drink," she said. "I can't..." And then she fell suddenly and heavily to the rug, hitting the floor with a violent thud. Emma leapt out of bed, and the two women struggled to get their employer onto the mattress. When she was flat on her back, she gazed upwards, trying to keep her eyes open. "He's faking, you know," she managed to say. "He's faking everything except the mathematics. Unless... unless..."

"Unless, what?" Lizzie asked, shaking her shoulders. "Mrs. Welles, you must tell me."

The woman fluttered her eyes one last time, breathed out, "Two equals Zero," and then fell soundly unconscious.

Lizzie thumped Emma's arm and announced, "We must take our positions immediately."

"Where, Lizzie? Oh, this is too horrible."

"It is almost over. Come with me to the Professor's study. We have so little time before it all comes to an end." With a sudden dramatic gesture, she extinguished the kerosene lamp, leaving the two to fumble their way through the darkness towards the staircase.

They slowed near the bottom, and then noiselessly glided into the study.

The room was very dark; the soft moonglow coming through the windows was not sufficient to light their path. Lizzie knew her way by habit, groping across the floor, until she arrived at the desk, her fingertips lightly touching the familiar inkwell. She picked it up and felt its comforting contours. It was heavy and seemed a good weapon to have in her hand in case of attack.

They stood there for what seemed like an eternity. For all the crazy talk about time speeding up, for Emma Borden it certainly seemed to be slowing down. The remaining fifteen minutes they waited in darkness and silence dragged on endlessly and offered so much fear that Emma's legs were buckling from the strain of standing.

"Emma," Lizzie whispered, her voice almost invisible. "The light, do you see it?"

A thin flicker appeared at the top of the stairs and began to work its way down. The two girls stood frozen as it grew in size, and they could just make out the quiet shuffle of slippers against the steps' carpeting.

"Here he comes," said Emma.

Almost immediately, from behind them, came a high pitched cackle, an almost insane laugh that struck the girls, as would a hammer being slammed at them from behind. Emma instinctively let out with a loud scream that ripped through the room, betraying the darkness with its volume.

"Watch out!" Lizzie cried, and there was a rushing noise, like something being swung violently through the air, cutting the space like a scythe, followed by a shattering crack on the other side of the room as glass was being hit with a violent force. There was a crazy series of screeches as the gears in the mantle clock, fractured by the projectile, came to a sudden halt.

The light that had been moving in the outer corridor suddenly burst into the room, filling it to the far corners with a yellowish glow. Just as soon as it entered, it fell rapidly downwards, clattering against the floorboards. Whoever had been holding the light had quickly placed it down to free up both his hands that now emerged out of the hallway shadows clutching what looked to be a huge bow and arrow.

"So," Lizzie said, "he is here." She pointed at Professor Welles, dressed in his frayed dressing gown, his hair sticking out at odd angles from his skull, his eyes wild with delight; he was framed by the doorway, holding aloft a composite Ibex horn bow. An arrow trimmed with blue feathers about the shaft was drawn within it. His fingers shook as they contained the tensile strength of the weapon.

"I am also here," came the voice behind them.

They whirled about to see an incredible sight, a second Professor Welles in an identical gown, down to the golden tasseled cord, holding an exact replica of the composite bow, except that his arrow had red feathers fluttering from its shaft.

Lizzie momentarily pondered the peculiar situation, but then her face was awash with amazement, as if something dark and ponderous had just been lifted from her. Her body straightened and relaxed, her eyes sparkled. She stepped forward towards the study door and said boldly, out loud, "Professor, I believe we have arrived at the Zero Point."

The man moved slightly towards her and Emma, his eyes lining up the shot. "Fear not," he said. "I am not going to harm you. The arrow can never reach anything I fire it upon! Zeno was correct when he created his paradox. I shall show you!" The bow and arrow angled directly at Lizzie as she stood proudly holding her inkwell.

Emma was paralyzed with fear. Deep within her, she felt a dread that surpassed anything that she had ever felt before. The care for her own safety fled and was replaced with the most intense desire to protect her little sister. Years before she had promised her dying mother that little Lizzie, then almost three years old, would be in her protective charge for the rest of eternity. Nothing would ever hurt little Lizzie; Emma would see to that.

"The arrow can most certainly reach her!" said the Professor Welles behind them. "I have conquered the infinitesimal quantities. I have exhausted the area under the curve of time! Watch and you shall see!"

Emma's mind was in danger of flickering out like the flame of a candle being blown by a strong wind. She wanted to disappear, to close her eyes and discover that nothing was happening at all, that she was back at home, safe within her room, feeling silly that her biggest problem in life was that her younger sister had to walk through her room to get downstairs. How trivial and base seemed all the problems of the world compared to this.

But here she was in the Professor's house, and not home, and the Professor had split into two men, insane men at that, bent upon killing each other, or killing Lizzie, or killing Emma herself. What a paradox, and how unbelievable. The Professor moving backwards into his own future will meet himself as a traveler from the future moving backwards into the past. And it is the Zero Point at which they would meet, two infinities coming together at the exact center that was Lizzie.

But they cannot be the same, she said angrily to herself. *Something must be different. Think, Emma! Lizzie needs you.*

Something in her remembered a strange puzzle. A match, a candle, a lamp, and a log. Which do you light first? Lizzie had posed such a question not to teach her what to do when literally confronted by such a situation, but to teach her how to think, how to factor out the mystery to arrive at an obvious truth by exercising the most elegant way of thinking. It was like one of those imaginary number lines that the Professor had talked about, not traversing the X-axis or the Y-axis, but moving at a right angle to both of them, moving like an arrow outside the cycles of time.

"Yes," she thought. "Yes."

"Lizzie," she shouted, and as her sister glanced in her direction, she moved her face towards the framed portrait of the whaler on the far wall. Then she glanced down at Lizzie's hands. The Girl Detective understood immediately, and with a savage heave, hurled the inkwell into the air in the direction of the canvas. Both Professors seemed frozen in their tracks, suddenly distracted from their deadly experiment, and followed the arch of the inkwell. It hovered for a fraction of a second right before the murky canvas as if it were trying to make up its mind about crossing the remaining space towards its mark, and then, with a surprisingly light crackling noise, the glass broke and black liquid splattered across the face of the captain.

"No!" cried out the Professor with the blue-tipped arrow. "What have you done?" His bow dropped from his hand, the arrow tumbling forward after the loss of its tensile strength, and clattered onto the floorboards. "You have destroyed my masterpiece!" The ink was spreading across the canvas, dripping downward as if the captain's face was melting black wax. He raced towards it, spreading his hands across the painting as if trying to halt the progress of the defacement. With a single deft and athletic movement, quite unlike anything Lizzie or Emma had witnessed before, the second Professor from the other side of the room darted like a swift deer across the space between them, and clobbered his double across the back of the head with his composite bow. There was a strange sound, as if a mill throstle had become unwound and all the cotton threads were being spun crazily into the empty air. Then the assaulted man staggered with a groan only to fall flat on his back, his bushy mustache blowing upwards towards the ceiling as the air escaped from his lungs. He rolled on his side and fell into darkness.

"I never liked that piece of plug-ugly junk anyhow," the other Professor quipped, looking up at the defaced painting. His bow went to his side and he stepped forward to put a kindly hand on Lizzie's trembling elbow. "Now, my dear, don't be afraid. Sydney won't hurt you. If I were you, I would call for Humphrey to come and detain this man until the police can arrive."

Lizzie glared at him with startled eyes and said, "Professor John Wellington Welles?"

"At your service," he said, with a slight dip of his bald head. "Miss Lizzie Borden, I don't believe we have ever met. But I have heard about you during my long absence."

Emma marveled at the scene. "This wasn't the Professor?" she said, pointing at the body on the floor.

"No," Lizzie said, not taking her eyes off the small man with the funny mustache and the even funnier grin. "I don't think the real Professor has been here ever since he left Brown University."

"Oh," the sly Professor winked, "I spent a few days at home here and there. Of course, I did send this damned painting on at his request. What a silly vanity, and how unlike me. Well, it's a miracle that my wife ever agreed to consult with a detective, but I believe that was part of his plan, to murder me and win her over, as if she would never guess the switch. And of course, he coveted my life as a world-renowned expert on the mathematics of trivial infinitesimals. When there was talk of revoking my expulsion from the University, I suspected he figured out a way to kill me and take my place."

"This was all his doing?" Lizzie asked, still trying to comprehend the bizarre events of the evening.

"Why, of course. At first, it seemed like a way to cure his lunacy, his belief that he was moving in epicycles, that he was actually becoming me on his retrograde motion through time. I thought at first that this would be… uh…good for his mental health. Of course, we changed places just about a year ago, and I fed him the mathematics by post. Sometimes I would come into the house disguised as a handyman, and leave papers on his desk. He memorized my lectures and formulas and grew obsessed with the idea of refuting my Zero Point theory. He wanted to believe so desperately that infinity could never be crossed, and man would never, ever arrive at his destination, either on the physical plane or in the realm of the heart and the spirit. He was forever an infinitesimal distance away from his desire. Perhaps that's the painful truth of all artists."

"But how could he believe such a thing," Lizzie asked with a shudder. "He was preaching exactly the opposite to me over the last week. He believed in the Zero Point theory."

The Professor clicked his tongue and shook his head. "You really think he wanted to finish the theory?" he said, quite humored at the thought. "He was delaying the answer, ready to sabotage the entire enterprise. He knew that he had till midnight of tonight to finish since that was the point at which I would return. He didn't foresee the possibility that the detective hired to solve his murder before it happened would actually be the very person who would also complete the mathematics."

"Me?" Lizzie said. "I solved the refutation of Zeno's Paradox?"

"Of course I have to recheck all the calculations," he said, poking through some papers on the desk. "But if you were able to calculate the precise moment of my return through my brother's somewhat psychic ability to sense the future, then you have indeed puzzled out one of the most perplexing aspects of my life's work. Perhaps one day, my dear Lizzie Borden, I shall explain it to you."

"Professor, where have you been this past year?" Emma asked, feeling a bit uncomfortable and trying to change the subject.

"Ah," he said, coughing into his fist. "Yes, well, that's my little secret. But let's just say I got a lot of fresh air and I created a good deal of very bad paintings."

"Remarkable," Lizzie announced. "But before I wrap up this case, I wish to enquire about the safety of your good wife."

"She shall be fit as a fiddle, I have taken care to give her just the right amount of a tincture of laudanum to put her out for one hour."

"Your wife didn't know about any of this?" Emma asked, the magnitude of the situation gradually dawning on her. "How could she not know that another man was impersonating her husband?"

"She suspected, of course," the Professor said, cheerfully. "But Mr. Humphrey knew my secret and kept an eye on her to make sure she would not suspect. Of course, surrendering the amorous pleasures of life was a necessary step. I suppose if Sydney had tried to take advantage of poor Julia in the bedroom, then she may have realized."

"How so?" Lizzie mused. "By the touch of his hands upon her, the quality of his affections, the tender movements that only a wife can detect in a loving husband?" For a brief moment, she imagined the touch of a man's fingertips on her cheek and shuddered.

"I suppose," the Professor chuckled. "But you do know that in many ways, Sydney and I were always two inches off from each other."

"Oh!" said Emma, raising her hand to her ovaled mouth as Lizzie stared down awkwardly at her feet.

The silence was broken by the arrival of Mr. Humphrey who seemed to slide into the room between his mutton-chops, dragging his permanent frown with him. "So," he said, blankly staring at the prostrate Sydney, then raised his stiff chin at the Professor. "It is accomplished," he added, his voice trailing off to a low pitch.

"Yes, my good man," the Professor laughed. "You have played your role well. And many thanks for the telegram telling me the exact moment and location indicated in Miss Lizzie's notes. The bow and arrow turned out to be a valuable bit of advice."

"I strive to render impeccable service," Mr. Humphrey explained, then gave a low stare at Emma who shrank a bit from his presence.

"Time to leave Miss Emma alone," the Professor said, waving an assured hand at her. "We will find a new maid. In the meantime, Humphrey, be so kind as to ring round the police station and fetch an officer. Sydney here may not be long in waking."

By the time the arresting officer arrived, they had tied Sydney Welles to the chair behind the desk. Officer Bence, who knew Lizzie quite well, and so wasn't surprised to find her in so strange a circumstance, gave a perplexed look at the crazy old man holding the large hunting bow, and at the other man who looked exactly like him bound in rope and slumped in a chair.

"Lizzie Borden," Bence said quizzically, "what trouble have you gotten into this time? And at so late an hour?"

"I have solved a murder that never took place," she said proudly, and went on to summarize the events as she understood them for the benefit of the policeman.

"Yes," the officer said, shaking his head a bit as if trying to dislodge a thought that was stuck on one side of his mind. "If I can follow any of that, I suppose it is the Professor tied to the chair that I must arrest for attempted manslaughter. Let's get him up and see what he has to say."

Bence slapped the bound man a few times on the cheeks, arousing him from his unconscious state. At first, Sydney was confused, barely able to focus his eyes, and then he saw the police helmet atop the clean-shaven face glaring at him. "I suppose you are here because of the murder," he said groggily.

"Which murder?" Bence asked.

"The one I am going to commit in twenty-three minutes time. I have been planning it for a year now, methodically and to the last detail. I cannot convince you otherwise, I suppose. It is a brilliant plan, one that my brother will never suspect. I have even arranged for a girl detective to investigate afterwards, but she will find nothing. She will come into this house posing as my assistant, but she will not find a single clue, because the poor girl will be moving backwards in time. There is no way she could solve the murder because she will be here before it happens. And it will happen you know, all in twenty-three minutes time."

"He's now moving away from the Zero Point," the Professor said, pointing towards his brother's sullen face that was collapsing back into sleep. "I suspected as much. He is no longer any danger to any of us."

"Professor," Lizzie said, holding out her hand, "I must congratulate you on a clever scheme well-executed. But I must ask you a very important question."

"What's that, my child?" he asked, his hands taking hers.

"You could have stopped this at any time. Why did you take such a risk and let yourself come very close to being murdered by him?"

"Yes," said Emma, enthusiastically. "And Lizzie and I were in grave danger as well. How could you, with all clear conscience, put us at so much risk?"

"Risk?" the Professor said, genuinely puzzled. "My brother believed that the arrow could never conquer Zeno's Paradox. His arrow never would have reached any of you, or me for that matter."

Lizzie fell back a pace, suddenly feeling a bit uncomfortable. She looked at Emma who was starting to open her mouth, but who also fell silent. Finally, Lizzie nodded and mused, "I suppose it no longer makes a difference; it is all twenty-seven minutes in the past by my reckoning. As we move forward, it will be more and more a thing of the past, swiftly to be forgotten."

The Professor raised his eyebrows. "Time does fly, doesn't it?" he quipped.

AFTER THE END

The next morning, the two sisters walked back down Rock Street, down the Hill towards their own familiar neighborhood, where the smaller houses nestled against each other were separated by small lawns and modest picket fences. Emma had taken off her maid hat and side pockets, and had deposited them in a midden heap behind the police station. Lizzie kept her proper gait and straight-backed appearance, clearly proud of herself. After a few blocks, she stopped and looked pleasantly at Emma.

"I don't believe I could have done this without you," she said, tenderly.

"Do what? Solve the mysteries of time and space? Refute Zeno's Paradox? Tell me, Lizzie. How many show-kettles did you buff this week? How many chamber pots did you empty into the privy?"

"I know you feel you have gotten the proverbial short stick, but I do assure you that in the end, dear sister, I believe you did something that is so precious and so dear on this earth, that I cannot imagine it having been done by any other person," said Lizzie.

"What's that? Measure out the ox gall to brighten the bed sheets?"

"No, Emma," Lizzie said, reaching forward and touching her sister's cheek. "You saved my life. No greater love..." She stopped herself short, noticing that a slight tear had appeared in the corner of Emma's eye.

"I did," she said. "And I do ask one thing in return."

"Anything, Emma. I owe you all the world."

Emma closed her eyes and took a few breaths, then opened them to face her sister. "Only that in the future, you ask me..." She stopped and closed her eyes again. "That you ask my permission before you use my room as an office for your detective business."

By the time Emma had opened her eyes again, Lizzie was laughing. "Of course," she said. "And I shall knock on your door before leaving my room so as not to disturb or startle you."

"Fine," Emma said, shaking Lizzie's hand. "Perhaps this is a start. Let's get home and catch up on our errands. I'm sure they are quite numerous by now, and the day is still young."

Lizzie produced her pocket watch, lifting it high, startled to see that the hands were not moving; it was frozen at midnight of the night before.

"Odd," she thought. "But curiously fitting."

Arriving at the front of 92 Second Street, Lizzie and Emma found Mrs. Borden, their stepmother, by the side of the house, holding some pails. She was surprised to see them, and couldn't stop staring at Emma's shapeless dress.

"I was the Maggie," was all Emma could say by way of explanation.

"Well, you can stay the Maggie for ten more minutes," Abby said sternly, handing her the pails. The water inside was brackish and smelled terribly. "Empty these and get me some fresh water."

"Ten more minutes won't hurt you," Lizzie said. "They will go by in an eye blink."

"And you," Abby said, poking a finger into Lizzie's shoulder. "Go fetch some more wood, we are going to make a fire. Your Father has a terrible cold and must stay warm."

Lizzie nodded and raced for the wood bin, dancing across the lawn, happy to feel her own family soil under her feet. By the edge of the stack was a hatchet, its gilt already faded, the handle threatening to splinter her hand. She stared at it for a moment; then lifted it up towards her inquiring eyes.

"Two equals zero," she thought. Like an axe moving backwards from two pieces of wood, and causing the two halves to fly into each other, merging into one. It all seemed so absurd. How could time move backwards? And how could anyone or anything travel across an infinite number of points?

She raised the hatchet over her head, feeling its heavy weight pulling backwards, the density of the metal, the earthiness of the wood. She always felt, when raising a hatchet for domestic chores, to be seized by some deep instinct that commanded her to wield the weapon with a savage justice, to look upon the target of her attack as a deadly menace that she must destroy or else all was lost for her, her family, her city. Perhaps as Fall River's pre-eminent Girl Detective, this menace was the bad men who plotted evil, who tried to control others against their will, or simply could not mind their own business without ruining the safety of their fellow citizens. Either way, Lizzie wished that in some small way, she could wield the hatchet in an act of justice against the dark and dangerous criminals who thought nothing of taking a life, or seizing another man's property. Would she ever reach that goal? Or was it ever an infinite number of steps ahead of her? She could do nothing but try her very best.

She fixed her gaze intently on one single log of wood that protruded from the stack, a solid half foot beyond the rest. It seemed so vulnerable, so open to attack by any weapon that would come flying through space, bringing a final judgment with its treacherous momentum.

But yet, she thought: Would the hatchet ever strike its goal? How will it conquer the paradoxes of infinite space? To test her burning curiosity, she swung the hatchet through the air, over her head, down towards the wooden log.

It seemed to take an eternity.

THE
TRAUMATIZED
METALLURGIST

1876. Fall River, Massachusetts.

Vantage Point

The Wampanoag Iron Works consist of a series of granite buildings grouped in a majestic compound along the curve of the Taunton River at Mount Hope Bay. The walls, which had originally been hewn from the quarry beds of a nearby cascading stream, define with precision the Iron Works' machine shops, engine rooms, furnaces, forges, and administrative building. The collective whole of these purposeful spaces breathes in the rich ore of the Earth, and from thence exhales the artillery cannons, barrel hoops and nails, iron castings, and ammunition which are destined to be consumed by other industries for other human activities. Like the textile and cloth manufactories that cluster against the river shoreline and back along the stream, the Iron Works bear witness to the indomitable will of their human creators and their unquiet domination of the once-primitive land.

Now consider this industrial enterprise from the perspective of the spiraling goshawk, who, breaking from the New England wilderness in search of the perfect crag on which to perch and survey its dominion, thus comes across this tangled plain of brick, wood, stone, and metal. What can be happening here? In times past, this landscape was a furry carpet of wood, a sprawling forest of cedar and oak, cut through by a falling stream, all bearing little evidence of the strange animal called man. Now the trees have been beaten back; instead, the great granite edifices that belch the hot breath of smelting iron arise in the clearing, themselves surrounded by a dense and filthy hive of ground dwellings. From such structures an army of servile men, women, and even children, emerge each dawn, their faces bent towards the dusty ground, joylessly marching through the gateway of the compound and not reappearing until the sun has set beyond the western horizon. To our long-tailed hawk, this entire cycle of human labor must be baffling indeed, being so against his free nature and unbounded spirit.

By coincidence, the sentiments of our airborne observer are being shared by a man who stands in the upper-floor window of the administration building, his attention fixated upon the rail yard and the small trains that puff and clatter, bringing their heavy loads of iron product to the shoreline and the cargo steamers that await their burden. The man in the window stares at the yard stacked with pig metal and coal bins, his eyes widening as if he were seeing for the first time a world he previously would not have thought possible. Perhaps he, like the hawk above, had also gazed into the wide plain off Mount Hope Bay, expecting to find familiar fertile earth, fresh water, lush trees, deep green, and blue skies, a bountiful land that would feed the needs of his species; but he has instead discovered the crowded dwellings and the polluted refuse of human life. The biblical Adam has not left the garden, but the garden has been transformed about him into one of blasted earth and painful labor.

Let us examine this human observer for a pace, pondering his immaculate cotton suit, his fine threaded pants and shiny leather shoes. Let us take note of the gold ring on his left hand, and the resemblance he bears to the suited figure in the mighty oil painting that dominates the eastern wall of his office. We quickly recognize that here stands the owner, president and chief agent of the Wampanoag Iron Works, Colonel Richard Ulysses Anthony: grandson of a legendary founder of Fall River's industry, and one of the wealthiest men in Bristol County.

Now that we have identified him, let us wonder why his face has turned sullen and distraught; and why he suddenly turns like a startled child, racing from the window, his legs folding beneath him as he curls on the floor beneath his desk, his knees to his chest and his eyes filled with anxious tears.

What can be the matter with this man that he should tremble so? With all his power and wealth, should he not be content and joyful in his existence? As he sobs, he reaches out with one hand towards the window, as if yearning for something forever beyond his reach.

This is a mystery that we must ponder.

THE PHYSICIAN'S ADVICE

June, 1876.

The Colonel had not been seen all morning, but it was known to his administrative staff in the outer offices that he was hidden behind his bolted door. He had arrived at nine on the clock, his furrowed brows, framing very odd facial twitches. He withdrew into his office, saying nothing, but having established a gloomy unrest amongst his clerks and accountants as they continued with their labor, all the while gossiping in hushed voices. "What can be wrong with the Colonel?"

After a time, they knocked politely, hoping to hear his familiar voice, but receiving only silence. So they pounded harder, barking petitions for him to come forth and demonstrate that he had not been hurt in any way. Sensing possible danger, his executive secretary had finally called for Doctor Ames, the only man who was allowed to discuss delicate matters of health with the Colonel.

The doctor alighted from his horse-drawn buggy before the red-bricked administration building and walked stolidly through the arched entrance, his black satchel by his side, a pince-nez straightened across the bridge of his steep and narrow nose. A rigid beard jutted outwards, itself a hairy extension of an enormous chin, and preceded him as he walked forward. A group of nervous factors followed him up the main stairs and through the outer rooms. "He has not been himself," they told him hurriedly. "Such moods he has shown." "His demeanor has been sullied!" "You must help him, Doctor Ames!" And so on, straight to Colonel Anthony's door. "He won't open up," confirmed the chief day clerk. "We've tried everything short of battering it down."

The doctor grasped his leather satchel with both hands for assurance, and then let forth a battery of knuckle raps upon the wooden panels, shouting at the margin of his lungs, "Richard, you'd best open up or I shall treat you quite indelicately at your next physical."

Within a moment, the bolt unlatched and the door was quite easily opened. The doctor raised a hushed finger of silence to the gathering crowd of workers before slipping into the office, swinging the door shut behind him. Once inside, his eyes began to adjust to the harsh contrast between the dark mahogany of the furniture and the sunlight streaming from the tall bay windows. The room was replete with wooden cabinets stuffed with ledger books, with endless bundles of accounting reports, and with large leather-bound volumes whose slightly unpleasant smell testified to how many years they had been sitting unopened on their shelves.

The Colonel was standing like a wounded child in the center of the room, his back slumped, his knees weakened. "Help me," he said plainly.

"My dear Colonel," the doctor said, appearing calm. "Whatever could be the matter?"

"I only wish I knew," the man lamented, staggering for a chair that rested against the side wall. The doctor helped him into its seat and then touched his anxious patient's forehead.

"You are cold as ice. I surely hope this is a purely emotional affair. Your health has been impeccable and I intend to keep it that way."

The Colonel pushed back his forelocks. "Ames, you and I have known each other for many a year."

The doctor's smile was small and slanted. "Your entire life, in fact. I caught you with both hands when you leapt into the world." He lifted a tight fist. "Why man, where has fled the zeal and optimism of that primal moment? You stand before me like a ghost."

The Colonel turned his face towards the sunlight, revealing watery eyes. "It happened suddenly, at midnight. All these years, all the bone-crushing work, the endless hours laboring to build this enterprise, to please the stockholders, to balance my interests against the operatives and the labor agitators. It all came crashing down. I can no longer think of it. No, my mind cannot go there!"

"Go where?" Dr. Ames asked, solemnly. "No one is asking you to go anywhere."

"Not a place, but a word. I cannot utter the word any more, nor look upon the hoops and nails and cannon into which we have cast it."

A beam of understanding came over the doctor's mind. "You mean the metal upon which this factory has been built?" The Colonel nodded, his face trembling. "Don't worry, Richard, I won't utter the word. But you must explain: it truly terrifies you? Surely this is the result of a prolonged and painful stress. Your job has driven you to the ground. I suggest you get away from it all. When did you last spend a day with your family? Or at a watering hole doing some swimming? Since when have you spent an afternoon on the shore of Gardner's Neck practicing your artistic skills with the paint brush?"

"Such pleasures are beyond my reach," the Colonel admitted.

"How long have you felt this?" asked the doctor, sternly. "You have been hiding it from me?"

The Colonel lowered his eyes ashamedly. "Do you recall when the operatives took to strike, and filled the courtyard waving their hammers and I hid myself in an abandoned reverberatory furnace? At the time, I explained my behavior by claiming I had been struck on the head with a ball-peen and had become senseless. However, it was far more than that. I was in my rational mind, of sorts."

"Do the workers frighten you so?" the doctor asked, his voice softening.

"No, it is not the workers I now fear; it is not they whom I am unable to look upon without being consumed by horror. It is the metal, the product." He turned his face and raised a forearm over his eyes. "Do not make me speak of it, if you treasure my humanity!"

Doctor Ames let out with a hearty chuckle. "Richard, you are showing your humanity at last. There is nothing inherent in the substance in question nor any product of your factory that will harm you. Your mind is producing danger where no danger exists."

"But it is all around me," the Colonel shivered, drawing in his knees. "I dare not leave this office for fear of confronting it everywhere. In the wrought fencing through which I must pass to get to the street; in the frame of the buggy I must ride to reach my home; in the railing that leads to my upstairs bedroom; in the nails that hold my family portraits upon the wall! Indeed, that substance is one of the most common elements upon the earth, and the molten core of this planet is said to be swimming in it. Alas, the meteorites from the furthest stars show that the Heavens are composed of it, and perhaps God himself is cast in moulds beyond our imaginings. No, Doctor Ames, there is no place on Heaven or Earth where I am safe!"

The doctor's mustache twittered as he removed his glasses, fogging the lenses with his open mouth and then wiping them with a noserag. "Richard, I understand such anxiety, but I can assure you that you are in no such danger, these being merely irrational emotions. The cure is not to retreat into a rarified world where the substance does not exist. You merely have to take a vacation to calm your nerves."

The Colonel ran his fingers over his flaccid face. "Eh, what?"

"Two months in Europe shall do you well. Yes, that would be my perfect prescription. When you return, you'll see that your tolerance for the substance shall be restored to normalcy, and you can once more drive your buggy, ascend your staircase, and hang your family portraits with joy in your heart. And upon your death you may enter the Kingdom of Heaven fearing nothing from the metal framing the pearly gates."

"But I can't abandon my business," the Colonel said, desperation seizing his voice.

"Nonsense, there is no time like the present to just abandon it all. Everything will be here when you return. There is no matter of business that is so important that you should risk your sanity over it."

"Yes, yes, you are wise, Ames, I see that now. Oh, what a fool I have been! How ingenious the under-pinnings of the human mind are, that it would make something so repellent to us we would flee from it, even if there is no danger. Ames, I feel the courage now to test this theory. Say the word, freely and unhindered as if you have never played witness to my anxiety."

"Iron," said the doctor plainly.

For a moment, the Colonel held his stoic ground, his face frozen in the aspect in which it had hung before the syllable had been uttered. Then, with little transition, a broad panic erupted on his brows, and he let loose with a harsh yelp. Before the doctor could stop him, the Colonel had dashed across the room, his long legs flapping about him, as he scurried for the velvet window drape, far to one side of the expansive bay window, behind which he sequestered his body.

"It is no use," he wept, "I cannot abide to hear it. To Europe I shall go, and pray that my ship shall not have any railings or wrought fences upon its decks! Oh, Ames, I am lost without you."

"I concern myself solely with your well-being," the doctor announced, lifting his pince-nez. "Is there anything else I can do for you?"

The thin voice came from behind the curtains. "Yes, send in Rogers. I'll need him to take my place and organize my affairs in my absence. And find Latham the Furnace Foreman."

"Latham," the doctor said ominously. "Isn't he the agitator who led the strike?"

"Yes, yes, but you see the extent of my mania, that I would rather face the strike leader than even catch a glimpse of...I cannot even say the word. Bring them now, man!"

Doctor Ames cleared his throat and quietly opened the door to the office. Standing before him, staring at him madly with various degrees of concern, were the assembled staff crowding the outer office. With a few hasty words, a boy was dispatched to the factory floor. After several nervous moments filled with ambient mutterings and stifled questions, two men appeared and approached the doorway. They were of very different demeanor, one being a stormy-browed, well-suited man with oiled hair and a wide tie. The other man was short, stout, and calloused, his rough face showing the harsh years, the cloth cap and baggy trousers revealing his relative rank in the hierarchy of the mill. Just outside the door to the Colonel's office, they halted and peered uncomprehendingly at each other.

"What's he doing here?" shouted Latham in a muffled Yorkshire accent.

"Is this a strike?" asked Rogers the sub-agent, rigidly. "I'll be damned if this is a strike!"

"The Colonel wishes to see you," Doctor Ames said, lifting his palm towards the open office door. Once they were inside, they stood confused at the empty space behind the desk.

"Where is the Colonel?" Rogers asked the doctor, as if talking directly to Latham was a forlorn option.

"I am here," came the voice from behind the drapes, now gaining in confidence.

"Is this a joke?" Latham asked, as Doctor Ames closed the door, cutting off the curious eyes and ears of the office crowd.

"I admit this is an awkward situation," the doctor consented. "It is too complicated to explain at the moment, so I would suggest you just listen to the voice of your employer."

"Thank you, doctor," the Colonel said again from his hidden nest. "The short of it is that I will be going away, far away, for quite some time, perhaps a couple of months, perhaps half a year. Rogers, you are now charged with complete and absolute power over the workers and staff of this mill. You are to act with decisiveness and unity of will."

The sub-agent blinked, as if facial movement was a prerequisite to mental understanding. "As you wish," he began to say. "But..."

"There is no but, you have to perform exactly as I described. Latham, you are to receive a doubling of your current salary if you promise not to cause any more labor unrest. Double, man!"

Latham stared blankly into the red texture of the drapes, raised a finger and opened his mouth, but then remained silent, his finger trailing downward as if it were representing the thought that had just dissipated in his head.

Rogers scratched his chin. "I don't suppose I can get double my salary as well?" he asked.

"Absolutely not, you are not indispensable to me, nor do you threaten my business on a daily basis. Latham here is intelligent, infinitely patient, and cruel in his long-term plans. Like a glacier during the age of ice, he moves slower than the human eye can detect, but in the end, he destroys landscapes. You, Rogers, are weak and derive all your virtues by imitating my gestures. In that respect you are like a monkey to my organ-grinder. No, you are to remain at your current salary and your only directive is to keep the profits flowing and the workers happy. Do you hear me?"

"Yes, I hear you," Rogers replied. "But I still don't understand why you're hiding."

"That's my business!" came a cruel howl. "Now get back to work you two and I'll see you in the winter when I return. Begone!"

Confused, the two men stumbled to the door and the doctor dispatched them back into the outer office. Once the door was bolted again, the Colonel walked shakily from his perch and gained the relative safety of his desk chair. "Do you really think Europe will do me good, Ames?" he asked.

"Splendidly," the doctor replied. "Go to Italy and take in the ruins of Pompeii. And perhaps the island of Elba, where a man who once conquered the world became a powerless prisoner. Ponder the transient nature of all human vanity. Visit many ancient tombs and destroyed cities, and view the broken pottery of history's most glorious empires, now gone in the dust of time. Yes, make it a tour of power's consequence. Soak in the lessons that the vanished empires have to teach us. Then you shall see that all this…" and the doctor waved a hand towards the window, his fingers extending towards the granite buildings beyond, "…is but wind…yes, but wind."

"Perhaps," the Colonel said, wiping the sweat from his brow with his cotton sleeve. "But keep an eye on Rogers and Latham for me. They don't take such a lofty philosophical view of things. Make sure they don't kill each other."

"I shall," Ames said, peering at the door, and imagining the scene that must be playing its course in the outer office. Then the two men fell into silence, interrupted only by the beating pulse of the metal works that vibrated in the floor beneath their feet, the walls about them, and the entire building, a surging and repetitive roar of a beast wallowing in liquid fire.

THE WIZARD OF PROSPECT STREET

September, 1876.

"They call me a boy inventor," boasted the petulant young man, seated with a comforting mug of medicinal sarsaparilla at the front table of the apothecary shop. A bowler hat bestrode his forelocked head as his almond eyes danced merrily over his inner thoughts, more so than upon the pretty girl before him. "But," he explained, "much of my work is the invention of small improvements to existing technology, such as an optimized relay in a telegraph machine. It's more accurate to call me a scientist, as my father does, and true, I use the scientific method, rigorously and with tremendous results. But I aspire to more than just being another inventor or scientist. I want to be a Wizard!"

"That's precisely the type of arrogant nonsense I'd expect from you, Homer," Lizzie Andrew Borden, the Girl Detective of Fall River, snorted, with a spoon balanced in one hand and a lump of ice cream melting in a glass before her. She had never heard Homer wax so pontifically, nor with such self-assertive luster in his voice. "I don't suspect you could even define the word 'wizard'," she challenged. "To me, it evokes a picture of a tall bearded man, his cap and robe decorated with astrological symbols, holding an ancient manuscript that describes methods to turn metals into gold."

"No," answered Homer Thesinger, excitedly. "That's some farcical court magician. My Wizard is a man who can control the elements, harness the powers of the water, divine the secrets of electricity, and provide insight into the nature of light itself! I'm talking of men who are shaping the new world that we live in, men like Thomas Edison, the great electromechanician, who is performing great miracles in New Jersey."

"Never heard of him," Lizzie sighed. "I swear, Homer, you produce the most unusual and obscure people."

"Edison is far from obscure. He's experimenting with electricity to provide an alternative to the oil lamp, one that will run automatically on a current of energy. No more shall we butcher the whales of the world's oceans to illuminate our nights. Soon, we'll merely toss a switch, and the light will flow from hot wires; you shall read your book upon a midnight without any oil at all, and no fear that the wind will blow the fire upon your sheets."

"Perhaps," she said between licks of her spoon. "I'd rather take my chance with an oil lamp than have a hot wire dancing about my head. And besides, how does making a wire hot make you a wizard?"

Homer held up his hands to the air before him and grasped the emptiness. "Can you touch the light? Can you move it around and make it do your will? Try that, and then tell me that a man who can conduct the course of light rays is not a true wizard."

"But he hasn't done it yet," she was quick to exclaim. "By your own admission."

"Well, he already invented the Quadruplex telegraph. From your puzzled frown, I conclude that you have never heard of a Quadruplex."

Lizzie forced her puzzled frown to dissipate. "I know what a telegraph is," she announced. "True, it is a remarkable device to carry words across vast distances. But there is nothing remarkable about this, certainly not anything to cause this man in New Jersey to be so adulated."

"Mr. Edison's Quadruplex," Homer said, breathlessly, "can carry four telegraph messages across one wire. Can you imagine this?"

"But I'd only want to send one at a time," Lizzie shrugged. "Where is the advantage?"

"Think of a world network of wires," he mused, "bringing the human word across vast distances, across oceans!"

"This is what you want to do with your life?" she asked. "It sounds rather lofty for a boy from Fall River."

"And Edison was just a boy from Milan, Ohio," Homer smirked. "Now he has a big contract with Western Union and a marvelous laboratory in New Jersey. Where would any of us be without ambition? The acorn would never become the tree. Lizzie, think of what you can do with a Quadruplex? What if you are in a situation where you must send a message to four people at the same time?"

"I shall send them all telegrams," Lizzie huffed.

"No, four telegrams would need to be drafted; that would be laborious. Imagine that you could enter some words into this machine, and then with one press of a button, you would send those words to four separate people."

Lizzie peered downwards, dropped her spoon into its glass, and drummed her fingers on the tabletop as if she were composing type. "So let us say that I must tell my sister back on Second Street what meat to buy for supper. I should merely compose the words as if I were setting the type, and then..." She reached over beyond her lunch and stabbed the table cloth with a forceful fingertip. "I shall send the message along its path, on the wire, and my sister and others shall receive it if I will?"

"Yes," Homer nodded, enthusiastically. "It becomes more marvelous than that. One day we will even abandon the typed words and shall harness sound the same way that we will harness light. The human voice, political speeches, entire pieces of music, will be carried over networks of wires moving into all the towns across America. We shall even send the signals across the trans-Atlantic cable. One orchestra playing Beethoven's Fifth in the Academy Building will be heard by the entire world!"

"Who will be conducting?" Lizzie pondered. "That matters, don't you think?"

"For artistic purposes, yes. But Mr. Edison will create machines that will capture the music, encode it onto sheets of metal, and then be capable of playing it back, long after its recording, long after the orchestral players are lying in their Oak Grove tombs. The ordinary man shall carry this music around in his vest pocket, and bring it out and listen to it when he chooses."

Lizzie sat back against her chair. "Well, Homer, while all you wizards go off on your great visions of scientific conquest and playing Beethoven over the Atlantic ocean, I'll still be carrying in the milk, ironing the laundry with my flats, and complaining to the Maggie that the morning muffins are burnt. Perhaps I'll be amazed when it happens, but until then…"

"We will all benefit from the coming revolution," Homer concluded. "And I'm not talking about socialism! Excuse me; I'll get us more sarsaparilla."

He marched from the table to the front counter where A.E. Dobbs, the proprietor and inventor of Dobbs' Medicinal Syrup Water and Sarsaparilla Health Notion, stood in subdued conversation with two bowler-hatted gentlemen. Lizzie watched Homer cautiously, subtly agitated by his arrogantly optimistic philosophies, by his masculine pomposities that were straining through the undergrown limbs of a mere boy. From the growing industrial culture about him in Fall River, Homer was learning how to desire power on a vast scale, to think in a large way that tried to encompass the world and all its powerful forces. It seemed only yesterday that Homer was merely tinkering with some rubber tubing and Bunsen burners in his father's barn on Prospect Street; now he was shouting about sending the human voice around the world over electrified wires. It had not been enough to fashion himself an electromechanician, toying with electricity and machinery. Now he was a wizard transmuting metals in his alchemical alembics.

It all comes down to metal and power, she concluded wistfully. They want the metal in their money, in their telegraphs, in their mighty ships on the river and in their cannons for war. The world of men is the world of metal. I'm glad that women have cloth and linen and silks to balance them out!

Homer returned from the counter, visibly distracted, his hands empty and tense by his side. He pointed towards the front counter, where Dobbs was putting down his wipe rag and joining his two new customers before the counter. Several more persons came in from the street, accompanied by a babbling buzz of voices. Through the dusty window, Lizzie could see that many men and women had gathered, and seemed to be staring down street, all talking, some pointing with puzzled looks as if they had not a clue as to what was happening.

"What's this?" Lizzie asked.

"Trouble at the Wampanoag," Homer said. "A.E. heard that someone was murdered."

Lizzie stared before her, seemingly focused on nothing, then started to pull on her cotton gloves. "Yes," she said. "I suppose my planned afternoon of dress shopping must give pause, for I believe I shall be of service to Fall River once again as a Girl Detective. Homer, I beg your leave: I'll see you again on Thursday, for more banter about the marvelous machineries of the future."

"You're going to the mill?" he asked, incredulously. "The police will take care of this. No need to put yourself into danger."

"Your sense of wonderment comes from the sciences," she explained. "Mine comes from the unsolved mystery. This murder at a mill may yet prove to be unsolved."

"It sounds very serious," Homer said, fidgeting with his hat and peering about at the gathering crowd. "I'd best accompany you."

"If you wish, but I doubt that the man was strangled with a Quadruplex wire. More likely it was something more mundane, a stabbing or a bludgeoning with a monkey wrench. It all seems so beneath your marvelous wizardry."

They joined the growing stream of people heading off down South Main. There were pedestrians of leisure, servants with armfuls of groceries, peddlers pushing their carts off their beaten paths, and business owners leaving their establishments puzzled over why so many people were abandoning their shopping and heading towards the river. They filed past several granite mills, where the thundering noise of the looms shook the earth under their feet, and where sad-eyed girls and blank-faced older women stared plaintively out the tall windows on each floor, unable to either enjoy or afford the commerce of Main Street, or take part in the curious march towards the Iron Works. A calm afternoon enjoying sarsaparilla was not their luxury. These mill women, enslaved by the machines of their masters, could not find the time to gossip about marvelous inventions in fantastical futures. They could only spare a fleeting moment to watch the migration of people westward, all that would be allowed by their foremen, and then turn back to their ever-demanding looms, the silhouettes vanishing from the windows as the thunder of industry continued unabated.

The sidewalk before the mill was obscured by the crowds that had gathered, and Lizzie and Homer had to elbow their way through to the main entrance. What magnetic energy has drawn them all here? The very talk of a murder was but a visceral pull that drew them into a wide-eyed tangle, buzzing like a hive before the gates. With reluctance, Lizzie tried to imagine what it would be like at her father's small house on Second Street, so quaint and unassuming, if the Borden home were ever the scene of a dramatic killing. So many neighbors clambering to get a view of the body, so many policemen crawling like insects about the rooms, entering her closet, disturbing her dresses. In less than a second, she had wiped the unsettling image from her mind, focusing on the situation before her.

Several policemen were holding back the crowd at the gate, the officers growing impatient and braced for action. Lizzie recognized Officer Beck, the bushy-faced man who had so generously helped her during the case of the Portuguese Reprobate. She caught his attention with a wave of her hand, then pulled Homer forward by the flap of his jacket.

"Miss Lizzie," Officer Beck said gravely. "This is not a place for you; go on home where it's safe." He tipped his hat at Homer, flashing little recognition.

"Most of Fall River is here," said Lizzie, pointing a gloved finger at the crowd. "Why should I be the exclusion, particularly since I have experience with crime detection?"

"There's no business here for a detective," Beck said, biting his lip. "Chester Rogers, the acting agent, took a gun and shot John Latham, the furnace chief, dead in the skull. Happened in front of everybody, so there's no doubt as to the course of events."

"I'm sorry to hear it was so simple," Lizzie commented, noticing that Homer's face had gone pale upon mention of the shooting. "Do you know the motive for this murder?"

"Well, that's a bit of a puzzle at the moment," Beck confessed. "But I don't think we have to stretch our imaginations too far. Latham was one of those English agitators, always stirring up trouble with the operatives. Straight Yorkshire tradition, and as socialist as you can paint him. I suppose poor Rogers just reacted to his politics in too expressive a manner."

"So this Rogers hasn't made a statement?" Lizzie asked impatiently.

"No, he's as quiet as a rock, I expect stunned to silence. The only thing he's agreed to is to identify the dead man and admit that he was holding the gun when they caught him."

Lizzie frowned. "You said a moment ago that he was seen by everyone. Now you are saying that he was caught with a gun. Did anyone witness the murder or not?"

"Oh, Miss Lizzie this is not one for your casebook, believe me. It's a simple act of murder." His cheeks twitched and his eyes softened. "Or so they say."

"Officer Beck," Lizzie said, a pert little smile dancing across her lips. "you are holding something back from me."

"Well," he confessed, "there's some poppycock I've heard that doesn't make any sense. They say that Rogers pulled the trigger and shot the man dead, but they also say he wasn't the one holding the gun. None of this adds up, believe me. But there were witnesses; and good ones too."

A solid bewhiskered man in a broad officer's tunic came forward, his shiny boots stirring beneath him. Officer Beck shrank back, visibly outranked. "Marshal," he said, tipping his hand. "I was just talking to Miss Lizzie Borden here…"

"Yes," said the City Marshal in a deep-toned voice. "I'm familiar with the Borden girl and her peculiar occupation."

"I was telling her that her services may not be needed," Beck said, nervously. "We got a real cut and dried one here, don't you think, Marshal?"

"Perhaps," he said, wistfully. "Or perhaps we can use an extra set of eyes and ears. Miss Borden, do you have a few moments to talk to a very apprehensive mill agent?"

"I don't have any other pressing engagements," she said. He motioned for her to follow him into the building and she moved forward, pulling Homer, whose face was still deathly white, behind her. The Marshal paused and cast a crinkled brow at the young boy. "This is my assistant," Lizzie explained, chuckling. "He's writing my adventures up into short fiction for a very prominent women's magazine."

"Perhaps," the Marshal said, stepping down to Homer, who seemed to grow shorter in height as the officer approached. "You're the Thesinger boy, aren't you? You distilled guncotton in your backyard.

Homer nodded and said with a whiff of pride, "Nitroglycerine, to be truthful."

"Either way you phrase it," the Marshal said, "you were in violation of city ordinance. And I turned a blind eye because you claimed you were... uh...making a 'valuable contribution to science that the brutish behavior of policemen should not corrupt.' I believe those were your exact words."

"So they were," Homer laughed nervously. "But it was a most valuable contribution."

"One that ended with a thunderous explosion which propelled an oak tree ten feet into the air, a tree which came crashing down on your neighbor's backyard privy, smashing it to bits."

"Yes, well, that was a mistake," Homer blubbered. "I'll be more careful next time."

The Marshal nodded to Lizzie then turned darkly to Homer, holding out a finger towards the boy's trembling face. "I'll let you in this mill, even into the crime scene, but you keep in mind I'm watching you with every eye in my head."

"Yes, sir," Homer said, then sank forward, his knees weakened, and trailed Lizzie and the Marshal in through the front gates of the Iron Works, away from the increasingly agitated crowd.

THE SINGLE BULLET

The administration offices of the Wampanoag Iron Works were elegantly designed and tastefully decorated. Lizzie, who had visited the board rooms of banks, was impressed with the beautiful interior, the burnished oak and maple furniture, the paneled walls boasting a few framed art prints depicting Biblical scenes in an Italianate style, desks and swivel chairs, and filing cabinets and potted palms all competing with one another for wall space. The clerks, accountants, and secretaries had a calm, studious environment in which to work, quite in contrast to what Lizzie had always imagined inside an iron mill. There were no odorous heaps of slag, or half-naked, sweating workers scorching their forge clamps and pounding their hammers upon tremendous anvils. Instead, Lizzie witnessed the white-shirted day workers who moved paper and totaled numbers, who labored with their brains, not their brawn, who came from good stock and wealthy families. These were academy graduates and university scholars, who, despite their academic calling or degree in life, were still sacrificing their daylight hours in service to the manufacture of metal.

The staff was standing at attention behind their desks as the City Marshal paraded across the expanse of the outer office, leading a smirking young girl and a frazzled school boy. His mature gait resembled a morning drill, giving the day workers another dramatic moment in a work day that had started so uneventfully, but which had since been transformed into a mystery play, with a plot that unfolded with each passing moment, complete with a gruesome murder and an endless roster of colorful characters.

The Marshal approached the open door to Colonel Anthony's office and motioned for Lizzie, Homer, and Beck to follow. Two men were standing inside, silhouetted against the sunlight of the bay window. As Lizzie's eyes adjusted to the contrasts in light, the two silhouettes gradually crystallized into two men, dressed in gray and brown worsted suits with high collars and string ties.

The broader of the two, sporting mutton chops which were slapped onto the sides of his face like metal plating on a gunboat, erupted with a furious bellow whose energy seemed to slam shut the office door behind them. "You have brought in children! Mere children! Mr. Marshal, are you mocking us?"

"Mr. Brayton," the Marshal addressed him, "I introduce you to Lizzie Andrew Borden, the Girl Detective. With the understanding in mind that you expected a mature investigator of the male gender, I ask you to consider that this is a girl who lays claim to great reasoning ability, and a sharp mind that may well penetrate the mystery that confronts us."

"Who's the other one," asked the shorter man in a nasal tone that bespoke a lingering head cold. His pin-pointed eyes were huddled together, both ever so slightly out of balance.

"Homer Thesinger," answered the boy, stepping forward and extending his soft hand. The two men stared at it with cold detachment until he withdrew it. "I am Miss Borden's biographer," he added.

"What do we need a biographer for?" Mr. Brayton said, raising his palms to his lapels. "This is not child's play, this is…"

"Mr. Brayton," the Marshal interrupted. "I understand your trepidation in this delicate matter, but I do assure you that I have brought a most excellent detective, and she shall hear testimony in a manner she sees fit. Lizzie, I introduce you to Mr. Thaddeus Brayton, chairman of the Wampanoag Board of Directors, and the mill's legal attorney, Mr. Conrad Twillie."

"I am most honored," Lizzie said, bending her head. "I assure you both that I will take this matter with the utmost seriousness. I have done great service to private industry, the people of Fall River and our duly appointed law enforcement officials. One must only be reminded of the Case of the Portuguese Reprobate or the Affair of the Unexpected Exhibitionist to register confidence in my abilities."

"You brought down Livermore," Mr. Brayton said, peering forward, his brow tightening. "I confess that the man's actions were reprehensible and un-Christian and I do give you credit for exposing his darker deeds. But I hold great suspicion against you. I don't know your loyalties."

"My loyalties are to justice," Lizzie said proudly. "I abhor all crime."

"I'm not talking about crime," Mr. Brayton said, impatiently. "I see you as a woman who hasn't worked a day in your life. Neither has your pale companion here. This case involves a subtle knowledge of the cunning philosophies adopted by labor and the moral complexities confronting management. There is a war of constant turmoil below the surface of our enterprise, Miss Borden. Many powerful men who bear your name in this city struggle with it every day. We must keep constant vigil, or else the forces of anarchy will overwhelm and strip us of the wealth and property that we have forged over these past seven decades. That danger is at the heart of this murder."

"You are saying," Lizzie said in a measured tone, "that I am not qualified to understand the political dynamic between the killer and the murdered man? In that case, how would a detective who is on the city payroll understand any of it better than I? He, too, would be neither labor nor management."

Mr. Twillie's eyes floated closer together. "A decidedly clever girl with quite a belligerent arrogance. Perhaps she is a useful resource, Thaddeus, what say you?"

"I say throw it all before her!" Mr. Brayton hoisted his arms upwards. "What can come of it? Either she solves the murder or she doesn't, and those are odds that would apply if Marshal had brought in the entire police force. Forge and foundries! Throw it all to her!" He turned his back and walked to the window, locking his fingers behind him.

Mr. Twillie coughed into a fist and with the other hand brought forth a silk handkerchief to wipe his palm. "Miss Borden, I ask only that you refrain from disclosing anything you learn about the internal workings of the mill or the unfortunate murder that has occurred here today. This is to be undertaken with strictest confidence. The same applies to your biographer. This is one chapter he shall not be allowed to write. Such restrictions will be lifted should there be a determination of guilt and a public trial. But until this becomes a public affair, you have no freedom of press."

"That is not an issue," Lizzie said, nodding towards Homer. "Should I fail to solve the case, I shall not be interested in publicizing its details."

"Granted," Mr. Twillie said, his face lengthening into a bold, stark statement of indifference. "I shall monitor all and provide legal punctuation as I deem fit. Mr. Brayton shall also bear witness to the investigation."

"Agreed," Lizzie said. "Having said all this, I wish to start with the murdered man and the weapon that killed him."

"Yes," the Marshal said, gesturing towards a door against a far wall. "Both are within, but I must warn you that Mr. Latham's visage is quite disturbing."

"I have seen many a cadaver in my day," Lizzie said, waving for Homer to follow her. They all filed into the smaller chamber, which seemed to be a private meeting room dominated by a long polished wood table fringed with high backed chairs. No doubt in this space, without windows and having only one communicating door between itself and Colonel Anthony's office, high level meetings of great sensitivity were conducted that decided the fates of hundreds of employees and shareholders. Now, upon the table, where many a secret financial report and profit statement must have been displayed, was a long white sheet stained with much blood in the area that gracefully curved over what seemed to be a man's chin, nose, and forehead. They nestled about the table, squeezing themselves into the space for a closer examination.

"The man was shot in the outer office," the Marshal said grimly. "He was brought in here to prevent ghoulish onlookers from watching the attempts that were made to save his life. Unfortunately, there is much emission from the wound."

The Marshal pulled down the sheet to reveal a face locked into a contorted state of horror, the eyes closed, the mouth distended, the tongue slightly protruded, and the cheeks twisted. A bullet wound punctuated the right temple, a clean opening that showed all signs of being a point of entry. It was the damage to the head down below, just behind the left ear, that told the gruesome tale. Small, sharp fragments of skull had fallen like cracked eggshell to the table, along with some brain matter and coagulated blood which had seeped down from this larger wound. Lizzie bent to look at it, but Homer kept his distance, his face whitened and non-expressive. She examined the man's head quite closely. "Clean face, other than the blood." She pressed a fingertip to the skin just above the wound on his temple, distending it from its natural shape. "In through the front, and out through the back," Lizzie noted.

"And there is the weapon that Rogers was holding over the body," the Marshal said, pointing towards a wooden tray that had been laid out at the foot of the table. Upon it was exhibited a shiny hand-firearm, an inert piece of metal that radiated its own haunting messages of turmoil. "You may examine it," the Marshal added. "The bullets have been removed, but take note that there were five left in the barrel. Only one had been fired."

Homer broke his trance and stepped forward to place his hand upon the gun. "Colt .45," he said, lifting it by its dark wood handle, the muzzle pointed towards the ceiling. "Single-action revolver, beautifully manufactured. Army issue," he proclaimed as he pointed it upwards, peering up the barrel and cocking the hammer. Lizzie lurched upwards on her toes for a brief second as he fired the trigger and a sharp metallic burst clanked in their ears. "They call it the Peacemaker," Homer said, snapping open the loading gate and examining the barrel. "I would not want to be staring into its orifice," he concluded, and placed the weapon back on its tray.

"There is no other entrance to this room?" Lizzie asked, gazing around at the three walls that were quite occupied with everything other than doorways. "Then at least we know the killer could not have possibly escaped through here."

"The killer escape?" Mr. Brayton glanced angrily at the Marshal. "What have you told this girl?"

"Not much," the Marshal replied. "Perhaps we'd best retire back to the crime scene, and there we can brief Miss Borden upon the perplexities that confront us."

THE STONE BRIDGE

The east wall of the main office was dominated by the large bay window overlooking the central complex of the Iron Works. Here Lizzie stood, staring through the glass begrimed on the outside by the vaporous pollution of the furnaces. Below, the various buildings, workshops, and furnaces glowed like a cluster of firebugs within a jar. The sounds of vast enginery, metal upon metal, echoed from the machine shops, and teams of men moved about on the pathways, some pushing carts of pig iron, others pausing in their tracks and looking blankly up at the window where Lizzie stood. She marveled at the many laborers, men who were engaged in such arduous toil that her daily tasks seemed petty by comparison. How readily would they trade their livelihoods for her comfortable world of domestic trivialities, to instead have a roof over their heads without having to count the pennies for their rent and to obtain a salary from how many metal casts they can perform in an hour. The value of their lives was measured by the tons of steel placed into the shipping yards of the Anthony family, a brutal equation from which there was no escape. She withdrew from the window, troubled by such thoughts and feeling reluctant to be observed by any of the workers below.

"To begin," Lizzie said, seating herself in the polished swivel chair behind Colonel Anthony's desk, "I need to know the facts, as they stand."

From across the room, Mr. Brayton and Mr. Twillie examined the young girl with frowns, offering more puzzled silences than answers.

The Marshal sensed the stressful pause. "Facts," he began. "One would hope that facts are solid things, like rocks or doorknobs, presenting a surface to the world that is hard and impermeable, and not subject to refutation. But here we have something troubling that causes us to question the nature of facts. There are indeed facts in this case: Mr. Rogers and Mr. Latham were seen through this very door quarreling. There are ten witnesses alone who saw Latham pull a revolver from his pocket and swear that he would do the deed. Six witnesses saw Latham point the gun straight at Rogers' head. And one witness saw the gun explode."

"So *Latham* pointed the gun at *Rogers*?" Lizzie asked.

"Correct, according to six witnesses."

"And Latham pulled the trigger."

"Equally correct, according to one witness."

"But it was *Latham* who was found with a bullet in his head."

"Yes," the Marshal affirmed. "And Rogers standing over him, holding the gun."

Lizzie drummed her fingertips on the desktop. "Could Latham have misfired, and Rogers grabbed the gun from him?" she asked.

"That was our first impression," the Marshal confirmed. "But according to the witnesses, only one shot was heard, and our analysis of the murder weapon shows only one bullet was discharged from the barrel."

"Is it possible that the Colt was not the weapon that was fired?"

"It was still smoking when Rogers was caught holding it aloft over Latham's corpse."

Lizzie pondered this for a moment, her eyes resting squarely in front of her as if she were trying to recreate the scene with her imagination. "So Latham fires a bullet in the direction of Rogers, but somewhere in the course of the bullet's travel to Rogers' forehead, it reverses direction and kills the man who fired it."

"The six witnesses," Mr. Twillie suddenly announced, "swear that Latham was holding the gun point blank at Rogers."

"Did anyone see Latham fall?"

The Marshal shrugged. "As soon as they saw Latham aim the gun and heard a cry of 'No!' from Rogers, they fled for their lives, thinking that the gun would be turned on them next. And yet, one minute later, when the security guard on duty entered the room, Rogers was standing over Latham's body holding the gun, with one bullet discharged. Latham was lying on the ground, his skull shattered and his life removed from his mortal remains."

"So one discharge, one bullet, one dead body." Mr. Brayton emphasized. "Nothing can be clearer."

"There is a definite narrative here and gaps to fill in," Lizzie stated. "We need to know how Latham arrived at the office, how he got into the room, and what was his business with Rogers. Perhaps we should begin with the executive secretary."

"That would be Miss Borden," said the Marshal. "We have her waiting downstairs." He snapped his fingers at Beck, who stood in some vaporous cloud of thought. Then the officer jumped to the occasion and fled out the door.

"What were the two men quarreling about?" Lizzie asked.

"It is undetermined," Mr. Brayton said. "But there is no doubt that labor agitation is behind this all. Latham was an old-time 'ten-hour' man, a supporter of universal suffrage. Back when he was a young mill worker in Pawtucket, he was a prominent member of the Dorr Rebellion. And he wrote anti-capitalist tracts for *The Monitor* all throughout the troubles. There was no rougher beast than Latham when it came to speaking up for the rights of operatives. Print cloth or iron, no matter the industry, he claimed to be the spokesperson of all the oppressed."

The Marshal scratched his beard. "Personally, I would not know whether to vote the man to be President of the United States or to have shot him myself."

"What is that supposed to mean?" Mr. Brayton said, his eyebrows flaring.

Lizzie ignored the chairman's comment, and asked the Marshal, "We believe that Rogers was arguing with him over some principle of workers' rights?"

"Hard to imagine, but the passions were undeniably strong," the Marshal said, staring down at the blood stains on the carpet.

Officer Beck reappeared with a small, peevish woman, bespectacled and awkward. She wore leg-o-mutton sleeves, tapered waist, and modest bustle. Her eyes widened when she laid them upon Mr. Brayton, and her body shrank back towards the door.

"It's alright, my child," Mr. Brayton said, paternally. "You may speak your mind and tell the truth."

"I shall do that and more," she said, her voice expressing a hesitant confidence.

"Miss Elizabeth Borden," Beck announced, "Miss Lizzie Borden."

"My," Lizzie said, holding two finger-tips to her smiling mouth. "It seems we are close in name as well as blood. Are you from the Richard Borden branch?"

"No," Miss Borden said. "That's a different Borden."

"And you are executive secretary to Mr. Chester Rogers?"

"Yes, or at least I am now, since the troubles with Colonel Anthony."

"Troubles?"

"Yes, Colonel Anthony has been working day and night on this mill since he inherited the ownership from his father five years ago, and I fear that he underestimated his own capacity for endurance. Three months ago, he suffered a nervous breakdown, right here in this office. He became morbidly afraid of iron, couldn't even say the word. He had to be whisked away to an Italian retreat to recover his senses."

Lizzie took a sideways glance at the Marshal. "Were you aware of this?"

The Marshal nodded. "I had some understanding that the Colonel was not well. We were told to keep an eye on his house for an indefinite period."

"Morbidly afraid of iron?" Lizzie said, suppressing a giggle. "How does this happen?"

"The demands of his job created tremendous stress in his mind," Miss Borden said, her face as blank as a fresh sheet of paper. "There is nothing more horrible than to feel your humanity sinking under the weight of industrial responsibility."

"Why?" Lizzie added, "Did the Colonel actually mine the ore? Did he work the furnaces? Did he pour the casts? Did he engineer the trains to their shipping destinations?"

"No," Miss Borden sighed. "But I'm afraid that there are other ways of feeling the weight of the business. His entire family fortune was resting upon his success, and the pressures on him were enormous. Not to mention he took a highly personal role in the labor disputes. Confronting the very people who toiled for his wealth, whose physical stamina determined the success or failure of his investments, was quite taxing on him."

"Any man in his position would feel a weight of responsibility," Mr. Brayton added. "There are many concerns suffered by management that are simply swept up in the undertow of labor agitation."

"Mr. Brayton," Lizzie said, holding up a palm. "I am asking questions and expect the answers to come from Miss Borden. Please curtail your commentary." She nodded to the secretary. "You may proceed."

"His nature was truly sensitive," Miss Borden continued. "He never meant to be elevated to such a position, and to be in a field where the laborers worked half-naked over burning furnaces, pouring hot liquid metal, toiling in the fields with their dynamite and drilling tools ... well, I should add that the irony of it all did not escape him. He was looking for redemption, for a way out of his predicament."

"But he did not wish to lose the money of his investors?"

"I don't believe that was a consideration for him in the end. He was haunted by what had once been his dream, which was to be a romantic poet."

"A poet?"

"Yes, he was a big admirer of Wordsworth, Shelley, and Keats. He even admired William Blake, despite the man's revolutionary beliefs. Yes, Colonel Anthony was a true poetic soul, and would much rather have been far from these Satanic mills, instead enjoying the bounty of nature and dancing with the wood nymphs rather than cracking a bull-whip on the backs of men who were his social inferiors. He had also meditated deep and hard on the moral implications of the cannons, ammunition, and armaments supplied by this company to the war effort, and the amount of human blood shed by our product. Despite what many may think, Colonel Anthony's true nature was closer to an angel's than to a murderer or a man capable of enslaving others."

"That's quite a claim," Lizzie said, "considering that the Wampanoag Iron Works has tripled its output and profit shares in the last year alone, due to a decrease in wages and the additional unpaid hours forced on the workers. Can a poet at heart be so calculating and profit-driven?"

"That was a decision by the Board of Directors," Miss Borden admitted. "And not one that the Colonel took to heart. In fact, it was that very directive that led to his breakdown."

"So he had a soft spot for the operatives," the Marshal said bemusedly. "You would never know it from his behavior."

"Not quite," Miss Borden said, staring blankly. "The Colonel kept his feelings to himself. Perhaps that was his undoing, and a circumstance leading to his gravest crisis. The day that he had his collapse, he was curled in a ball like a child, under his desk, refusing to talk to anyone except his physician, Doctor Ames."

"Was he examined by this Doctor?" Lizzie asked.

"In this very office, and immediately the Doctor prescribed the trip to Italy. As far away from the production of iron as the Colonel could possibly go. He suggested the Colonel visit ancient ruins so he could ponder the vanity of man's existence. The Colonel knew the poet's words quite well. 'Look on my works, ye Mighty, and despair!' Shelley."

"I always wanted to see the shores of Calabria," the Marshal mused, tugging at his mustache. "It would beat the hell out of Rocky Point."

"What is your recollection of the actual shooting?" Lizzie asked Miss Borden.

"Alas, many of the pertinent details I did not hear or see; however, I feel my narrative could prove valuable. It was early this morning, just as the ten o'clock whistle blew, and Mr. Rogers came into the office late. Then he quickly gave me orders to leave him alone until further notice. He closed the door, and was silent for a time."

"For how long?"

"I would say half an hour by the clock. Then Mr. Rogers suddenly flung open his door, looking all angry and fierce, waving his arms and calling out for me to get Mr. Latham immediately. Then he said something unusual that I have not forgotten. He said, 'Tell Latham to make haste to the Stone Bridge! No dilly-dallying!'"

"Dilly-dallying?" Lizzie repeated. "A curious phrase. What do you think he meant by the Stone Bridge?"

"I am not sure of the exact allusion, although I took it all to mean that Mr. Latham should expedite his arrival. *Tout de suit*, as the French would say. So I dispatched a boy to find Latham down in the machine shop, since he was on shift."

"Did you tell the boy to repeat the phrase, word for word? Including the Stone Bridge part?"

"I did everything that Mr. Rogers ordered me to, word for word, most assuredly."

"How long did it take Mr. Latham to arrive?"

"About five minutes, I would say. I have no understanding if five minutes constitutes 'making haste to the Stone Bridge.' but Latham seemed to rush into the office, paying no attention to myself or any of the other assistants, and walked quite confidently up to the door. Without hesitation, he opened it and stepped inside, leaving it just barely ajar behind him."

"The door was not wide open?"

"Not at that point. But we did start to hear the shouting, muffled shouts with both men talking over each other in a heated way. We all became concerned and it was myself who swung his office door open. My concern was entirely with Mr. Rogers' safety. I did not care what Mr. Latham thought or felt of my actions."

"How far open did you swing the door?"

"Almost completely, as far as it would go. Far enough for me to see Mr. Rogers by the desk and Mr. Latham standing before him holding the gun."

"How was he holding the weapon?"

"Outward, like this. Almost point blank. Several of us screamed at that point, I must confess. It was truly a gruesome sight. I never hope to see such another."

"So at that point, you ran?"

"Yes, I did run for the door to the outer office. I did not care to be in the general area when the firearm was discharged."

"Did all the people witnessing this with you run at that same time?"

"I believe we ran in stages: some of us at first, the rest upon the following moments. But I did not make it out the door to the hallway before I heard the shot."

"So the interval of time between your witnessing Mr. Latham holding the revolver towards Mr. Rogers, and your hearing the gunshot, was a mere matter of minutes?"

"Not even a minute. I would say as long as the time it would take for me to run halfway to the hallway."

"What happened then?"

"There was a frightful silence, like all time had come to a halt. Then we looked back, frightened, at the office. The door was open, and Mr. Rogers was nowhere to be seen. But neither was Mr. Latham."

"Both were gone from sight?"

"Yes, at first I took that to mean that Mr. Rogers had fallen to the floor, possibly mortally wounded, and that Mr. Latham had somehow fled deeper into the room. But then we saw the poor man's feet on the floor. And then Mr. Rogers appeared back where he had been, holding the gun, looking startled. He glanced down at the body, then at the weapon in his own hand, and then at us. He spoke to us: 'Have no fear,' he said. 'He is no longer a threat to us.' This filled us with a tremendous sense of relief, and we all felt safe enough to enter the room."

"Everyone entered into the office at this time?"

"Yes, about ten of us. We all wanted to know if Mr. Rogers was unharmed. His body was certainly in prime condition, but his mind seemed a bit frayed, as if he had just been through a terrible ordeal and his nerves were sundered."

"And that is when the police were called?"

"We didn't see any resistance to the idea from Mr. Rogers. In fact, we all thought it to be a clear case of self-defense." Her eyes darted swiftly towards the Marshal. "Apparently, our opinion was not shared by those who had the authority to declare it so."

Lizzie quickly asked, "Who was the last person to actually see the two of them before the gun was fired?"

"That would be Mr. Howard," the Marshal jumped in. "The Pig-Iron Puddler."

"A Puddler?" Lizzie asked, curiously. "He was standing in this office?"

"I had first noticed Mr. Howard just before the explosion," Miss Borden continued. "He ran back into the office with us and stood over Mr. Latham's body, staring down at it like it was some curious artifact he had found during a naturalist hike. He did give me a nervous shudder."

"Did he speak at the time?"

"No, he remained silent. And yet..." Miss Borden paused, her voice wavering as she raised a finger towards her cheek. "There was something peculiar going on. Mr. Howard was standing over Mr. Latham, and yet when I turned away, feeling greatly disturbed over what I had witnessed, I happened to peer into that mirror—"she gestured towards a slanting oval mirror that stood sentinel next to the office coat rack, "—and I saw Mr. Howard over by the door, standing behind the crowd, moving backwards as if he were inching his way across the floor."

"Was it at that point that he left the room?"

"I suppose so," answered Miss Borden. "I'm not quite sure why it struck me as odd. Perhaps he had gotten to the door a bit too fast, like he had run from the body. But a moment later I turned around and he was still standing in the room, talking to one of the office staff and pointing back towards the body. It was as if he couldn't decide if he wanted to flee the scene or not, which made me suspicious of him. Very odd behavior."

"Why would he want to flee?"

"I have not a notion on that. However, I am positive he was in the outer office when the shot rang out. He is not the killer, I am certain of it. I just remember how strange it felt when I saw him in that mirror..."

"I have one last question for Miss Borden," Lizzie announced. "Do you believe that Mr. Rogers had any true motivation to murder Mr. Latham?"

"I know they were not on the best of terms because of Mr. Latham's agitation, and how he wrote vitriolic diatribes against mill management in the columns of *The Monitor*. And he sent angry letters to *Iron News*, which has the audacity to publish them. I can think of many men of Mr. Rogers' social standing who would like to have seen Latham rotting in a jail cell or dangling at the end of a rope."

Lizzie put her fingers together below her chin. "But even if we take that as motivation for a murder, why would Mr. Rogers do this in broad daylight, in front of so many witnesses?"

"It was not characteristic of Mr. Rogers," Miss Borden observed, "to have put himself at such risk, or to have murdered anyone for that matter. However, even if he were to contemplate such a heinous act, I do not believe he would have done so with his own hands, even if those hands belonged to the man he murdered."

A muffled cough was heard and Mr. Twillie spoke: "Pardon me, Miss Borden, Mr. Brayton and I have taken note of some of the dubious allegations in your account, yet we are willing to overlook these due to the tragic nature of the events. However, we have a question of our own, one that Miss Borden here, no doubt, cannot ask because she does not even know that the question exists."

Lizzie raised an eyebrow, trying to comprehend Mr. Twillie's statement. "A question that I do not know exists?" she asked. "That is very odd."

"Most definitely," Mr. Twillie continued. "But now I must pose it to Miss Borden: are you aware that Mr. Latham was said to have been a member of a strange society, one that would stop at nothing to overthrow the owners of this mill, and to surrender the very means of production to the hands of those who would destroy it?"

Miss Borden's face went slightly pale, her cheeks thinning. "I know nothing about such a society," she said, "except strange rumors, and I certainly do not know if Mr. Latham had any involvement. But when I did witness Mr. Rogers and Mr. Latham poised to combat each other, I thought immediately that something unspoken had been brought to a boil, that the conflict between them was symptomatic of that deeper conflict."

"This is most interesting," Lizzie said, stroking her chin. "A secret society within the mill?"

"One dares not speculate," Miss Borden said plainly. "As I have already told you, there are only whispers."

A long pause followed her statement, while all the inhabitants of the room eyed each other with the strange anxiety that overcomes a group of intimates who suddenly feel that everyone else has become incomprehensible strangers. Lizzie swatted some dust from the desktop. "I will follow up on your suspicions."

"That is entirely your affair," Mr. Twillie cautioned.

Miss Borden nodded with a faint trace of respect, and then jerked a thumb back towards the outer room. "I must return to my desk," she muttered, glancing furtively at Mr. Brayton. "I fully expect to be relieved of my employment and sent home without a job within the hour. Truthfully, that shall be a relief, if you must know." And then she vacated the room, leaving behind a shadow as if she were still standing in the path of the slanting sunlight.

"A secret society," the Marshal said, breathlessly. "Of all the confabulations..."

"What do you know of this?" Lizzie asked the stoic lawyer. "If such an organization is behind this murder, you must tell me immediately."

"We were not suggesting we knew anything about a secret society," said Mr. Twillie, hastily. "We were merely asking if she had any such knowledge."

"Even so," Lizzie said firmly, "you have taken a perfectly coordinated and balanced interrogation and derailed it with your political paranoia. I must ask the two of you to remain silent from here on in."

"I have even a better idea," the Marshal said. "Hide inside the meeting room."

"What?" Mr. Brayton said, tugging at his mutton chops. "I have to remind you that I represent the presiding board of this mill and I will not tolerate your impudence."

"Regardless," the Marshal said. "Behind the door, both of you. And speak not a word. Be grateful that I am allowing you to hear anything." The two men looked at each other with skittish alarm, and then tromped to the meeting room, Mr. Brayton muttering a few syllables while Mr. Twillie gave the Marshal and Lizzie purposeful stares. As soon as they were secure inside the room, the Marshal pulled the door to within an inch of being closed.

"What do you make of that?" he asked Lizzie.

"I'm not sure," she mused. "When we embark on the murky sea of secret societies, simple facts take on even more insubstantiality than that which we have previously suspected. Indeed, each fact does turn into its opposite, and all hope at recovering a solid truth can be lost."

"But we are not talking about the supernatural here," Homer said, sliding from his chair and advancing to the center of the room. "Even in science, forces that appear to be ghostly and beyond our physical senses do, upon closer examination, begin to follow rigid laws that enable us to make predictions. Although we cannot see a secret society, we can yet detect its presence and trace its behavior."

"In my mind," the Marshal added, "the society does not even have to exist to exert a force. The mere rumor of its existence causes people to behave oddly. It is an angry ghost haunting the mills, turning brother against brother, manager against operative."

"Careful," Lizzie said, jerking her head towards the meeting room door. "As we proceed, we must determine for ourselves if this is a deception, or whether Mr. Twillie actually does have cause to be paranoid."

"One cannot blame him," the Marshal sighed. "If iron mongers can become morbidly afraid of their own metal and discharged bullets can turn about in mid-flight, anything can happen. Where do we go from here?"

"It is time to visit the exact moment of the crime," Lizzie asserted, "or as close as we can to it. I believe we must now speak with Mr. Howard, the Pig Iron Puddler, he who is described as being the last witness. In his words may lie the answer to an unfathomable mystery."

THE BATSTO GHOST

The man who entered the room accompanied by Officer Beck was medium in height, unassuming, swathed in overalls, clutching a cloth hat between his hands. His mustache drooped down towards rough stubble on his wide chin. "Thomas Howard," Officer Beck announced, and the man dipped his head in deference towards the Marshal and the girl behind the desk.

"By your leave," he said with a lumpy voice. "Mr. Marshal, you do me proud. Interrogated twice in one day, what an honor!"

"Mr. Howard, at this hour I am a mere spectator," the Marshal announced, thrusting out a gloved hand towards Lizzie. "Here is your inquisitor."

The man's eyes sparked and he raised them towards Lizzie directly. "I'm sorry if I seem a bit twitchy, but you caught me at a delicate moment. Seeing what I have seen isn't a common occurrence. And now to have to take off my hat to a young girl who has more authority than the City Marshal, that's quite hard to fathom."

"You show respect to Miss Borden, Howard," the Marshal cautioned.

"Yes, I shall." The man rotated his hat between his dirty fingers. "I didn't mean to imply I won't take part in this interrogation. I suspect she'll review the same points of order that I've been revisiting over and over with various policemen and investigators down below. Unless, of course, she's creative and has some new angle to pursue."

Lizzie suppressed a smile and folded her hands on the table. "I admire your pluck," she said. "I'm not sure if my questions will compete in originality with the other investigators, but they are my questions, not theirs. To start, from where do you hail? You don't have a local accent."

His lips pulled back into a slanted smile, his teeth obscured by his mustache. "Yes, that is indeed a different sort of question. No, Miss, I'm not from around here. Rather I hail from the bog-lands of New Jersey. I'm an old Batsto man working the furnace in the Pines, you better believe it. I spent twenty years hauling the bog iron out of Batsto. I bet you never had to spend two decades of your life lifting rocks, did you Miss Borden?"

"I have not been alive for two decades," Lizzie said with a giggle. "But I assure you, I have nothing but the utmost respect for your labor. The fantastic marvels of today's modern age would not be possible without the selfless work that you performed in the bogs of New Jersey."

Howard rubbed his chin and said blankly, "Perhaps I did contribute to fantastic marvels. Perhaps some houses up on the Hill have some banisters cast from my bog-iron, or some cannonball I gave birth to in the furnace actually won a battle for General Grant. But in actuality, the only fantastic marvel I experienced in my day was to get a dollar into my pocket at the end of the week, so I could buy food for my family. And even that didn't last long. Pennsylvania came around with its fancy furnaces, and we were out of business. We left the Lake, and even now the bog-iron's growing back, but no one wants it. They just want the Lake water for drink in Philadelphia. And suddenly there's no more Lake, no more Pines, no more village. So me and my wife and my poor son had to come here, to work for the Colonel. We live in two rooms and the landlord takes everything we got. But I keep pouring the casts, and tending the puddling furnace. Is that fantastic enough for you, Miss Borden?" He grinned widely, crinkling his cheeks.

After a nervous silence, Homer Thesinger, seated in a guest chair against the far wall, cleared his throat. "Mr. Howard, that furnace at Batsto that you so diligently kept burning for two decades. Did you run this by a water wheel?"

"Why yes, we had our dam, and the spillway turned the wheel."

"And you fed the charcoal and the ore through the top?"

"Yes, layered with shell flux, and it would melt down to the crucible. We'd grab the run-off from the bottom, and paddle it into the casting shed."

"I saw a picture of this in a trade journal, and I believe it was the Batsto Furnace."

Howard's face soured. "What do you care about these furnaces? You're but a boy, never saw one in your life."

"But I examined the output of your fine castings," Homer said, gleefully. "My family has a whole collection of kettles and skillets from Batsto and I so admired the craftsmanship I did some research into the manufacturing process. In the library stalls I discovered a monograph on the Old Jersey Furnace that explained the entire process to my great satisfaction. Indeed, I have enjoyed many a meal made in your hallow-ware."

The man's eyes moved closer together. "How do I know you're not fabricating this story? My kettles couldn't have been distributed this far north!"

"Indeed they have, and I invite you and your wife and your son over to my father's home this very evening to enjoy a fine meal and an elegantly brewed pot of tea from the implements we are discussing. The meal will be delightful and the tea will reach a fine degree of subtlety, all enriched by the iron products in which they are to be cooked. And that, Mr. Howard, is a fantastic marvel, more lasting and more valuable than any fancy beds or staircase railing up on the Hill."

The old bog-iron man looked at the boy with a twinkle in his eye, parted his lips as if he meant to reply, then turned sharply towards Lizzie. "I have my own supper plans, thank you kindly, so I'll have to turn down that offer. In the immediate, I'd like to answer this young lady's questions, if you please."

Lizzie nodded towards Homer. "Mr. Howard, I would like to return to the moment in question, when Mr. Latham is quarreling with Mr. Rogers and he pulls forth a revolver with the intention of murdering him. You witnessed the actual shooting?"

"As sure as daylight streams through that window, I can see that gun pointed straight into the face of Mr. Rogers."

"But you did not see the actual moment of contact?"

"No, I can't say I did. I was too busy running for my life. I didn't have enough passionate curiosity to watch a man die."

"But you heard the report of the gun?"

"Surely, I did. We all heard it, but no one was clear whether it had gone astray or not, and we all kept racing towards the door."

"You heard the explosion while you were running for the door?"

"Most definitely. I would not be standing there like a slack-jawed fool, knowing that the bullet would fire at any second."

"Mr. Howard, I ask you one more time, did you actually see the bullet leave the gun?"

His mouth twisted under his mustache and he blinked cryptically. "Well, how can someone see a bullet leave a gun at all? It travels so fast, you wouldn't see it even if you stared at it. When I said I saw the gun fire, I suppose I was condensing a bit."

"So your answer is no, you did not see the gun fire."

"I heard it sharp and clear, Miss Borden. As for seeing the bullet suspended in space long enough for me to identify it as a bullet, I can't vouch as clearly. But you can believe me when I say that barrel was taking a long hard look at Mr. Rogers' face, and within a second or two of me turning to run for the door, there was an explosion, only one. Only one gun was fired and I know who was holding it and to which point of the compass its barrel was pointed."

"After you heard the report, you came back. You even entered this office and examined the body?"

"Why, yes, I was following the crowd. Mr. Rogers was holding the gun, and we weren't afraid of him, so I examined the scene."

"Did it strike you as odd, after what you had witnessed, that it was Mr. Latham with the bullet in his head and not Mr. Rogers?"

"It's not my business to puzzle that one out," Howard said, "being that I'm just reporting what I witnessed."

"Mr. Howard, why were you here in the first place?"

"To feed my family of course. A man must work."

"No, I mean why were you up in the offices of Colonel Anthony? You work on the casting floor, your crew make nails and hoops and kitchen ware from the iron that flows from the furnaces. What were you doing on the third floor of Colonel Anthony's administration building?"

He stared grimly at her. "Why do you ask?"

"It's an innocent question, I believe, and quite fair in my estimation. You merely have to state your business with Rogers, or anyone else in the office."

"If you must know, I was determined to ask for a pay raise."

"Was it typical protocol to leave your furnace down below and to walk up to the private offices of the executive Agent of the mill at mid-day to ask for a pay raise?"

Howard's face tightened. "My father brought me up to be direct and to raise my eyes to the man in the big house. When we were unhappy at the Lake, we would march right up the road to the owner's front porch and confront him as he sipped ice tea with his daughters. Put the man on the spot! Demand your due! I may be in a New England mill now where a man's labor isn't worth the metal that our pay is stamped upon, but old habits die hard."

"Yes," Lizzie said. "Quite so. I do admire your gumption."

"May I go now, Miss Borden?" Howard asked, scratching behind his ear, and nodding towards Officer Beck. "If my interrogations are over, I'm planning on taking the afternoon off, being that my foreman is dead and my boss is under arrest for murder. I don't suppose casting some barrel hoops would be profitable under these circumstances."

"Good idea," the Marshal said, his smile broadening. "Enjoy the afternoon sunlight."

"Can't say I'll see much sunlight," he said. "I have some business to discuss with the wife, in light of all this. Not often that we're both at home at the same time, it may be an enjoyable experience." And with a wink of his eyes and a flurry of his cap, he paraded out the door, pushing his fists into his pockets and whistling a casual tune.

"There's something about that man that's not quite correct," the Marshal said, peering at the empty space where the Puddler had stood.

"How so?" Lizzie asked. "Was his story consistent with his earliest interrogation?"

"Decidedly so. Except for the part about asking for a pay raise. Earlier today he told us that he came up here to resign his position, that he wanted to 'spit in the face of the man who drove him like a slave.' Yes, those were his exact words, weren't they, Beck?"

The officer who stood like a sentinel near the door, stirred into motion. "Yes, sir. When we first nabbed him down on the floor, he made it sound as if he were ready to kill the man himself."

Lizzie's eyebrows lifted. "You nabbed him on the floor? You mean, he went back to his station?"

"He was the only witness who didn't wait around for the police," the Marshal explained. "Beck had to go fetch him."

"Why did he leave the scene of the crime?" Lizzie said, puzzled. "And why did he change his story?"

The Marshal shrugged. "Prestige, perhaps. His one moment to shine in the light instead of hovering in the shadows of the machine shop."

Lizzie glanced over at Homer. "Would you really have had the Howards over for their supper?" Lizzie asked. "Without consulting your parents, you would invite over a complete stranger?"

"Without a doubt," Homer beamed. "He would have made a great smash with my mother. She always boasted about how she had the sturdiest and most excellently crafted iron skillets in all of Bristol County. Indeed, the entire Commonwealth. Meeting the man behind such a beloved work of art would have been her greatest pleasure."

AN AGENT'S SECRET

Chester Rogers was slight and nondescript, his thin face revealing little of the turbulence that must have been crackling like fire within him. The two policemen who flanked him, the Marshal who stood behind him and

Officer Beck who guarded the office door, both seemed fidgety, as if at any moment they expected an outburst or a threatening move. They could hardly be blamed for their vigilance: before them sat a man who only an hour earlier had fired a bullet into another man's brain. His calmness, under such troubling circumstances, was what was most disturbing about him.

The irony that his interrogator, a young girl of no seeming consequence, had the outrageous audacity to sit behind his own desk as she questioned him, did not escape Lizzie. She began carefully, "I have been informed that you were engaged in an argument with Mr. Latham, and, in the resulting confusion, the poor man has been shot in the head. Can you deny this?"

Rogers eyed the Marshal. "Where is Mr. Brayton? Who is this girl? I don't know her, why should I speak to her?"

"You'll answer her questions," the Marshal said with measured tenseness, "as if I were asking, do you hear me, Rogers?"

"At least tell me her name."

"I am Lizzie Andrew Borden," she said proudly. "And I suspect you would have heard that I fared very well in the past investigating crimes both high and pedestrian. In the Case of the Purloined Curio, I brought about the downfall of Livermore, the mill agent."

A strange light appeared in Rogers' eye, and he looked at her intently. "Livermore," he said. "Even more of a reason why I should not discuss anything with you."

"Why would you be so critical of my actions in that case?" she asked. "Do you condone murderers and would prefer to see them go unpunished?"

"Many crimes have gone unpunished," Rogers said with a sneer. "Why should that one have been different?"

"Because the man who Livermore murdered was a good man, while Livermore was vile and uncivilized. Just because he was a mill agent doesn't mean..."

"I don't care if he was a Methodist minister," Rogers snapped. Then he paused as if asking her to contemplate his words carefully. "I have nothing further to say about that," he added.

"What do you mean?" the Marshal asked, his brow furrowed. "What do Methodist ministers have to do with..."

"I think this can all be reduced to a simple question," Lizzie said, shelving the snippet of conversation in her mind for future examination. "Did you or did you not shoot Mr. Latham in the head with a Colt .45?"

"You mean the Single Army?" Rogers said, disdainfully. "Latham brought it into my office and made all sorts of threats."

"What kind of threats exactly?"

"I have nothing to say about that, or the whole incident, except that the gun went off during a struggle."

"Who fired it?"

"I have nothing to say."

Lizzie hesitated, waiting for any further comment, but the man had closed his mouth and turned his face to the door. "There is a witness who saw Mr. Latham pointing the revolver in your direction," she explained, "almost at point blank range. Then a second later there was a loud report from the discharging of the gun. So how did the bullet not reach you? What magic did you perform that would have reversed its course and sent it spiraling into Mr. Latham's head? Are you a magician, Mr. Rogers, who can bend the course of a piece of metal hurtling at close to one thousand feet per second?"

"No," he said. "I'm not."

"Then what happened? Can you put our minds at rest and show us what transpired in that brief second after the revolver was fired?"

"No," he repeated.

"Can you at least tell us the reason for your quarrel?"

He breathed deep, considering some inner thought, then proceeded. "We received a rather large order from New York, of such a magnitude that to fulfill it would tax our resources. To meet the order, I directed that the teams were to work overtime, one extra hour a day, with no increase in pay."

"And Latham, as fiery as his agitation was, opposed this directive?"

"He loathed it, said that I was a harsh monster who should be destroyed."

"Would you disagree with that assessment?"

"I was put into this position suddenly, without warning, forced into a system of responsibility for which I cannot take blame. It is my duty to keep these mills running, and to turn a profit for our stockholders. I recognize the humanity of the men and women who labor in my name, but I cannot simply let empathy for their plight ruin the production of the iron."

"But the men and women who produce that iron for you are human beings, and they have families to feed."

"They are free to come as they please, and to go as they please. They are not slaves."

"No," Lizzie said, pondering. "I would not think they were slaves. But how can they go as they please when they have no other place to go? That's like telling a man who is deposited without a boat in the middle of the Atlantic Ocean that he is free to swim to shore if he chooses."

"I am not here to argue politics," Rogers said. "I have had enough of it listening to men like Latham."

"So, are you pleased to see him go?" Lizzie asked.

"I was staring down the barrel of a gun," Rogers said. "The weapon was aimed to kill me and I had to act fast."

"No man can act as fast as you claim to act," the Marshal shouted. "It's physically impossible."

"How do you know how much time had expired?" Rogers answered. "Because of a few secretaries and clerks who barely understood what was happening? Why do you favor their memories over mine? Latham pulled the gun on me, and I had no choice but to turn it back upon him."

"Through the power of your mind alone?" Lizzie asked. "Somehow, you reversed the direction of the bullet?"

"I will answer no more questions," Rogers said. "If you wish to arrest me for murder, that is your prerogative. However, if you cannot prove that I pulled the trigger, if you have no witnesses, and by your own admission, I cannot possibly have fired the gun, then you'd best let me go this instant and judge Latham's death a suicide." He closed his eyes with a brief flutter. "I shall say no more until you make your own decision."

"Make our decision?" the Marshal cried, his voice thundering. "Why, of all the impudent..."

Lizzie took a breath and rose to her feet. "Mr. Rogers, what is the significance of the Stone Bridge?"

Rogers gave no answer, but his brow furrowed. Lizzie walked to the front of the desk, her dress trailing about her, and leaned in close to Rogers' left ear. "The Stone Bridge," she repeated. "Was this some kind of code? Did he bring a gun with him because you had somehow instructed him to bring the gun?"

"Why would I tell him to bring a gun?" Rogers said, keeping his eyes shut. "That would be suicide."

"Suicide for you?" Lizzie asked. "Or for him?"

"It was merely an expression," Rogers said between tight lips.

"There is a stone bridge that connects Fall River to Aquidneck Island, is there not? Can that be the bridge in question?"

"I have no idea of the origin of the expression, I just find it useful when asking a man to double his pace and make haste. I leave the history lessons to others more versed in the events surrounding that bridge."

"Mr. Rogers, I have an important question for you, and I am most eager that you will supply your very first answer, since you have effectively avoided giving any up till this point. I have heard rumors about a secret society in this mill, perhaps a workers' conspiracy, one designed to seize the means of production from the owners and to give it to those who toil to create the wealth. Do you have any knowledge of such a cabal?"

"It sounds like rank socialism to me. I pay no attention to those European political fads, although I suspect Latham, being from England, had some knowledge of it."

"Was that the subject of your quarrel? Did such talk provoke him to pull a revolver upon you?"

"Discussing politics with Latham was an ineffectual experience. When I attempted to reason with him, explained to him my position, defended the

economic system that drives society, I might as well have been talking to a brick wall. He was unwavering in his beliefs to the point of losing touch with the blunt realities of life."

"You didn't answer my question."

"I suspect I have," Rogers said, his mouth slightly twisted. "I have answered every one of your questions, perhaps too much so. May I go now? Or shall I be put into shackles and dragged to the police station to sit behind bars and shout my innocence to the mob below my solitary window."

"Mr. Rogers, what do you know about Thomas Howard the Puddler?"

His eyes darted away. "He is of no consequence to me."

"What was he doing in your office at the time of Mr. Latham's death?"

"Perhaps you'd be best off asking him. I know nothing of his business."

"Did you see him in your office after the shooting?"

"Yes, I did, in fact. He came in with the rest of them, ghoulishly observing the scene."

"Did you not think it unusual that he was there?"

"I paid it no mind. My attention at that time was occupied with more important matters. I had no truck with a puddler. But wait, yes, I did have a thought in my head regarding him. And it was this: Why is he here in my office, and not at his furnace station increasing my wealth? Yes, that was my very thought, but it was as brief as a single moment, a fleeting thought."

Lizzie turned to the Marshal and waved a diffident hand. "He is entirely at your command."

"Damnation," the Marshal said, pulling forth a pocket watch and noting the time. "Mr. Rogers, I cannot find any means by which I can link you to the crime. There is no material evidence, outside of the fact that you were holding a smoking gun over a dead man's body after it fired a bullet into his brain. You are free to go, for now. But don't leave town. We may require you for further questioning."

Rogers smiled and got to his feet, his cheeks blushing. "I'm happy to have helped in any way to illuminate this affair. Now that you have given me the pleasure of my freedom, I do have a statement of fact to make, one that I was unwilling to make when I assumed that my fate lay behind bars."

"And what may that be, Mr. Rogers?"

"One bullet cannot come from two different directions; it is a sheer impossibility. A gun can only be aimed in one direction. If the bullet came from a direction that was contrary to the direction in which the bullet was fired, then either the gun was not in the position where it is believed to have been, or the bullet itself was not as it seems. Both gun and bullet came from a furnace of fire, and back to the furnace they shall go. And there may be a puddler at both ends of the affair."

Lizzie, Homer, and the Marshal simultaneously blinked and pondered his words, attempting to straighten them out in their heads. "That's what you call a 'statement of fact'?" the Marshal asked. "I have half a mind to beat the truth out of you, Rogers!"

The sub-agent sauntered to the door. "I have no more to say except that upon my arrival at home, I shall consult with a lawyer, and next time you shall find me better prepared to not answer any more of your useless questions." He took one last glance about his office as if to soak up a scene that was not confined to memory, and then disappeared from view.

"What do we make from that?" the Marshal huffed. "Not exactly a signed and sealed confession, is it?"

"On the contrary," Lizzie said excitedly. "I believe we did hear something akin to a confession."

"What, you think he pulled the trigger?"

"I am not inclined to reveal my theory as of yet. There is another person I will need to interrogate."

Her thoughts were interrupted by the sight of Brayton and Twillie standing in the meeting room doorway, their proud faces stoic and silent. They advanced into the room like synchronized dancers, or perhaps bonded Siamese twins, afraid of stepping apart lest their connection to each other be compromised.

"We have listened and observed," Mr. Brayton boasted. "And we must restate our suspicion that dangerous and secret forces are at work within the mill. Perhaps this man Howard knows more than he is saying, or Miss Borden is in collusion with the conspirators. Whatever transpired in the small amount of time between Mr. Latham's firing of the gun, and the arrival of the bullet at his forehead, is not of any consequence. Our only concern is that Mr. Rogers defended the mill, its principles and well-being, against dark and savage conspiracies."

"Perhaps," Lizzie said. "Or perhaps your theory about the secret society is mere paranoia."

"There is no proof to confirm that," Mr. Brayton said, clanking his cane against the ground. "Your science and deductive reasoning are of no use here. We highly recommend abandoning the case, and simply letting the lack of evidence decide the outcome. Let it be determined in a court of law. A guilty man is dead, an innocent man and defender of the faith is walking in his liberty. Is that not enough to redress the balance and put all this to rest?"

Lizzie rubbed her forehead as if to stimulate further thought, turned to the Marshal and Homer for some modicum of personal support, then leveled her gaze at the two well-suited men and answered with a plain and unassuming voice, "No, not really."

"Eh, what?" Mr. Brayton huffed.

"A man lies dead," Lizzie said, pointing to the room behind their backs. "His life stolen from him. For all your pretended proclamations of justice and the role of your business in the larger affairs of mankind, I fear that the integrity of your iron mill and the safety of your investments is not a consideration here."

"Such talk is not trivial," Mr. Twillie said. "We can order you off the premises as a suspected member of the secret society. You will never be able to disprove us."

"Nor can you prove such an allegation," said Homer, unexpectedly. "Sir, I am but a young boy, steeped in science and not quite as well-versed as you may be in the practical affairs of industry, although I do follow the technology in various trade magazines. So my opinions may fall short of intellectual profundity, but it does seem to me that regardless of whether this secret society exists, and regardless of whether it played a role in the killing, you have hosted in your factory today a highly publicized murder. The entire city is witnessing these events unfold, and all revelations will be subject to public scrutiny. If you fail to present to them a solution to this mystery, word about ill-doings in the mill will spread about the city, perhaps the entire commonwealth. Agitation will increase, for Mr. Latham will have become a martyr, a common working man murdered by management, and management will doubtless be perceived as having heartlessly allowed his murderer to go free. So, I think you should permit Miss Lizzie to pursue this investigation to its proper conclusion, lest you turn your factory into the spark that would light the fires of revolution, perhaps even on a global scale. Do you want to be known as the industrialist who initiated the downfall of industry?"

Mr. Brayton's eyebrows had somehow joined above his nose. "Not particularly," he answered. "No."

"Then perhaps," Homer concluded, "Miss Lizzie should be allowed the run of the mill. Let her work her magic."

THE CRUCIBLE

The thundering of the steam hammers and the relentless roar of the furnaces, beasts of burden groaning under a yoke of unimaginable heat, filled the hallows of the factory floor, drowning under its tidal wash of energy the singular voices of the men who labored at the machines. As Lizzie walked with her company across the wide open floor, crowded to the walls with piled machinery, immense castings and moulds, and jagged mounds of slag, she raised her hands to her ears, attempting to quash the pressure that was building inside her head. Both the Marshal and Homer made some gestures to her, perhaps to redirect her course, or to convey some information, but their words were lost in the deafening din.

A row of workstations against the northern wall was manned by workers who stood holding long strips of metal that they were awkwardly feeding into hungry machines. The men were constantly making adjustments to the angle of the strips as the metal teeth ate at them, thereby spitting them into a hopper below. What emerged were metallic spikes that Lizzie took to be nails. Often she had seen her father procuring these nails for his furniture business, but now she marveled at their birth, seeing how they were cut from whole metal by the machines, and so quickly, to produce hundreds of them within minutes, ready for use. She ran to one of the hoppers, to the surprise of the worker who manned the operation, and drew forth one of the spikes, holding it before her in the light, and smiling. The worker gestured for her to get out of the way, tilting his head towards the machine as if warning her about a dangerous creature.

The next stage of the factory floor was populated with a variety of unfamiliar machines that were all stamping and shearing, cutting and stripping. The cacophony of noises rose like the ear-bleeding murmur of several off-key choirs, dancing in rhythm but continually slipping about each other's measures. It was more bearable, more fluid, than the nail factory, but nonetheless taxing upon the ears.

A worker maneuvering a wheelbarrow of machine parts appeared before Lizzie, blocking her path. He stumbled for a moment, angling to get around her, then stood firm and straightened his back. For a moment, their eyes met, and Lizzie felt a strange wash of feelings. Acknowledging the presence of this man felt wrong, as if she were establishing the grounds for a confrontation. He clearly wanted nothing more than for her to get out of his way to give him easy passage to a particular area of the shop, but Lizzie somehow felt as if he were angry, thrown into ill humor by her dress, her frilled hat, her gloved hands and rustling skirt. She was as out of place on the factory floor as a sunflower would be growing from the middle of a board room desk. With her will paralyzed and her body frozen into place, it was left to the Marshal to step forward and gently guide her onward by pushing her shoulders.

As they approached the furnaces, the air grew hotter, smokier, and more rank with the vapors of metal. Blasts of heat made their breath more labored, pressured the surface of their faces, reddening their cheeks, warming the floor, indeed the entire earth, beneath their feet. Liquid metal, spitting off embers in sprayed arcs, poured down chutes, directly towards large moulds, there to be cast into various shapes. Men stripped to their waists, dirt-crusted and dripping streams of perspiration, channeled the metal with long poles that they deftly stroked with all the vigor of a gondolier moving his precious cargo through a canal.

Other men raced to and from the large banks of fiery machines, pushing before them their barrows that glowed with the white-hot metal, itself comprised of ill-formed bricks and logs with crude edges, of unpounded spongy fire masses that belched embers as they sped. One wheelbarrow full of coal, navigated by a scurrying worker, nearly ploughed into Lizzie; she just managed to step aside, her hand flying to her open mouth, her shoes tripping on her long skirts.

"The Devil!" the man cried out. Was his frantic gaze, his rapid pace, merely to work the iron, to get it from the furnace while it was still burning hell-fire and malleable enough for hammering? Or was his sense of panic more acute because his foreman had been murdered and he was not allowed to stop production? These men, who had labored under the supervision of Latham, knew he was dead, and that his body was lying mutilated by an iron bullet, perhaps of their own manufacture, in a meeting room above. Yet, here they were, still working, still driving the wheels of industry. What manner of place would not even allow one of them an afternoon of contemplation, or even of grief for the tragic loss of one of their fallen men? What irony would put them right back into the rolling wheels of producing wealth for the very man who may have murdered their boss, their fellow worker, their friend?

She turned to the Marshal and gestured that she needed to talk to him, but he insistently pointed onwards, driving her towards an area past the furnaces. Beyond the full blast of heat was an array of workers settled at their anvils, lifting their proud hammers aloft and driving them down heavily upon the burning products of the casting floor. Some had helmets and goggles, some braved it alone with bare sun-burnt faces. Their random clanks and hammer strokes all played against each other in a symphony of metal clashing against metal.

Lizzie absorbed all the sights and sounds about her with a wide-eyed naiveté, as if she were experiencing the birth of her own awareness of the world. Here was the origin of so many of the things she took for granted. The anvils, kettles, skillets, and nails were being born in a painful agony of cutting, shearing and pounding. Bins of pig iron lay inert, waiting to be re-melted and transformed into casket hoops and fencing. Common sense had always told her that the manufactured items about her, whether they were at home in her kitchen on Second Street, or in some public place like Dobbs' Apothecary, were made in some factory—she was always mindful of this; however, the industrious labor before her was also colorful and adventurous. The flowing metal; the searing heat; the seemingly random, but highly organized flow of men and workers and machines; the ingenuity that was deeply invested in every moving part; the centuries of labor and skill and accumulated knowledge on how to work the metal, on how to transform its state to liquid, on using heat to change its nature and qualities, working its shape and stamping upon it the forms of the things we need in the world, all this activity and knowledge and hard physical labor, all whirled in a vortex of mind-numbing, tremendous energy about her.

Homer too gazed about him like a child in a confectionery shop, his mind awash in lightning-quick observations of the gear cranks, the fly-wheels, the steam hammer fittings, the flying belts, catwalks, ladders, and furnace designs. He had never seen such an industry of labor and technology working together on such large a scale, and was embarrassed to admit that he had lived in relative ease in the same city where such labor was being driven, yet had never even glimpsed any of these scenes before. These men were not a group of comfortable middle-class dabblers in scientific observations and experimentation, nor were they students trying to impress young women with Bunsen burners and chemical reactions inside test tubes; they were brawny and lusty men who savagely swung the hammers, pumped the bellows and paddled the burning metal with precision and skill honed to the level of art. Here was the end path of science, the practical application of its principles, the user of its chemistries and physical laws of nature to effect the production of goods. In his library books, in the privacy of his own studies, he had known such worlds existed, but to stand in the midst of it while it danced about him, his mind and imagination turning with the fly-wheels, was a most extraordinary experience. For a moment, in the center of the blasting room floor, he was spell-bound. He gently extended his arms and closed his eyes, feeling the vast power and industrious magic happen about him.

"Move on," the Marshal shouted over the din. To the policeman, the scene about him was about as aggravating as one could experience during the course of a working day. And yet there was a sense of comfort in witnessing the precise regularity with which the workers turned the wheels and kept the mills rolling. If only the men who drilled under his command would be so machine-like, what benefit they could be to the city. It was very well to patrol the streets for lawbreakers, investigate murders, track down criminals, and hobnob with politicians; but, in essence, the ultimate mission of the Fall River police was to maintain a lawful balance, to ensure that the wheels turned, the mills rolled, the assembly lines produced, and that the daily labor did not stumble. The Marshal glanced at Brayton and Twillie, who walked across this floor as if it were a front lawn and they were about to chastise the gardener for not trimming the hedges properly. Their only concerns seemed to be whether these half-clothed Vulcanists about them were focused enough on their work. Did they even consider what equilibrium was being held in check, what forces of anarchy were being contained in their Pandora's Box, and how petty their profit margins seemed in the face of such chaos? All life, mused the Marshal, was a constant tight rope walk between the towers of Order and Disorder, and money had as much to do with it as a carrot dangling before the mule had to do with the purpose of the cart ride.

They passed down a long corridor, echoing with the steam hammers and anvil strikes, then came to a larger cavernous area. There hordes of finished product, small parts and larger complete machines, lay about in rows and columns. To Lizzie's untrained eye, these were packed shipments, ready to be rolled off to train cars that were visible through a tremendous opening in the wall. Beyond the freights, she could see the tracks that curved in towards the glistening water of the Taunton River. The schooners were at dock, the water was glistening, and the vast assemblage of iron product, now having reached the end of the production line, huddled like uncertain immigrants about to embark on a perilous journey to some unnamed continent.

"Where's the Howards?" Mr. Brayton snapped at a thin dock foreman who stood with an inventory book. The foreman waved towards a far wall where a small glowing furnace flared and fizzled, angrily eating the coke and ore within. Before it sat a small child, barely six years old, on an upturned barrel, his body clad in overalls, a cloth cap atop his begrimed face, and his coal-stained hands holding a shaft of iron which he turned about, examining it like it were a creature of strange fascination. He lifted his face warily towards the odd assembly of policemen, mill management, and youths who approached him, expressing no small agitation of mind.

"Erasmus," said Mr. Brayton abruptly. The boy snapped to his feet, tossing aside the iron shaft which clanked against the ground, sending an uneven echo through the cavern of the room. "Where is your father?"

The boy's eyes darted to and fro, as if trying to calculate the dangers inherent in his potential answers. The Board Chairman asked his question again with a harsher bite, bringing the boy, it seemed, almost to the verge of tears.

"Erasmus?" Lizzie asked, glancing at Mr. Brayton, who nodded. "Erasmus," she repeated, kneeling down so her face came level with the boy. "You work this furnace? What do you do here?"

His lower lip trembled, then withdrew, as if he were attempting to stifle his own words. Then he muttered, so faint that Lizzie had to tilt her ear inwards to hear, "We get rid of the slag." Then after a pause, he added, "And the broken bits."

"You melt the slag?" Lizzie asked, and he nodded his trembling head. "Where is your father now? Did he go home? Why didn't you go with him?"

"Not allowed," he said, darting his eyes frantically at Mr. Brayton. "I'm a bad boy if I go."

Lizzie walked closer to the furnace and peered into the fire tongues that danced in the heat blasts. Picking up an iron stoke, she shifted it around inside the belly of the machine, turning about chunks of coal and ore, causing a run-off down into a crucible where the molten metal bubbled and burned. Evidently, quite a bit of slag had been melted down in the past few hours. She tossed the stoker aside, and backed off, brushing down her skirts, assuring herself that no fiery ember had nested inside her clothing.

"This child is in much danger," she said directly to Mr. Brayton. "He should not be manning this station, or at least he should be clothed for protective measures."

"It is very safe," said Mr. Twillie mechanically, as if repeating a speech that he had made on several occasions. "Do not fear that he will burn or be injured by the furnace. If it happens, it is because of his own negligence."

Lizzie felt her own breath cease, and she looked immediately towards the City Marshal. His eyes were dimmed, his lids pressed half-closed, his stern face telling her that her argument was best left for another time, another forum. She slapped her hands together and said loudly over the grinding roar of the factory: "I believe I have solved the murder!"

Her audience all stirred, glancing at each other, their faces flushing with expectation. "At least the mechanics of it," she added. "But now I have one last detail to fill in, which, with a little bit of luck, will tell me the identity of the individuals involved."

"Involved?" the Marshal asked, surprised. "Mr. Latham and Mr. Rogers were the individuals involved."

"Not quite," Lizzie said. She lowered a hand towards the mouth of the furnace. "I need to see the Howard boy's mother. She is the key to this entire mystery."

"Mrs. Howard?" Brayton bellowed. "Are you serious? What has she…"

"Yes," Lizzie said, proudly. "I am quite serious. I believe a few questions posed and a careful consideration of the answers will reveal to us the length and breadth of it all, including who pulled the trigger that launched the bullet that ended Mr. Latham's life."

"How would she know that?" the Marshal asked. "It was her husband who was present at the scene of the crime. Do you suspect that he confessed the truth to his wife?"

"I believe," Lizzie replied, "that Mrs. Howard knows more than we think, but understands little. Now, Officer Beck, if you would please take charge of this young boy and entertain him for an afternoon. Buy him some ice cream at Dobbs' Apothecary, get him a proper outfit of clothing, a scrub bath at the police station, and then return him to his home. Charge all expenses to my father at Borden and Almy's on South Main. After his proper grooming, I shall induct him into the Lizzie Andrew Borden Trust Fund for Destitute Children. My charity shall provide what his parents have withheld."

The young boy looked up at her, his eyes widening, his cheeks trembling. Then he lifted a blackened hand and poked out an index finger, his other fingers curling against his palm. With his mouth he made the sound of a small explosion.

"Pop," he said.

"We shall see," Lizzie said, her smile vanishing.

THE MOUSETRAP

Two separate buggies transported the company up the steep slope away from the mill, turning onto Columbia Street to where homes grew more clustered, huddled together as tents would be placed in a strike camp, fraternizing against the oncoming winter cold. The buildings rose upwards, some floors seemingly accessible only by way of unsteady wooden stairs that snaked up against the windows. The streets were eerily empty, in sharp contrast to the crowded Second Street where Lizzie lived with her family. The men of this neighborhood were all absent, away at their machines in the various mills, as were perhaps the women and children, too. Whoever remained here enjoying the privacy of their homes between the factory bells was no doubt busy with washing, ironing, cooking food, dusting, scouring, chopping wood, chipping ice, tending to small children (only the tiniest were exempt from the mill work), and otherwise engaged in activities that their spouses could not perform when they returned from the prolonged work day, exhausted and half-dead.

They alighted on the street before a house that rose upwards several stories. The wail of a mourning dove cooed over the backyard fence; Lizzie caught a glimpse of the wings as the creature ascended beyond the neighbor's yard. It was as if some part of her own spirit had flapped outwards and away, the unbounded part of her beating heart that dreaded witnessing under what conditions the Howards actually lived.

As they ascended the front porch towards the main door, a haggard face appeared in the second-story window, a round but fleshy and begrimed face. A bolt of recognition crossed Lizzie's mind: "Mr. Howard!" The face twisted into a state of panic, the eyes bulging and the mouth widening into a silent scream, and then withdrew so quickly that they all blinked as if doubting what they had seen. "That was Mr. Howard," Lizzie repeated. "But..." she said, closing her eyes and attempting to see in her mind's eye what had been wrong with the face. Perhaps it was that he had been wearing spectacles? Or that he had shaved his beard stubble?

"He didn't have his mustache," the Marshal said. "By Jupiter's Scepter, he went right home and shaved off his mustache. Now, does that strike you as a perfectly innocent thing to do after being the main witness at a murder?"

The Marshal banged upon the front door. After a brief but hushed argument from within the building, one that was barely loud enough to distinguish any words, or to determine even how many people were disputing, a thin and humorless woman opened both the door and the screen. She had on a plain gingham dress with a dirty apron, upon which she wrung her hands; and her eyes were reddened with distraught tears. "You are here to arrest my husband?" she asked, immediately spying the Marshal's brass buttons and authoritarian mustache. "He will cooperate, I dare say he will."

"We interrogated him at the mill," Lizzie said. "Has he explained to you the situation that we face?"

"He is not a murderer," she said, her voice disintegrating, her fingers rushing to her cheeks. Upon the buckling of her knees and the start of her downward spiral, the Marshal stepped forward, cradling her as her posture disintegrated.

"We shall be destitute," she was muttering. "All is lost!"

"Get her off the street," the Marshal said, and the officers, with the help of Homer, carried her into the front hallway and up the staircase to the dank kitchen on the second floor.

"The bed," Lizzie commanded, and they followed the rapid movement of her eyes towards a door that led deeper into the apartment. Lizzie noted, with dark forebodings, the faded rose wallpaper, the splintered furniture, the coarse and matted rugs, and the variety of insects that raced down the hallway on scuttling legs. Here, in these impoverished and destitute quarters, lived the Puddler and his family. This was the abode of a man who scooped the slag and poured the molds needed to create the cheap trinkets destined to decorate the homes on the Hill; a man whose credibility and veracity she was threatening to destroy; a man who had never done her any wrong, and, indeed, seemed to be engaged in only one activity: the provision of security for his family through the hard work that a pampered middle-class girl like Lizzie could never comprehend, far less execute on her own. The reaction of Mrs. Howard to their arrival bespoke a misplaced guilt, of a good man trapped in untenable circumstances.

By the time they had laid Mrs. Howard out on the lumpy mattress in the bedroom, under a painting that appeared to be the single attempt at decoration—a lighthouse astride a seashore hill at twilight—Lizzie had regretted her approach. What comfort could she afford this innocent woman now that she was here to implicate her husband in a savage murder?

"Mrs. Howard," Lizzie said, tapping the back of the woman's hand. Her eyelids fluttered and opened, focusing on Lizzie's slight smile and large soft eyes. "We do not wish your family any ill will, but we need to discover the truth about the affair at the mill."

"He is not my husband," the woman said, and Lizzie noticed that Mrs. Howard's eyes were not resting on her, but on something over her shoulder.

"What?" the Marshal shouted, and the two police officers joined in his outburst. All was fury and flailing arms, while the assembled lawmen scrambled for the dusty shadow that had unexpectedly darted across the room towards the kitchen door. The Marshal's arm hooked around the runner's neck, while Homer, darting downwards, grabbed his knees, forcing him to buckle and collapse. There was a brutal mêlée of men, of uniforms and hats, all clattering apart and together, and next an outcry from an unexpected and unfamiliar voice, then a groan and a gradual settling. All of the men present were splayed on the floor, breathing heavily, seemingly secure in their capture of the now-succumbed individual. Lizzie was puzzled to see that the subject of attack was Mr. Howard, the Pig Puddler; only at this moment, he was snorting hotly over a bushy mustache that somehow had managed to adhere itself back to his bristly face.

"Can't a man leave his own home!" he was barking. "I won't stand still for another interrogation; you have all you need to know!"

"Except for who you really are," Lizzie said. Noting that the man was pinioned by the assembled lawmen, including Homer, who was still clasping him tightly by the shins, she knelt down, rustling her skirts, and picked with nervous fingers at the man's facial hair. For a fleeting moment, the man struggled with his nose, twisting it sideways as if attempting to prevent Lizzie's actions; then, realizing that he had no physical way to halt her, he sighed deeply, his two eyes coming together in the center of his face as Lizzie peeled away the mustache, revealing a rudely shaven upper lip.

"God's wounds!" the Marshal cried. "What is the meaning of this?"

"I can tell you the meaning," Lizzie said, holding up the strip of hair as if it were a trophy. "But I think we should allow him to speak, should we not? You will not be of any more trouble to us?" she asked politely.

"No," the man said, his limbs deflating, his rigidity vanishing. "I will not struggle, let me go."

With some reluctance, the men released their prisoner. Realizing that he was being afforded his freedom, the man shook his limbs to test their agility, and then, along with several lawmen, scrambled to his feet. He stood before them, wiping the dirt from his vest, smoothing over the creases in his pants. "I will no longer resist in any sense of the word."

The Marshal looked at the man and froze, his body stiffened into an awkward pose of disbelief. "Begging your pardon, Colonel Anthony," he said, his voice crackling with uncertainty. "I may need to arrest you in a moment, but feel free to provide an explanation for this behavior."

"Thank you, Mr. Marshal," spoke Colonel Richard Ulysses Anthony, thrusting his chest forward in its denim worker's shirt, his hands outward in a gesture of good faith and show of non-violence, and his eyes perched stonily upon Lizzie. "I require an equally compelling explanation from Miss Borden."

Lizzie was about to respond when a rustling at the kitchen door turned all heads towards another man, previously unseen, walking slowly across the creaking planks.

At first, the figure seemed a replica of the Colonel, dressed in his worker's threads but sporting the bushy mustache. A closer look at the pock-marked face, the crinkles around the eyelids, and the grizzled chin, collectively confessed the identity of Thomas Howard, Pig-Iron Puddler. He stood stock still and apart, blinking at the tableaux before him. "So," he said in a whisper, "is it over?"

"Evidently," the Colonel responded, his hands patting his sides. "And I don't see any need to put your good wife through any more of this torment."

Howard nodded, took a glance at his trembling wife, whose face was already radiating a profound sense of despair, and then, with grappling fingers, reached up to his bushy facial hair. With a deft twist of both his hands, Howard pulled the mustache from his lip. Without the hair, he looked no closer to the Colonel in aspect or general flesh tone, but Lizzie could now see how the addition of the mustache on both men could deceive the executive secretary or a startled accountant whose awareness of a passing stranger's facial hair would be secondary to the event of Mr. Latham's murder.

Mrs. Howard, stirring from her troubled swoon, gazed at her husband's bare lip, her mouth shutting tight, her eyes widening. "Thomas," she said, in a voice surprisingly calm. "You look ten years younger, I dare say."

MELTING POINT

The two men, the Mill Agent and the Pig Puddler, sat behind the kitchen table facing the company, their faces as contrasted as night and day. Mr. Howard's cheeks were drawn with sorrow and long labor, while Colonel Anthony's smile was crookedly smug and confident. Before them lay the two bushy mustaches they had pulled from their lips, displayed as if they constituted evidence being offered in a courtroom trial.

"I find it amusing," Lizzie chuckled, absorbing the scene, "that they can only resemble each other with the fake whiskers. It shows how the human mind does filter out what it chooses not to see."

"It was damned hot during the castings," Mr. Howard complained. "I'm glad to be done with it."

"You did the correct thing," she replied. "How you must have suffered these past three months, knowing that your life has been compromised for the benefit of this murderer."

"Murderer?" said the startled Marshal, his hands grabbing at his belt. "Do you mean to suggest the Colonel?"

"There is no need for me to be evasive," the Colonel said. If he were haunted by any guilt, his countenance and tone of voice did not betray it.

"I did kill Latham with my own hands, and I shall sign a confession to that effect. I only ask that you send for Doctor Ames immediately, for he is the only person who can guide my tortured mind back to a position of equilibrium. Until then, anything I pronounce is under the provenance of a deranged manner of thinking. Isn't that right, Mr. Brayton?"

The Chairman, slumped in a corner upon a three-legged stool, held his face in his hands, making slight billowing noises. His lawyer, Twillie, standing by his side, his face thin and expressionless, with one hand upon his employer's shoulder, appeared to be jolted by the Colonel's inquiry. "There is little I can offer you, Colonel," the lawyer said, "except to advise that you have already stepped beyond the boundaries of my purview. I can offer no more than minimal advice on how to proceed from here."

"The Iron Works shall be dust," Mr. Brayton whispered through his fingers. "Dust in the vapor of time."

"More for that anon," Lizzie announced. "What we need to do now is untangle the knotted evidence and reveal this plot for what it is. For, although I am confident of the mechanics of the crime, it is only the Colonel who can explain to us the motivations that drove the affair. And I suspect that it will be harder to extract that confession of motive than it was to obtain the confession of having committed the deed itself."

"Hang it all, you think I care a fig for why?" the Marshal said. "If he will sign a statement to the effect that the gun smoked in his hand, I'll stop asking for the why."

"Yes," Lizzie consented. "That would be sufficient, but we can at least piece together a rather simple explanation from a complicated set of evidence. For future plots and murders may depend upon our work here today. If Mr. Brayton is correct about the conspiracy within the mill, then this murder may be symptomatic of a wave of violence that may engulf the industry. And in that context, the motivation behind this is of great interest to us."

"Granted," the Marshal added, humbled. "Far be it from me to discourage the uncovering of a criminal society. Proceed."

Lizzie glanced at Homer, as if trying to draw inspiration from her silent friend. He stood under his bowler by the bedroom door, one elbow drawn up to the wall, one leg casually crossed over the other. However, when Homer saw Lizzie's face with its so-familiar expression of a dam about to burst and thereby reveal the secrets of its contained water, he stood to attention, adjusted his hat and placed his hands at his sides. "Edison," he repeated. "It started with Mr. Edison."

"Yes," Lizzie said. "And the idea that a signal can flow in multiple directions at once. Pure information, unencumbered by what that signal actually means. A telegrapher sends off the message, 'Come quick, I need you!' in a series of electrical dots and dashes. To the metal wire on which the signal moves, that message is merely a change in current, meaningless to the untrained machinist. What is needed at the other side is a human mind to place those dots and dashes back into a set of symbols that have actual meaning—such being the nature of words."

"You are a born Electromechanician," Homer complemented her. "Edison could not have explained it better."

"And for every transmitter," Lizzie said proudly, "there must be a receiver. Observe Mr. Howard and Colonel Anthony who we see before us. Both were Pig Puddlers, one in the management office, the other in the furnace room melting and casting the pig iron. The highest office and the lowest dungeon. And a flow of information between them. 'Tell Latham to make haste to the Stone Bridge! No dilly-dallying!' Why was this message sent? And what exactly is the Stone Bridge? These questions I asked myself.

"I do not think it wrong to assume that Mr. Latham never pulled that trigger. But a bullet was fired! Was it Rogers himself? How did he get the gun? It is very simple: the gun seen in Mr. Latham's hand was not the gun that had been fired at all. And the gun found smoking in Mr. Rogers' hand is not the same gun that was in Mr. Latham's hand. There were two guns in that room, and the one that fired into Mr. Latham's forehead was in the hands of Colonel Anthony."

"I confessed," the Colonel said hotly. "Is that not enough?"

"No," Lizzie said. "I want to demonstrate how you did it, to dispel any notion that it was a miraculous piece of magic. There was nothing magical about it, it was mere mundane luck, dreamed up in the flash of a moment, executed with little thought, and then covered up with some simple deception. Once I explain the mechanics of it, you will seem more of a lackluster mind, than appear a criminal genius."

"I did not aspire to criminal genius," the Colonel said. "I simply acted, and then I ran. Yes, like a rank coward. But now, I wish to face my fears, look Madness and Death in the eye, and so laugh at their dark mysteries."

"Your fears," Lizzie echoed. "Like the fear of metal, the irrational terror brought about by the very substance that creates your wealth? Perhaps the metal is just a substitute for a deeper fear, that of the workers themselves who fire and cast the metal for you into products that you can sell. The metal represents, at least in your mind, the accumulated hatred and violence building in their hearts as they labor day and night to grow your fortune. You are more afraid of them than Death itself, and all that fear was poured into the casting mold of your imagination. So you decided to conquer your fears by taking on the guise of a puddler and working the metal yourself. I have seen this before, men hurtling themselves directly at the very situation or person who troubles them most."

"I thought you were in Pompeii," said Mr. Brayton to the Colonel, his eyes darkening, "looking at dead people to remind yourself of the ephemeral nature of life. That is what you said."

"That is what my doctor suggested," the Colonel said defensively. "But do not fault Ames; he is innocent in this affair. He counseled me, and I saw a way of tending to two problems at once, my own mental breakdown, and the rumors of a secret society of syndicalism within the mill. I have previously built up a rapport with Mr. Howard, being that I studied well in the history of the bog iron industry, and Mr. Howard had much to contribute to the subject. I met with him secretly, and conversed often about the furnaces of New Jersey, from the days before the anthracite flowed out of Pennsylvania and the face of modern iron production changed forever. Remember, Thomas, the many hours we sat with our corn cobs before the fire and wove endless tales of pulling the iron from the bogs, of pouring the shell flux, or of crucibles and boshes, of charging the furnace, of rolling and slitting the sheets? How we envied our ancestors who pounded the hammers on the anvils to produce the perfect nails for wardrobes and cabinets and chairs. How free they were, producing with their own hands, callusing their palms and fingers to produce the goods that they would then sell directly to the customer in his humble home. Those early men of metal forged a revolution, Thomas, building an iron industry to flout the British with all their manufacturing. We were no longer a nation of cash crops, tobacco and cotton; we were now makers of iron! And steel! Yes, Thomas, we talked of steel, and the new processes and blends that would help this nation grow to gigantic proportions. How we dreamed of our metal plated against the hulls of giant ships crossing the Atlantic, of metal capable of defying the icebergs of the frozen north, of buildings in the midst of our cities rising to fifty stories tall, of hardened war machines that would fright the souls of fearful adversaries and drive our conquests home! Do you remember, Thomas? Say you do, and I shall be vindicated."

The other man at the table eyed him furtively, his lips tightening, then said, "If I had known what you are capable of, I would have found a place to stuff that corn cob pipe."

"Now, Thomas," the Colonel said meekly. "That is unkind."

"Nonetheless," Lizzie continued, "a devil's pact was made between the two, and instead of fleeing to the Mediterranean, the Colonel went straight to this home. Here, he confided in Thomas his plans to work the metal. Tell me, Mrs. Howard, was this the time, three months ago, when your husband decided to grow his mustache?"

The woman stirred, at first hardly aware she was being addressed, then flashing recognition of Lizzie's question. "It came suddenly, almost overnight. I did not question, for I am a simple woman, and know little about men's ways."

"It did not strike you odd that such a bushy mustache can grow overnight?"

"He gave a muddled explanation at the time," the wife observed. "With hindsight, it does not make much sense. Oh, what a fool I have been!" She lowered her face into her weakened hands.

"Do not draw out her humiliation," Mr. Howard implored. "I did explain to her, later in the month, that to carry out this deception with exactitude, the Colonel would need to take more liberties in my own home, eating dinner in my place, tutoring my young son his letters, even…" He paused for a moment, forcing his eyes upwards to daringly fall on his wife's crumpled posture. "…sleeping in our bed."

"My God," the Marshal whispered. "What perfidy is this man not capable of?"

"Do not judge me!" Colonel Richard Anthony shouted. "For I had a higher purpose in mind."

"Higher?" Mrs. Howard said, raising her face with a renewed sense of dignity born from outrage. "You call that a higher purpose?"

"Exactly," said the Colonel. "Once I was within the mill, laboring at the furnace with the pig iron, I began to gain more information about the society of which we have talked about only in whispers. It may have been a stray voice from the casting floor, or a rumor carried by train rail into the charcoal house, or a fragment of truth brought to me by a child stoker. But I incrementally came to gather my evidence against Latham and the evil forces that pulled his puppet strings. After a time, I knew the extent of his plans, the scope of the conspiracy, and I knew I had to act."

"And you forged a deal with Rogers," Lizzie said hastily, "for him to take the blame for the murder, did you not?"

"As I have already said," the Colonel bemoaned, "it was not well thought out. It happened all in a matter of moments. I brought the Colt to the office the night before, smuggling it past the guards, explaining it as some iron to be melted in the blast. I then brought it to the office, where I spent a sleepless night huddled behind my own curtains, strangely believing that the events of the past several months had been nothing but a dark dream. I wanted to rest in the halls of Morpheus, only to awaken upon the dawn seeing my tweed suit upon me, and my morning reports on my desk; it seemed as though it was June, and none of this nightmare had even occurred.

"Yet, I was awakened by Rogers entering the office. It was a strange moment, for I assumed he thought me to be Howard the Puddler, come with a gun to assassinate him in the name of the society. He would have raised the alarm from the start and forced me to abandon my plans, but I ripped off the mustache. By so doing, I assured him that all was correct with the world, and that he was in no danger of falling prey to any assassin's plot. It took a long time, but I slowly convinced him that the death of Latham was necessary, that it would send a message to all anarchist assassins everywhere their syndicalism would not be tolerated in our society. I described a plot in which Latham would be shot in this office and it would be believed that Rogers was the culprit, but that he acted in self-defense. To alleviate his fear of being imprisoned for the rest of his life, I cited several popular cases of the past where a man accused of murder would be set free after a dramatic and very public trial, found not guilty of all charges although common sense and even some hard evidence spoke otherwise."

"Nonsense," Lizzie snorted. "I know of no such cases. You are talking fantasy."

"You have not heard of the Reverend Avery," the Colonel said hotly. "Look into your own backyard history, Miss Borden. In 1832, a Methodist minister of Bristol strangled a poor mill girl in Tiverton. He had secretly made her pregnant, and she was in turn blackmailing him. One night he met her under a hay pole at a Durfee farm and tied a rope around her neck, killed her in cold blood. He was subjected to three trials, Miss Borden. Not one, but three, in Bristol, Tiverton, and by the elders of his own church. And in all three cases, despite the majority of evidence against him, he was set free."

"The Methodist minister," the Marshal echoed. "Rogers told us that to our face. He was reaching out with the answer and we were too blind to see it!"

"I have heard of the Reverend Avery," Lizzie said. "But he spent the rest of his life in shameful ignominy, living under assumed names and witnessing his own effigy burned in the streets. Why would Rogers agree to such a future?"

"We were in the midst of discussing that possibility, how we could effect the crime in such a manner as to instead establish him as a virtuous hero in the eyes of management. He would be the man who stood up to the society and cut it down at its root."

"You mean," the Marshal said bitterly, "you aimed to kill a man in cold blood and then let one of your inferiors take the blame."

"Latham would be a sacrifice," the Colonel said breathlessly. "One death would put an end to the society and avoid decades of warfare between labor and management. I asked Rogers to call Latham to the office, where we could shoot him at point blank range within the hearing of a dozen office workers. There would be no doubt that Rogers shot Latham in self-defense."

"But you did not expect," Lizzie said solemnly, "the Stone Bridge."

"Yes, the Stone Bridge. There was the crack in the scheme, the thought that Rogers was a member of the society himself. How agitated he must have been in that office, talking to a crazy man with a gun, knowing the plan was that he was to be arrested for murder on the flimsy promise that I would find lawyers to free him from prison." He cast an unctuous glance at Mr. Twillie, who was still nursing his pale employer.

"Let it be read into the record," Mr. Twillie insisted, "that I knew none of this. I honestly thought the Colonel to be staring into some dead volcano somewhere."

"But what is the Stone Bridge?" the Marshal said, pulling at his cheeks. "What message did that convey to the furnace room?"

"We may never know the meaning of the Stone Bridge," Lizzie offered. "Rogers will never tell, and Latham is dead. And the others that are part of this conspiracy will never cough up their knowledge, even under pain of torture."

"Rogers part of the conspiracy?" Mr. Brayton said, his face rising into sudden renewed interest in the proceedings. "Why, all the confidences I have made in that man! All the business secrets and development plans! They were being fed directly to the secret society?" He went deathly silent, and began to tremble as if an eruption of his intestines was imminent.

"No doubt," Lizzie speculated. "We evidently have here a group of scoundrels of no moral suasion. Confidences are betrayed as easily as children play games in the gutter. Such is the flow of intelligence through a network of spies and assassins. There is no honor amongst thieves."

"Rogers was part of the conspiracy," the Colonel conceded. "But I did not know it at the time; how foolish I had been! I had not heard of the Stone Bridge, nor the secret message within the expression 'dilly-dally.' Latham came armed, and the real Thomas Howard came with him, but stayed outside. I was sequestered behind my curtains, and watching this ugly scene unfold before me. Rogers engaged Latham in some sort of debate, shouting about production and lengthened hours; and Latham, knowing this all to be some sort of ruse, replied in kind and shouted about worker's rights and increased wages. In the midst of this charade, Rogers must have made some sort of gesture to indicate to Latham that the danger implicit in his Stone Bridge message was behind the curtains, at which point Latham pulled forth his gun and pointed it in my direction. To the witnesses looking through the door, they must have believed the gun to be pointed at Rogers, due to the angle at which they were watching. At this point, I had no choice but to fire. It was an act of self-defense, one can argue. If I had not fired, it would be me lying dead in the mortuary, not Latham."

"You fired at a very lucky moment," Lizzie explained. "When Latham pulled his pistol, the eyewitnesses peering in from the front office had started to run, fearful that they would be caught in a spray of bullets. With those witnesses, no one would guess that it was not Latham's gun that had fired."

"Excepting myself," Mr. Howard lamented. "I did not even believe that the Colonel could be in that room. I truly believed that it was Latham who fired. My hatred for Rogers was such that I held contempt for those investigating, attempting to prove otherwise, or so it seemed from my vantage. Now that I see the Colonel's plot so clearly, and my role in the matter, I humbly beg your pardon and throw myself at your mercy."

"No grudges there," the Marshal nodded. "But how do we know this to be true? We still have no witnesses but Rogers and the Colonel, and their words are suspect."

"Without a doubt, a forensics report from the coroner," Lizzie offered, "will reveal that there was no gunpowder burns or powder upon the victim, something that would have been quite evident if he had been shot at such close quarters. Add to this that the angle of the bullet from the bridge of the nose to an area right behind the left ear showed that it had not been fired at him from directly in front. Evidently, Latham was shot from the area by the bay window."

The Marshal huffed and paced about, grabbing at his mustache and muttering. Then he raised a gloved finger as if to make a point, but sighed and said, "So how did the Colonel, disguised as the Pig Puddler, get out of the room after firing the gun? And how did the gun get into Rogers' hand? And by Saturn's Rings, what happened to the gun that Latham was about to fire?"

Lizzie cast a glance at the Colonel whose strange smirk had returned. "Here he was clever," she said, "but still very simple. Taking advantage of the confused circumstances, and noting that there was not a soul in the outer office standing by the door, the Colonel came out from his gunmen's perch, and slipped the smoking Colt into Rogers' hand, all according to plan, although I doubt that Rogers had much time to consider his alternatives. Then he reached down to Latham's body and snatched up the gun – whether it was a Colt or not is something that seems to be lost to posterity. It seemed fitting to the Colonel to leave only one gun at the scene, and that it'd best be one that had been discharged. Then he just stepped back behind the open door, hiding his presence, as the returning workers, including Thomas Howard, entered the room. At this point, there were two Pig Puddlers present, and in the confusion, no one really noticed. Except for Miss Borden. I recall her one bit of testimony that Mr. Howard seemed to flip from one side of the room to the other. She noted this phenomenon in the full-length mirror by the coat rack but dismissed it as an optical confusion. Yet she actually did see two Pig Puddlers, and remains the only witness who did so."

"So there were two gunmen," the Marshal said, "but only one bullet fired, and it was not from the gun in Latham's hand. So, what happened to Latham's gun after it was snatched by the Colonel?"

"I can guess that it happened as follows," Lizzie said proudly. "The Colonel slips from the room, bringing Latham's gun with him, proceeds down the administration steps, into the hallway and up towards the furnace room. There he tosses the weapon into the fiery chamber tended by Mr.

Howard's young son, Erasmus, who by now must be quite confused over the true appearance of his own father, having spent several months being tossed back and forth between the real person and the subterfuge. By the time we have examined the furnace, all traces of the gun have been removed, the fire reducing its form to liquid, to be scooped from slag and drained into new moulds to provide domestic trinkets for Fall River households."

"You are all correct," the Colonel said. "That is exactly how it happened."

"Perhaps," Mr. Twillie said, raising a palm towards the Colonel, "we'd best keep our mouths shut from this moment on."

"The man who should be doing all the talking," the Marshal observed, "is Rogers. He can verify this story one way or another, if he tells the truth."

"I don't suspect he will be talking much," Lizzie observed, "for if he is truly a member of this anarchist society, then he will continue to protect its secrets. For example, you will be hard pressed to discover the true meaning of the Stone Bridge, or the hidden message inside the phrase 'dilly-dally.' Latham took that to his grave, and so shall Rogers or any other member of the society."

"Isn't it best," inquired the Marshal, "to take this man into custody on the strength of his confession, and to lock him away for his crime? Why should we chase after motive if the proof of his guilt is enough?"

"No doubt it is best," Lizzie answered. "Secret societies are difficult to detect, even more so to expose. And they will counteract our investigations with more violence. Yes, we shall heed the Marshal's advice; we must allow justice to balance what she can, and leave those political battles for another time."

As Lizzie finished with a flourish of her hands, there was a clattering on the stairs, and then the sound of heavy boots ascending. All eyes turned towards the kitchen doorway, where Officer Beck, his beard flecked with the white smear of vanilla, appeared. He was holding the hand of a small boy by his side whose entire mouth and nose were buried in a generous glob of ice cream on the top of a hearty sugar cone. Erasmus Howard had been transformed from the filthy waif of the furnace room into a bright, cheery, and well-groomed young lad, clad in checkered knickers, a clean pressed shirt on his torso hugged by suspenders, and his head bearing a flattened cloth cap. His skin was cleared, his hands a healthy flesh tone, but the biggest alteration to his previous incarnation was the broad smile that shined across his face on both sides of the ice cream cone.

"Pop!" he said, pointing towards the pocked-marked Pig Puddler at the table. The man, who since the arrest, had not smiled or cast any gentle eye upon any man, now gave forth a comfortable chuckle. He crossed the room, kneeling down to greet his son with a warm and intimate embrace.

"He has been cleaned and fed," Officer Beck stated, then glanced back upon the stair behind him, twisting his hands. "Yes, and there is one other matter. As I was procuring this iced delicacy for young Master Erasmus, a gentleman approached me and demanded audience with the Marshall immediately."

"What kind of man?" the Marshal asked. "What business does he have with me?"

"Not any particular kind of man," Officer Beck answered, staring with blinking eyes at the Colonel. "Sir, is that who I…"

"Don't be so agog, Officer," the Marshall said. "I'll explain later. Summon the man you speak of."

The Officer motioned down the stairs and a soft ascent was heard. The sound culminated in a lanky figure appearing at the doorway, his bushy beard thrust forward, his pince-nez balanced on his cautious nose, and a leather satchel clutched in his bony hands. "Doctor Ames," the Colonel whispered. "Dear Lord, you are my salvation."

"Not quite," the doctor beamed, making an odd hand gesture with two fingers before his chest. "Marshal, I would like to have ten seconds of privacy with the Colonel, if it pleases all and one."

"Ten seconds," the Marshal said. "You have petitioned your own time limit, proceed."

The Doctor crossed the room and stood beside the Colonel who stared at him with awkwardness. The physician then knelt down, and placed a cupped hand over the Colonel's ear. All the company could see his cheeks bellow with his lips and then he was silent, his hand removed, his form moving away from the Colonel towards the door. "Thank you, gentlemen," he said, then made a slight waggle of his fingers at Lizzie, who stood defiantly behind the seated Mrs. Howard. "And ladies, adieu!" And he was gone, departing with just a clattering down the stairs and a rusty creak of the front door of the house.

"What do you suppose that was about?" Lizzie asked, disquieted, then turned towards the Colonel. "Can you explain? What did he tell you?"

"Professional confidentiality," the Colonel retorted, gazing towards the begrimed window, pretending a profound disinterest. Somewhere in the far distance, a mill tower was tolling the hour, and Fall River was beginning to fall under a veil of dark northbound clouds.

The Last Cast

The young pair rode their buggy back to the apothecary on South Main Street, their intellects contented, a sense of justice having been served permeating their peaceful afternoon. The Girl Detective and the Boy Inventor strode into the nearly empty store, caught the eye of A.E. Dobbs, Proprietor, and demanded two more sarsaparillas to quench their late afternoon thirst.

"What did you hear about that trouble at the iron mill?" Dobbs asked, his hands behind the spigots. "Was it indeed a murder?"

"Truly," said Lizzie, proudly. "And I solved it."

The proprietor twisted his cheek and shook his head playfully. "I suppose I'll read about it in the papers, or get some stray gossip from customers, but I don't think I'll ever know the truth behind it all until I hear it directly from you, Lizzie Borden."

"*Il n'y a pas de quoi*," Lizzie said, taking her mug and turning towards their street-view table. When she blinked at Homer's startled expression, she explained, "I'm studying French privately, to prepare for my trip to the continent. Father keeps suggesting the Grand Tour." They sat together with their drinks.

"Europe would be quite illuminating," said Homer excitedly. "You can stop in at the Royal Academy in London. I hear that they are attempting to complete Babbage's designs for a computing machine that would carry out the processes of the human brain through electrical relays."

Lizzie looked distraught at his pronouncement. "Really, Homer, first the light of the human eye is captured by a machine, then the human voice is captured, now the human brain is being reduced to...a machine! Did not your trip to the Iron Works teach you anything about how technology dehumanizes people? If I go to London, I shall visit the National Gallery, and take a tour of nearby Windsor Castle. I shall witness art and architecture that is immortal."

Homer sipped at his drink, visibly dismayed by her comment. "I did notice the demands placed on the workers, as well as the unfair conditions and the political complexities that arise from such inequality of wealth and labor, but I also saw men who were putting their hearts into the work; I could see it."

"Perhaps," Lizzie conceded, "the truth is somewhere in between. We shall meditate upon this."

"In the meantime," Homer said, "I have a new chapter of your biography to compose. Yes, I shall record this case for posterity," he laughed heartily. "The Adventure of the Doubled Pig Puddler."

"One can think of a more sensible name than that," Lizzie suggested. "I'm afraid the affair didn't have the same sense of completion as my other cases, largely because we never discovered the true nature of what we may confidently call The Stone Bridge Society. It would have been a sweet moment indeed for me to have done at least that. For now, I feel as if I have solved the mechanics of the crime, not the motivation."

"What makes you so sure you solved even the mechanics?" said Homer, surprised. "You only think that the Colonel was the man who pulled the trigger."

"Why would you make such a statement? It's readily evident. Besides, the man confessed, you were there, you had ears in your head at the time."

"True, but anyone could have said anything. No one knows for a fact that the Colonel was walking around with a Pig Puddler mustache in that office room. What do you base that on? That Elizabeth Borden saw a reflection in a mirror? And even if we do put a puddler in the room during the shooting, how do you know that it wasn't Mr. Howard behind the curtains, and Colonel Anthony in the outer office?"

Lizzie felt a wave of tension along her spine, reaching her neck and tightening her face. "Homer, you are beginning to frighten me. Don't you think that the Colonel's confession is authoritative enough?"

"Well, let's examine for a moment what he said. According to him, he was in the office explaining to Rogers that they have to kill Latham, not realizing that Rogers was really part of the conspiracy. So Rogers gave some sort of signal telling Latham to come with Mr. Howard and to bring along a handgun for self-defense."

"And where is the fault in that scenario?"

"Who was sitting next to the Colonel when he confessed?"

"Mr. Howard, the real Mr. Howard."

"Right, and what if it was Mr. Howard and the Colonel who were plotting to kill Latham, not the Colonel and Rogers? Or what if Latham himself was plotting with Rogers to kill the Colonel but they didn't expect the Colonel to have a gun as well. What if, Lizzie Andrew Borden?"

Lizzie took a deep sip of her sarsaparilla, swallowed, and closed her eyes to accompany a long sigh. "I am going to totally ignore," she confessed, "everything you just suggested. I consider it all to be irrelevant to the case and more typical of your skeptical approach to life."

"Fine," Homer said, and crossed his arms. "Have it your way. The Colonel killed Latham after being betrayed by Rogers. It's a good scenario, and one that suitably accounts for all the facts."

"Yes," Lizzie said.

"And besides, the Colonel confessed, and will go to jail of his own free will."

"Correct," Lizzie said.

"Then why," Homer quipped, "did Doctor Ames have on a false beard?"

Lizzie lowered her mug and stared hard at Homer. "A false beard? How do you know this?"

"Because the real Ames is a friend of my father's and comes quite often to the house. I've had the pleasure of witnessing the man up close dozens of times. And I can assure you that the man who came to the Howard house this afternoon was NOT Dr. Ames."

Lizzie blinked and then followed the curved path of a fly over her head.

Turning towards Homer, she shut her lids, then fluttered them open as she responded, "I see little reason for you to lie to me, but given the fact that someone unnamed, no doubt a member of the Stone Bridge Society, has staged a hoax right under the very nose of the City Marshal as well as the Most Excellent Girl Detective of Fall River, would it behoove us to make light of this? Should we tell the Marshal? Would it make a difference even if the Colonel is acquitted on the grounds of self-defense? In sum, Homer Thesinger, does it matter a fig?"

Homer nodded briskly. "I don't suppose, but I did want to give you that observation."

"Yes, well, we can keep that observation under our hats for now. Besides, there's very little we can do about it." She drummed her fingertips nervously on the tablecloth. "Imagine, Homer. The case is still not solved. We don't know any more about what happened in that office during those few seconds than we did before the investigation. Should I be concerned about this? Will my reputation be tarnished? I had a perfect record of solving the crimes I've investigated, now I must live in shame that I am not perfect."

"Lizzie," Homer said. "In this particular case, we should just leave it well alone. There's politics and interactions here we can't possibly comprehend, and with which we should not be getting involved. There is a time and place for everything, and if this Stone Bridge Society does in fact exist, and if it is growing in strength and gaining a foothold in the mills, we shall hear about it again. And perhaps then we shall confront our Doctor Ames impersonator and rip his fictional beard from his face, exposing the conspiracy and bringing them all to justice. But now is not the time, I agree. We shall remain quiet and humble, in the light, but watching the shadows."

The bell atop the front door tinkled and a thin man in a gentlemen's coat entered, his eyes staring widely about as if he were attempting to test out his vision for the first time after a long blindness. A.E. Dobbs jumped to the service counter to see to the newcomer's needs, but the man held up a hand, forcefully, and sat down.

"I saw a terrible thing today," he said hauntingly, "and had a horrific vision."

"Would you like some sarsaparilla?" Dobbs enquired. When the man didn't respond, the proprietor shrank back to his seat. Lizzie called out across the table. "What was the terrible thing?"

"A man was killed today," the man said, his bearded face turning towards her. "In the mill. The Iron Works. "

"We have heard news to that effect," said Lizzie, solemnly. "What did you see?"

"I saw the body being removed," he continued. "The sight pierced me, and propelled me into a deep trance. I was spiraling over the city like a great hawk, and the human world was below me, in those dark mills along the river and the stream. I flew unencumbered by any ordinary restrictions, soaring over the heights, looking for a crag on which to perch. Yet I could not find anything but stacks and steam and brick and metal. There was no natural cliff, nor gorge, nor ravine, nor even a towering tree on which to perch. I circled and circled, longing to land, desperate to find in that valley of industry, some resting place that I could temporarily call my home before I migrated once again to the feeding grounds of the far north.

"Then, as I was bemoaning my plight, there was a mighty rush of wind, and a fire storm, and a great conflagration assaulted the city. The citizens ran to the streets, hoping to escape the inferno of their homes and places of business as they exploded in the hellish flames. But there was no escape. As they huddled against the river, attempting to save themselves from being burned alive, a terrible wind came in from the north and hurled the flames to the very lip of the river. Women died with their sons still clutched in their swaddling clothes; men of great wealth were consumed; children even, and animals also were all eaten up by the ravenous hunger displayed by the great storm.

"Then all was smoke and ruin, and not a living thing stirred. I alighted upon a singular stack still rising from the burnt rubble and rested my weary wings. There was calm once more, with all that belonged to man in ruins. All the human presence had been erased as if the entire race, with all its atrocities, its wars, and its art and science and culture had never even existed upon the planet. The forest was growing back; the mighty mills were sinking into the dust, ready to be cast forever into the timeless abyss of eternity.

"I could do nothing but weep, as only a hawk would weep when it sees no place called Home, but longs to be at rest. Yes, I will never again be the same."

The man's head sank to his breast and he heaved a tremendous sigh. Lizzie carefully stepped across the floorboards and touched a fingertip to his shoulder, causing him to shudder. "Forgive me, my young lady," he said, his eyes rising with an unexpected twinkle shrouded by watery tears. "I shall arrive on the other side of my melancholy, and anon be myself once more. Good day to you, gentle people. Good day." And he replaced his hat, adjusted his watch fob, and ironed out with flat fingers the creases in his jacket. After a final nod of his head that bespoke a reluctance to surrender to despair, he stepped out onto the street to the delicate tinkle of the apothecary bell.

"Don't tell me," Lizzie said, refusing to turn her countenance towards Homer.

"But I must," Homer said, no trace of pride or satisfaction in his voice. "Now you have met Doctor Ames."

"I gathered as much," she said, bemusedly. "I have solved the case, but I have not fathomed the mystery."

Then she turned, clapping her two gloved hands together. "Homer, I believe we must meet again next Tuesday morn for some more sarsaparilla and some most excellent banter about science and technology. Yes, I believe I would enjoy such a discourse. And I am most curious about the discoveries of Mr. Edison in New Jersey."

"I shall be delighted," Homer said, bowing slightly and replacing his bowler. The two paid their bill to the proprietor, and stepped out into the busy foot traffic of South Main Street. They then disappeared into the busy stream of traffic that flowed, as a river would into an ocean, into the endless parade of human life.

THE MELANCHOLY SCION

MAY 1927. FRENCH STREET, THE HILL, FALL RIVER, MASSACHUSETTS.

PRESSED IN LAVENDER

For Lizzie Borden, Andre de Camp will always be the Poet.

In all her sixty-six years on earth, she had never been known to pay such reverence, silent or otherwise, to any member of the male sex, whether to applaud virtue or to praise physical elegance. But Andre de Camp, scion of a wealthy French family that had relocated to Fall River in the summer of 1877, a tall, brooding and decidedly handsome bachelor of nineteen years, the product of private advanced education, brilliant, fastidious in his manly dress and precise in his manners and ethics, held a special place in Lizzie's estimation of the masculine half of humanity.

She first glimpsed him at a mid-summer charity event in the church hall of the First Congregational. Standing with his illustrious family—the father wearing proudly a decorated uniform, the mother and sister standing upright with pious concentration—Andre bowed his head towards Lizzie, just once, as if in humble supplication before a higher power. The gesture sent a chill through Lizzie's being.

She quickly became impressed with how the de Camp men were so very different from the money-driven barons who banked her city, the uncultured factors and industrialists who would never design a cathedral or build an opera hall lest they consider it "a foolish dollar spent." Andre de Camp may have been spawned from that same class, yet he brought with him all the cultured elegance of Paris and the dark mysteries of the southern Languedoc, locales that Lizzie had admired from afar through sepia photographs of the mountainous region with its lush outcroppings and deep-veined soil, a land she thought only existed in her dreams.

Andre was a graceful, aristocratic youth who, like herself, was more comfortable with the personal passions and the aesthetics of everyday life than with the complexities of commerce. She saw in him not the proud Marshals and Presidents of France's dusty past, nor the great Sun King in his splendid palace, but the simple shepherds from the paintings of Poussin, the noble musketeers of Dumas, and the provincial people of the tales of Flaubert. He embodied in his presence all the excitement, adventure and beauty that she had admired in the great French paintings and novels that made their way to various Fall River parlors. In her opinion, he far outpaced in every manner the grown men of his generation.

But for the rest of her days she would never speak his name aloud. Even as an aging woman of the Hill, secluded in her summer bedroom in the rambling Maplecroft, her manse and hermitage, alone as she looked back upon a dark and hidden life, she would only speak of Andre as the Poet, and then briefly, and then only to a chauffeur or a domestic who was not of her generation, who would never have heard of the de Camp family, or would never repeat her words to anyone in town who may have known them, and then only when she was caught off guard with some seizure of nostalgia for a Fall River that had once been and now was no more.

But when the glimmer came in her aging eyes, and she spoke of the Poet, when she made oblique references to faces and places now lost to time and memory, when she hinted that once she had loved and felt within her breast a singular passion the likes of which had never been repeated, it was the summer of 1877 and the Case of the Melancholy Scion to which her thoughts took her. Back to a time before she was the secluded spinster on the Hill, before she sat alone in church because no fellow citizens would occupy the pews adjoining hers, before she was accused of that terrible crime whose shadow she would never escape, back when she was young and fresh and alive; to the time when she walked the streets of Fall River with Andre de Camp, who also was young and fresh and alive, and who, despite her unwillingness to let her heart be so directly touched, had truly loved her.

Back when she was Lizzie Borden, Girl Detective.

Unsettling Revelations

1877. South Main Street, Fall River.

Andrew Jackson Borden took his pre-dinner constitutional from the front of his quaint little Greek revival house on Second Street towards the tonsorial parlor, the post office and the pharmacy to, respectively, get a shave, check for his mail and to inquire about the gastroesophegeal disruption pills his wife Abby needed for her burning chest pains. Threading his way through the narrow streets, surrounded by the bustle of pedestrian traffic, the whinnying of nags, the clattering of buggies, and the hawking of the fish mongers, Borden turned to survey the town that had given him birth and had nurtured him through his rise to prosperity.

So many estate properties, he thought to himself. *So many empty lots. If only I could possess them all, to have that locus of power over the domestic and commercial fate of every individual in Fall River.* He allowed himself this one pure moment of magnitude, imagining an inflated likeness of himself that lay unrealized by his business colleagues, and then with a wistful grin that barely moved the edge of his mouth pushed on towards the barber for his weekly trimming.

At that very moment, a short squat man with a bulbous nose and bristling mustache stopped in front of Andrew, ungraciously blocking his path.

"You're A.J. Borden, I believe!"

Andrew lifted his chin proudly. "I do have that honor."

The man's mouth made a strange mumbling motion and then before Andrew could take refuge in flight, the man bellowed an almost incomprehensible "Feeeyaaaah!" and a large wad of saliva came flying across the distance between them, landing with a sickening thwack on Andrew's cheek.

"Here's for your thievery and your damned Ullsworth!" the attacker shouted. "Take a rest in one of your own flimsy coffins, why don't you? Hang ye be to Arcady!" And then the man was gone, leaving Andrew to wipe away his indignity with a hastily drawn handkerchief.

Ullsworth? Andrew pondered as a few passers-by giggled and pointed. Could that be the family he had driven from the Anawan Street property? Better for them, they couldn't afford the rent, not on the cloth doffing salary that Tobias Ullsworth had settled for after the end of his whaling career. The wife and seven children were much better off as wards of the city, where at least they could be assured that they would be fed every day. But who had been his attacker? And what connection could he have with this Ullsworth? Surely it took a dedicated passion to accost and insult a prominent citizen in broad daylight before gawking pedestrians.

Andrew turned to head home but was surprised to see his young daughter Lizzie standing on the street corner in a pretty pink and white striped fantail skirt and polonaise fresh from *La Mode Illustre*, topped off with a cunning chip hat laden with silk pansies perched high aloft her curly hair. She was positioned by a lamp post with a far twinkle in her wide blue-gray eyes.

"Daughter," Andrew said, pointing in the direction of the fleeing assailant. "I am afraid you had to witness my unexplained ignominy."

"Father," Lizzie said, her voice thinner than usual. "I did not see anything, for I am adrift in a waking reverie."

"You are indeed adrift. I don't think that I have ever seen you in such ponderous daydreaming. What distracts you from your daily duties?"

"I have been to the charity event this very hour on Saturday past."

"Yes, indeed. You accompanied myself and Mrs. Borden. Emma, I believe, was home with a complaint."

"And at the Church I had occasion to see the party of Frenchmen who have recently joined our community from abroad."

Borden nodded, his mouth clenched. Rubbing his unshaven cheek, he explained. "The de Camp clan...mighty proud people. They bought the Durfee Estate and are in the process of establishing an import-export concern. The Comte de Rennes, the father, is an enterprising gentleman, albeit a bit taken with lofty matters such as art and music, subjects not quite befitting a man of his industrious character."

"They are highly cultured then," Lizzie said, her eyes widening. "Oh Father, do tell me that they are versed in all matters of aesthetics. Poetries, romans-a-clef, sonnets and concertos, painting and architecture. Tell me that young Andre can dance to a rondo as easily as he can recite Shakespearian soliloquies, that as a family they have that spark of creativity within which transcends the ordinary particulars of our daily labors and occupations."

Andrew heaved an unpleasant grunt. "If you mean do they listen to operatic clap trap, or read the ramblings of word mongers, then yes, Daughter. They are aesthetes."

Lizzie smiled, her face reddening in the afternoon sunlight. "I am glad of it. Young Andre has caught my fancy, but I think you must tell not a soul about my feelings."

Andrew struggled to process this evidence of his daughter's awakening womanhood. He knew in the past that she had been distracted by boys, but she always maintained a short temper and a feigned indifference, perhaps to avoid complications. And she had socialized with strange, undeveloped male specimens like Homer Thesinger the Boy Inventor who presented himself more as a child despite his recent attainment of standing six feet tall. But Andre, the handsome youth who had been introduced as Jacques de Camp's scion, he was altogether different. He was stern and determined, calm and centered. He was also several years Lizzie's elder, and seemed strong enough to conquer her coquettish behavior if such was his will. No, this would not do. The de Camp boy must be denied access to Lizzie by any means necessary.

"Daughter," Andrew said, his mouth tightening against the emerging words. "Need I remind you that the Count is a Roman Catholic? They attend Mass at St. Anne's, don't you know?"

"Father," Lizzie smirked. "By now you should know that when it comes to spiritual matters, I ascribe the choice of worship to be up to each and every man's conscience. Besides, I am told that the Count has a Protestant mother."

"Yes," he grumbled. "Well, what, then, would you say if I told you that there is much scandal surrounding young Andre?"

"Scandal?" Her eyes peered purposefully, trying to discern his meaning.

"What ever could you mean?"

"Much has been discovered about the family since their appearance in town. I have already heard word from my fellow stockholders at the Mill, who make it their business to investigate the background of newly arrived immigrants, that Jacques de Camp, the father of your beloved boy, has cleanly sailed through their careful scrutiny; but I fear to say that young Andre has not fared as well. The boy is known…" Andrew paused for dramatic effect "… he is known to frequent Houses of Assignation. He is a Sporting Boy."

Lizzie felt the fluttering in her head long before she could digest her father's statements. "Assig…" she muttered. "Sporting…" then she lifted a hand to her forehead and began her downward spiral towards the sidewalk. Andrew leapt forward and caught her in his arms. Her eyes were shifting violently back and forth under her lids.

A man in a bowler hat with trim mutton chops emerged from the moving traffic of pedestrians and offered his services. "Is this young lady aright?" he asked. "I am a doctor. Ah, Borden! I see Lizzie has taken ill."

Andrew recognized his Second Street neighbor, Dr. Seabury Bowen and watched breathlessly while the doctor brought a cracked tablet to her nostrils. She groaned, showing signs of life.

"Will she live?" asked Andrew grimly.

"Examine her pallor," said the doctor, pointing. "She has merely fainted. Nothing more."

Andrew scratched at his beard. "I suppose you want some brass for your services, Seabury."

"I am in your service," the doctor said, trying to haul Lizzie to her feet and tip his bowler simultaneously. "No coin required. Let us just get the poor girl home."

Andrew hesitated, assessing Dr. Bowen carefully. "You do not mean to clap me with a summation upon our arrival? I will not honor it!"

Dr. Bowen took a patient breath. "I have heard of you, Mister Borden. You need not fear any trickery from me. I am concerned only for the girl's health. Your daughter, I presume."

"Yes, it is Lizzie," Andrew huffed. "Be about your business, man. It is a harsh day when I confront an honest doctor. But I will tolerate your aid for my Lizzie's sake. Spring to it, man!"

As he helped Dr. Bowen carry Lizzie the two short streets to their home on Second Street, Andrew pondered Lizzie's reactions to the revelations about the de Camp boy. He felt a brief pang of guilt over distressing his daughter to the point of fainting.

"But my actions were all correct," he rationalized. "No good could come out of Andre de Camp. Not for my daughter!"

A Desperate Visitor

Lizzie awoke in her cramped bedroom on the upper floor of the Borden's modest Second Street house. Fully clothed and reclined on her bed, her forehead beaded with sweat, she struggled to make sense of the tolling of the church bell. The small walls and their flowered paper caved in on her as she fought for her breath.

"Lizzie Andrew!" came a sharp cry.

Springing to her feet, she felt a disorienting rush of blood to her head as she nearly fell back onto the mattress. Her shoulders were caught fast by two hands that emerged from below a thin and chinless face that was now coming into focus. Lizzie's elder sibling, Emma, was standing before her, a frown upon her brow.

"My Sister," Emma sighed. "Sometimes I fear that you have the falling sickness."

"No, Sister," Lizzie said, bringing the back of her hand to her forehead. "It is Fall River that has the falling sickness!"

Emma waggled her head as if trying to dislodge a disturbed thought. "I have ceased to attempt understanding your inane ramblings. One would think that you had been secretly dropped on your head when you were a child."

"Would that the act was repeated to clear my mind of these worries."

A flash of recognition came across Emma's face. "You are pursuing your consulting services again. I swear by all the heavens, Lizzie, that is all nonsense. Pay more attention to your proper duties."

"Emma," Lizzie said earnestly, "I have heard this day that our town is host to Sporting Boys. And where there are Sporting Boys…" Her eyes took a quick dart about the room "…there are Fancy Girls."

Her sister flinched with great discomfort at the phrases that she was hearing. "If such matters go on in this town," Emma said with a shrug, "it is the province of the law to sort it out and the mandate of the Almighty above to judge their sins. For now, all we can do is suffer our mundane tasks upon the earth."

"Mundane tasks?" Lizzie suppressed a spontaneous chuckle.

"Yes, mundane. Mrs. Borden has some paper wrappers for us to address. And I believe there is a buggy to bring to Swansea Farm. Do you not remember that today is Wednesday? Now be downstairs in a few moments, composed and alert." And she darted from the room, more frustrated than concerned. Lizzie stood alone, staring into space, thinking.

After changing her downstreet ensemble for a cotton calico and stout tie oxfords, clothing more suitable for scrambling after eggs in a chicken coop, Lizzie came down the front stairs of the house to find her stepmother, Abby Borden, by the front door. Abby was a plump woman of fifty-two, with a dour and haggard face, as if she had spent the better part of a lifetime trying to feign cheerfulness with little reward.

"I am glad to see you well," Abby said cursorily, handing her a stack of paper wrappers. "Mr. Borden is hiding in his room fearing Dr. Bowen's summation. One day that man shall be the death of us."

From the sitting room door emerged a smart and handsome man, his warm eyes twinkling above his mutton-chopped mustache. "Miss Lizzie," he said, nodding his chin respectfully. "Dr. Seabury Bowen. I trust you are feeling much better."

"Very fine, doctor. I have never felt better. Are you the man who aided me in my time of distress?"

"I have that honor. Even I, a poor medical man attempting to establish himself with such modest resources, has heard of the great Lizzie Borden, the Girl Detective of Fall River."

Abby groaned, her hands fleeing into her apron. "What nonsense! Girl Detective indeed!"

"Your daughter is quite an accomplished woman, Mrs. Borden. I am pleased to see her fine and healthy. Now it is for her father I fear. He seems to be in a state of apoplexy, as if something is weighing upon his mind. He muttered about a man who accosted him in the street."

"I believe Father said something about it," Lizzie said, "but I do not think that I remember."

Abby sighed. "Your father does indeed have many enemies since he has elevated his station in life. No doubt many of them wish him harm."

"I believe it was an English bard," Dr. Bowen added, "who described the King that must wear the crown as having an uneasy head. Sleep comes dear to such a man."

"Amen," Abby concluded. "Now, Lizzie you have chores to run. Emma's in the barn harnessing the rig. I suspect she'll call for you shortly."

Dr. Bowen removed his bowler from the standing rack, bid the ladies good afternoon and took his leave. Abby bolted the door after him.

"There are some doctors in this town who are decent at heart, Mrs. Borden," Lizzie said smugly. "Don't let Father begrudge such a man."

"To your chores!" Abby quipped. "Don't dally, there's much to be done. It is Wednesday you know!"

Lizzie took the wrappers and entered the kitchen where the stove was ablaze and some papers were already burning. Staring into the grate, Lizzie could see that they were legal documents touching upon property estates. For a brief moment, Lizzie thought she could discern the name Ullsworth on one of the papers. Something flickered in the back of her memory. Something she had heard while drinking her Ayres' sarsaparilla at the pharmacy with her friends, something about a whaling man who had vanished and his indigent wife and children. She was about to reach in and try to salvage the paper when she sensed a fluttering in the air behind her. Spinning about, Lizzie was facing her step-mother who stood with her hands thrust into her apron, a look of astonishment on her face.

"Lizzie Andrew," Abby said, her voice humbled. "There is a gentleman to see you. I do believe he is a gentleman despite his garish appearance. Although I doubt your father would ever allow such a person into his home."

"Garish? Is he fancied up like a saloon performer?"

"No, he is…well, perhaps you'd best see for yourself."

Lizzie came back to the parlor to find a very tall man standing by the piano. He was jowly and broad, covered in a red brocade of fine military threads, his feet planted firmly on the carpet, his strong arms bent behind his back. A domino mask obscured his eyes and nose, and a broad cape flowed like a theatrical curtain behind him. His mustaches extended below the mask and stood firm and proud like they were testifying a profound Yes to the vagaries of life. And while his mustaches were displaying defiance against darkness, his jutting chin was mastering the art of adjuration, a proud opulence that spoke of an abandoned country and a melancholy exile. Here was a man that radiated energy, masculine and forceful. Lizzie felt self-secure enough to stand firm before him, and to extend her hand without diverting her eyes from his piercing gaze.

He gave a brief smile. "Miss Lizzie Borden, the Girl Detective."

Lizzie held out her hand and he gently pressed his lips to it. "Forgive my forgery of identity," he continued, "for I have a high position in this town's industry and I must keep it secret, even from you, my potential consultant."

"I am intrigued." Lizzie waved towards the pillowed sofa. "Please have a seat and explain to me how I can be of service."

"I prefer to stand," the strange visitor exclaimed. "It provides extra labor for the legs, but my circumstance is such that at a moment's notice I must spring like a lion for shelter. I cannot be too safe."

"I see," said Lizzie, occupying the sofa with a coquettish descent. "Please explain to me how I can be of service to you."

He executed a hasty cough, his mustaches quivering, and then he began: "I represent a rather large number of Fall River businessmen, many of whom are aware of my identity but none of whom know that I am consulting with you. Besides yourself, your most polite mother, and the coach man who is in my private employ, no one knows of my visit here today."

"That is Mrs. Borden," Lizzie corrected him, nodding towards the door that Abby was, no doubt, pressing her ear against. "She is not my mother." Lizzie raised her voice to proclaim, "My mother is dead."

"Ah, I see. You must forgive my faux pas."

"No offense taken, Mr…uh…"

"You may call me Chace. Yes, that name would be suitable. But I may resume with the narrative of my situation. I am in communication with a large number of European concerns that are investigating the Fall River market, primarily interested in buying up stock in industry here. Some of those concerns have ties with the royal families of Eastern Europe. As you may know, there is quite a fuss going on abroad due to the conflicts with the Ottomans over the Slavic lands. England and France are quite busy with their espionage and intrigue, both of them taking sides one way or the other with the Russians over this terrible conflagration in Bulgaria. The Russian army has crossed the Danube and is laying siege as we speak to the city of Plevna. The death toll is mounting, and there are those who wish to see a hasty end to this campaign."

Lizzie nodded. "I read the Fall River Herald on a daily basis, Mr. Chace, while I heat my irons. I have perused some editorials about the affair with the Turks."

"Then you are aware that Europe is now a powder keg waiting for a match to fall upon it. And when that happens, there will be a conflict such as the world has never before seen."

Lizzie sighed, meditating upon the foolish games of powerful men and all their silly armies and conflicts. "There does seem to be quite a large amount of consternation. I can imagine the outcome of such an imbroglio. But what has this to do with anything concerning which I can help you?"

Chace rocked on his heels. "A Russian noble of some reputation has bought up large amounts of textile stock in order to raise funds for a private army to fight the Turks. I was to be the liaison between the Russian and a certain European government. He has sent an agent, an inventor, to speak on behalf of Russian industry."

"What could this Russian possibly have to offer the foreign government that could be so valuable?" asked Lizzie. "And why Fall River?"

The eyes under the domino mask darted from side to side as if scanning the room for spies. "The Russian inventor has laid out the plans for a new self-acting Mule which, when it was combined with the new Hayes and Drumpet Throstle Spinner and put into production at his test plant in Moscow, quadrupled his yarn output and tripled his pick per yard. We intend to sell this patent for the self-acting Mule to the highest bidder in Fall River while retaining a commission on each yard spun using the technology. This particular Mule technology will revolutionize the entire industry. The first manufacturer who adopts it will become wealthy beyond his imagination and the Russian shall have his privately funded army to fight the Turks and raise the siege of Plevna."

Lizzie shrugged. "Personally, I prefer the simple pleasure of a summer's afternoon eating pears in the yard, but I can see that when money and power are involved, men will do anything to exploit the common mill worker."

"Yes, it is very true. But if Herr Marx should have his way...well..." Mr. Chace raised a handkerchief to his sweating brow. "That is a story for another time." He stared in reverie at the far wall, his mind lost in some anguished internal debate.

"So you tell me that this Russian inventor is in Fall River with the plans for his invention?" Lizzie said, picking up the thread of conversation.

"Yes, but there is one particular that he did not count on. His plans have been stolen!"

Lizzie raised her hand to her mouth. "My Lord!"

"Yes. There has been perfidy of the most sinister kind. This Monday last at ten in the evening, while the Russian inventor was asleep in his hotel, a scoundrel entered the premises and stole the plans."

"Did he not have them locked up somewhere for safe-keeping?"

"Ah, that is the embarrassing part. He had ingeniously stowed the plans inside a medical...uh...how do you Americans say it? A pessary? Which he inserted into a chamber of his own anatomy. Modesty forbids me to locate the particular chamber in which the pessary was stowed."

"I see," said Lizzie, blushing slightly. "I believe it is a suppository you are referring to."

"*Mais oui!* Yes, indeed. A pessary! The fiend put him to sleep with liquid ether administered with a cloth over his nose, and then went to work extracting the container."

"Such a hiding place would not easily be accessed," Lizzie sighed. "But when a man is unconscious, all sorts of violations are possible."

"Yes, that is exactly what I said to the foreign government. But they did not find such comments amusing. They told me I had twenty-four hours to find the plans, with or without the pessary; and that if I did not produce them before the arranged time for the meeting with the mill owners on Friday afternoon, I shall be removed immediately from my position as liaison. In such a case, I shall return home a ruined man, all my investments canceled, and my prospects in America reduced to nothing. Hence the desperation with which I approach you."

"Time must be of the essence," Lizzie suggested.

"More than you can imagine, Miss Borden," Chace confirmed. "Even more at stake than my own reputation is the fate of Europe. If the patent negotiations break down with the Russians, the balance of power will shift to those nations backing the Ottomans. All the stresses and tensions that are holding Europe in check will unravel and there will be a violent and bloody war amongst the nations. Shall I say, a world war, to coin a phrase."

The tall mysterious man paused for dramatic effect. Out in the street, a nearby church was tolling the hour. The clopping of horse hooves and the crying of the fishmongers lingered in the room. A darkness came over Mr.

Chace's masked face as he waited for her to respond.

Lizzie took a deep breath. "But why come to me?" she asked. "I am merely the youngest daughter of a furniture salesman. I have no particular aptitude with which to deal with industrial politics, far less military wars abroad."

"But you are Lizzie Borden the Girl Detective! Amongst the board members of the leading mills you are notorious for bringing down Livermore, the mill owner who killed his own plant manager. You have shown fortitude, intellect and powers of detection that some consider uncanny. I come to you as my last hope to save not only my paltry self, but to help maintain the balance of power in Europe."

"Yes," Lizzie shrugged. "I did perform quite well during the Case of the Purloined Curio, and I was commended by no less than the Mayor himself for the Adventure of the Antiquated Blunderbuss, but I still don't agree that you have to hide from me, Monsieur Jacques de Camp, Comte de Rennes!"

"*Zut alors!*" came the bellowing reply from the sturdy giant. His cheeks went slack, and his hands fell to his sides. "I am undone! How did you know?"

"It is simplicity itself," Lizzie proclaimed. "You are doing an appreciable imitation of an American accent, but there are certain nuances in your nasality that bespeak a French origin. Further, your mustache is of a particular cut that I have seen only in Daguerreotypes of gentlemen from the hills around Carcassonne in the Languedoc. And I do believe I see embossed on your forefinger's ring the characteristic coat of arms for the Merovingian lineage, long since vanished from the Franco-Monarchial scene, but forever bound with honor and respect within the de Camp line, which I have studied at my local lending library, exhausting its modest resources on the topic.

"As for all your tales of Russian and Turkish conflicts, one need not go further than the few scraps of articles that can be read while heating flats for a grand session of handkerchief-ironing to know that England is attempting to stop the Russians from going to war against the Ottomans, while France is wholeheartedly backing the Russians' campaign. Further, the French government has recently investigated land grants in the Taunton River area for possible development of mills that would be run by France's own interests. One cannot put all these facts together without deducing that you are indeed a French investor recently imported into Fall River, and the only French investor I know of who fits that description is Jacques de Camp, whom I have scrutinized at a charity event this Saturday past; and who has the same hair styling as you, not to mention the same mustache, jowls and green-gray eyes. The domino mask and the perfected American accent did not fool me one jot, for I am a Girl Detective!"

De Camp was thunderstruck. His mustache puffed with his cheeks. "How extraordinary," he roared, his French accent becoming more apparent. "And in one so young! How can you doubt your abilities after such a display?

The Russians are almost assured that their precious self-acting Mule plans will be retrieved. My commendations!"

He bowed low, almost to the ground.

Upon his upsweep, Lizzie said with a wry smile, "How delightful that a cultivated man of such stature should bow to me, a poor little girl in such a modest little house." She laughed and raised her hands to her mouth. "Oh dear, that is precious! Well, Monsieur le Comte, you may relax and remove your disguise. How may I be of assistance to you in this very strange affair?"

With all pretense tossed to the wings, the French aristocrat, with a sweeping gesture, removed the mask to reveal a handsome if not rugged face and deeply intelligent eyes. "I want you to find the Mule plans," he announced.

"But where do I begin? The thief must be miles from Fall River by now."

"No, I believe him still to be in this city. The only clue we have is this signet that was left behind at the scene of the theft, presumably by accident." De Camp lifted up a ring that glimmered in the sunlight shafting through the parlor window. Lizzie took it for inspection and saw a crimson letter A centered on the ring's face plate.

"I have not seen this before," Lizzie said, a shudder coming over her.

"I have. It is the sign of a secret society that operates right here in town. The Arcady Society. I'm not quite sure what their objectives are, but it seems likely that they are nihilists whose only goal is to topple the Czar from power and bring about a worker state in Russia. They have a vested interest in preventing the Russian expansion into the Crimea, and God alone knows what their plans are for Fall River."

"And this ring is a symbol of their Brotherhood?"

"Yes, the letter A is a symbol of the sudden violence that will erupt when the common man is ready to rise above his masters. They are no doubt influenced by Bakunin and his lot. I do believe elements of their society, inspired by the successful assassination of your President Lincoln in 1865, are planning the same fate for the Czar. They are aware that my mission in Fall River is an obscure but crucial step in the Czar's plan to reinforce his military victories."

Lizzie curled her fingers around the ring and sighed. "I find this all most fascinating," she said. "I would most heartily love to work on the case."

"I can reward you handsomely. Money is not an object. My purse is open for your use."

"No need. My consulting services are done purely for the good of all people everywhere. I have no material needs to compensate. I do, however, have a few questions regarding the robbery. How big is this container?"

"About the size of a peach pit. The plans, which have been printed on delicate tissue paper, are folded very tightly. But recall Miss Borden that the plans may no longer be in the pessary."

"I am aware of that. Of what material is it made?"

"Solid iron, embossed with the Romanov coat of arms and with a hinge that opens into its cavity."

"This Russian inventor, from where does he hail?"

"St. Petersburg. He has been sent straight by the Czar himself to secure the contracts with the Fall River businessmen."

"Where did the theft take place?"

"At the Hotel Wilbur, not more than ten minutes walk from this very house."

"Do the textile men know of the unfortunate robbery?"

"*Mon Dieu*, that would mean disaster. They are currently under the impression that we will be presenting the plans for the self-acting Mule by this time Friday morning."

"That is most unfortunate. This ring that you found in the hotel room of the Russian, was it simply lying on the floor? I find it unusual that a ring can so conveniently slip off an intruder's finger."

"Ah," de Camp said, screwing up his eyes as if trying to find the exact words. "The ring was not exactly lying on the floor. It had fallen off inside the Russian during the process of extracting the pessary."

"Oh," Lizzie said with a shudder.

"Yes," de Camp sighed. "Please do not ask for details on how we discovered it. I am not used to discussing such matters with a young lady. Needless to say, the Russian is mortified beyond words and for security purposes has been sequestered in a safe place far from this town."

"We shall save the details for another day," Lizzie agreed. "I would like to see the hotel room where the Russian was assailed."

"By all means. Be at the Hotel Wilbur this very afternoon. I must exercise discretion and disappear from the scene. So you shall rendezvous with my son, Andre, who will represent me in this matter. Report to the lobby of the Wilbur at three of the clock."

Lizzie's chest tightened. "I don't believe I have had the honor to meet your son before."

"Andre is a fine *garcon*, just turned nineteen. He has a bit of a fiery disposition and he is very strong in his opinion about foreign affairs. We often clash over such matters, but he is loyal to our *famille Languedocienne*. The bloodlines run very deep and he is a proud scion."

Lizzie rose to her feet. "I shall meet your son then at three at the Wilbur Hotel."

"Three o'clock!" The Comte de Rennes bowed once more, tucked on his domino mask, and ushered himself towards the front hallway. "*A bientot*," he said wistfully.

From up the hallway came Emma's thin voice. "Lizzie, I have rigged up

the buggy, with no help from you, thank you!" Then she appeared in the parlor, dressed in a flowery hat, just as the Comte spun on his axis. Emma had barely caught a darting glimpse of the man in the cape and the mask, when she let out with a bellowing shriek. All the color drained from her face and her hands raced towards his face.

"Emma!" Lizzie said, just as startled. But it was too late. Lizzie's older sister had bolted for the front stairs and was stomping upwards towards the safety of her bedroom, making strange whimpering noises.

"I am profoundly apologetic," de Camp said, with a nod towards Lizzie. "If I had known..."

"It's all correct, Monsieur le Comte," Lizzie said. "Emma is used to far worse."

Lizzie stared at him through the window of the parlor as he descended to his waiting carriage in the street. She sighed, thinking of the boy she most dreaded, and most wanted to meet.

THE SPORTING BOYS

The Wilbur Hotel was up North Main at Granite Street. Lizzie managed to get there without a buggy and arrived just before three as a work team was unloading water barrels from a horse-drawn cart. A large banner straddling the main entrance boasted of the hotel's finer qualities:

FALL RIVER'S WILBUR HOTEL
An Ordinary of Most Excellent Attributes

Today: The Boston Barkeep Furniture Corporation Conclave
Displays of Stools and Mirrors by Master Craftsmen

Fine lodging for transients and permanents
Beer, oysters and horse-keeping
Elocution lessons by Professor Joseph Maple, Esq. of New Bedford

Rooms Available
Restaurant Attached – Victuals At Most Excellent Prices

King Darius Wilbur, Proprietor
Samuel Samways, Bar Keep

The lobby was bustling with an influx of folk from as far away as Providence, Boston, and even from the wilds of northern New Hampshire, for the Wilbur was playing host that weekend to a convention of saloon-furniture salesmen. They paraded around the lobby, these men of varnished wood and beveled mirrors, their top hats nestled in their forearms, their mustaches glistening with wax, their rattling wives beside them. In the center of the lobby was a large casket, presumably filled with beer, and a burly bartender in a bleached cloth smock was handing out samples in hardwood mugs.

Lizzie was surprised to see her father wandering the crowd, not particularly connected to anyone, but occasionally giving a grim nod to a passing gentleman. He twitched imperceptibly as his daughter appeared before him, planting her parasol firmly between her feet.

"Father, I did not think that you took an interest in the latest fashions in bar stools."

Andrew twisted up his brows. "I am merely memorizing the faces. They are competition, you know. But what brings you to the Wilbur, Daughter? Certainly you have not been seized with the desire to sample Master Samways' Home-made Hops?"

"No, Father. I am on a case."

"That nonsense business you started. I sincerely hope that you are being paid well for your troubles. A penny worked for is a penny in the pocket. I wouldn't have it any other way."

Lizzie smiled as the nearby town hall clock tolled three o'clock. A thin beardless bell boy in a small hotel jacket approached Lizzie.

"Miss Borden?" he asked in a voice crackling with adolescence as if he were growing upwards before her very eyes. He handed her a note which she unfolded. Noticing her father staring at her intently, she reached into her purse and pulled out a coin which she tossed to the grinning bellboy.

"Here you are, my hard working lad—a penny from my pocket." He hopped away merrily as Andrew scowled at her wasteful habit.

"Room 209," she read, and then bade her father adieu with a tilt of her head. She headed for the staircase, leaving Andrew Borden fish-mouthed.

"My own daughter, not yet eighteen," he stammered. "Unescorted to an upstairs room. What more horrors can this modern world bring?"

As Andrew turned to leave, he spied in the corner of the lobby three young boys dressed in lean long broad coats, watch chains and high boots, laughing and spitting their cigar smoke into the choked air. Two of them were fitted out in bowler hats and the tall, lanky leader in the middle was balanced under a tall opera hat that served to exaggerate his height. It was the Sporting Boys, the nattering nabobs of Fall River, grinning and roaring with chummy ostentation. Andrew noticed that as Lizzie ascended the staircase, the Sporting Boys were poking each other and pointing in her direction, their eyes filled with boyish leers. They were commenting upon Lizzie's elegantly draped posterior as it sashayed up the staircase, much to their amusement.

Their thin leader pumped his legs up and down as if he were a strutting rooster. "B'hoys!" he chortled. "Need we neglect Miss Lizzie Borden of Second Street and the fine young hams she's leaving behind for our viewing pleasure?"

The Boys roared. "Get out me tape measure, my skenchbacks!" one of them shouted. "My, what gazing stock!"

"She'd make a good Bowery G'al at dragging time! I mind you!" the leader shouted.

Andrew bit his lips and took a few awkward strides across the lobby to where the Sporting Boys were posturing, staring them down as their laughter subsided. The leader in the opera hat patted his chest.

"Andrew Borden I believe," he said proudly.

"Who may you be?" Andrew bellowed. "Your countenance is vaguely familiar."

The boy tipped his stove pipe and grinned. "Frank Rivers, how may I be of service?"

"I have heard of you, Rivers," Andrew growled. "You and your associates here are mere sensualists. But I'm not afraid of your secret language and your fancy airs, and I am appalled by your rendezvous with women of fallen characters. Your libertine antics may go over in fancy cities, but not in Fall River; this town is full of respectable folk! Be gone immediately and take your rabble with you!"

The smile on River's face was defiant. He tossed a side glance to his two companions who seemed to be hovering around his facial expressions looking for guidance, then he plastered down his soap locks, stepped forward and leaned in towards Andrew's sinking eyes. "No time for curtain lectures, I have a right to be in this public place," he said wickedly. "I paid my coins for a room, and so did my B'hoys here. And don't go apple bonking our fuzzle talk. We adopted it right from Paradise Square in Manhattan Island and it's proper for all my skenchbacks."

Andrew raised a straining fist. "No matter where you obtained your wicked speech, I cannot allow your vulgar remarks touching my daughter."

The thin wobbly-eyed boy next to Frank Rivers stepped forward. "Hi hi, cousin! 'Ol' Frank here won't be remarking anything touching your daughter before he can remark on anything worth touching."

Andrew's head went hot and he shook a curled fist. "Don't go near my Lizzie or..." His eyes turned red with anger as he bellowed, "Or I'll twist off your heads!"

And then, having expended his courage and energy, Andrew seemed to vanish into the air only to reform at the center of the lobby, heading towards the street. Frank Rivers turned to his chuckling companions and smirked. "Lam him, B'hoys!" he howled. "I am trembling in my boots!"

At his lead, they broke into laughter as Andrew disappeared between the endless displays of bar stools and spittoons.

DEDUCTIONS AND ROMANCE

At the top of the staircase, Lizzie found herself looking down a long hallway that stretched southward between two parallel rows of doors. Halfway down, a man in a dark brown suit sat on a stool slanting backwards, humming wistfully to himself. As Lizzie alighted onto the landing, he straightened up, then scrambled to his feet and respectfully removed his hat. He was a large bear of a man, middle-aged and paunchy. His mouth was obscured by a dropping mustache. He wore a long dark-brown greatcoat that seemed unseasonal and was stained with the dust of the road.

"Miss," he said, blinking at her.

"Are you the detective from Pinkertons?" Lizzie asked.

"Pinkerton, Miss," he said proudly.

"I don't believe I catch your meaning."

"The name's Pinkerton, Miss. Fred Pinkerton of Pinkerton Brothers Private Security Firm."

"I see, your name does inspire confidence," Lizzie said, chuckling slightly into her gloved hand.

"The French boy is waiting," he announced.

On the door paneling behind him were the gilt numbers 209. With a soft touch, Lizzie pushed the door open and stepped inside.

The room was dark and stuffy. Only a few beams of sunlight slanting through the closed shutters enabled her to see a shadowy man standing in the corner. At first she considered her situation to be one of immediate danger, alone in a hotel room with a stranger who had not yet identified himself. After all, this was the room where the Russian inventor had been scandalized. But trusting in the delicacy of the moment, she swung the door shut behind her.

The shadow moved into a shaft of sunlight and Lizzie recognized immediately the bespoken Saville Row suit jacket, the youthful attempt at a military mustache, the twinkling eyes. Even the West Indies Bay Rhum that danced in the air between them whispered the name and title: Andre Louis Jacques de Camp, the Vicomte de Rennes.

"I know you," she said, remembering her father's ominous words about Andre's Sporting Boy life style. Why would the Comte send her into such a dangerous position?

"I know you too, Lizbeth Andrew Borden," Andre said with slight merriment. "I assure you that there is no danger here. Be at ease and join me in solving this wretchedly complicated and ever-deepening puzzle."

Lizzie's breathing came more easily. His voice was fine and equally well-mannered. This comforted her. "The name is Lizzie," she corrected him.

"Then Lizzie shall it be." He pointed towards the brass bed and the carpeted floor. "*Mais bien sur*, this is indeed a strange field upon which we are now treading. Here we have a room where a crime took place. A man was assaulted and something was stolen from him. What do you see in this room, Lizzie Borden? What scenarios can you deduce from the remains of Monsieur Tchakorov?"

With a daring flourish Andre drew back the shutters and let the bright sunlight flood the room. Lizzie was suddenly overwhelmed with an intense amount of detail. She paused, put fingers to her chin, and peered about. Then, while Andre stood at attention with a wry smile, she perambulated the length and breadth of it, peering into corners, examining surfaces, bending her knees to see beneath the furniture. She picked up nothing, but examined everything, maneuvering her body to change her line of sight before cuspidors, bed posts, cabinets, and the writing desk. She sat in a chair, smelled a bouquet of flowers in a vase on the dressing table, cast a winking eye at some framed pictures on the mantle, waved her fingers over a clump of charred wood in the fireplace, and pressed her shoes heavily against randomly selected floor boards. She nosed through the clothing lying on the rumpled bed sheets and the heaps of linen lying on the floor. A pile of papers in the waste basket occupied her attention for several moments. Lastly she inspected a painting that hung upon the southern wall, a copy of a rustic scene by Poussin of several shepherds gathered about a stone tomb. The painting stared back at her with an unsettling feeling of mutual fascination.

She came back to the center of the room and stood proudly before Andre. "I have comprised a scenario," she proclaimed. "For your amusement I shall state it."

Andre gave her a permissive wave of his hand.

"I did not know the name of the Russian until you just uttered it," she said. "But I can say with confidence that he is a proud man from a wealthy family that has recently come upon hard times. He was forced into the business of selling mill technology by the unfortunate death of his wife, which has left him with two small children to support."

Andre stared blankly at her. "Go on," he said.

"He was in this room for two days before his unfortunate assault. During that time he indulged in real estate speculation. No doubt he felt that migrating to America and bringing his children to Fall River would provide them with a future that cannot be realized in Czarist Russia. He also sees Fall River as an excellent town for his new bride-to-be since her career as an equestrian acrobat has come to a very tragic end."

"Excellent," Andre said with a reserved smile. "I can't imagine how you perceived many of the details in that portrait, but I did witness you examining the postcard upon the dressing table from the Louise Soullier Circus with the inscription from Marie confessing in French her deepest love and the prospects that await her in America."

Lizzie nodded towards the dresser. "Moreover, the clothing that you had laid upon the bed and the charming but sad bouquet of flowers on the writing desk have provided me the opportunity to reconstruct his recent past. As for the clothing, the fine quality of the suit shows a man of some means, but it has in the past year been washed so often its colors have faded, showing a recent downturning of his luck, no doubt happening simultaneously with the passing of his dear wife."

"What does the bouquet tell you?"

"Through a correspondence course with the Ophelia Society of Boston, I had the opportunity to study the fine art of florigraphy and floral management within parlors and sitting rooms. After completing the Home Guide To The Secret Language of Flowers, I had trained my eye to perceive the elegant messages that were being scripted within the combination of floral arrangements. Tchakorov, being from St. Petersberg, takes a very romantic European approach to this art. In this bouquet he has blended together crimson tea roses that show a melancholy loss, something that he has vowed never to forget. The presence of the scarlet nasturtiums led me to believe that there was a military death, perhaps a brother in the Bulgarian campaign, but the nasturtium also symbolizes patriotism, perhaps reflecting a period after the profound loss where he attempted to regain his emotional composure through world affairs. The pheasant eyes and blue periwinkles that are so mournfully laced at the corners show a sorrowful remembrance, that his feelings once so potent and devastating were mellowing into a sublime melancholy. The white Poppies whisper of a striving for forgetfulness, a moving on, so to speak."

"So far," Andre confirmed, "this is 'all correct' as you Americans are so fond of saying. What about the equestrian bride-to-be?"

"Ah, the full-blown red rose in the center that blooms above the rest speaks loudly of a return of hope and the dawning of a new happiness after a long sojourn in a wilderness, no doubt a wilderness of a mental nature. One can only guess that Tchakorov has felt a new love dawn. The enthusiastic postcard from the French horse woman that bespeaks a life together in America fulfills all my florigraphic interpretations."

"And the real estate speculation?" Andre asked.

"The caked mud on his boots is peculiar to a lot that is being developed just around the corner from Anawan Street, one that Mister Southard Miller has put up for sale. Near this lot is a tobacco shop that sells the Louisiana Perique that has a moist vinegary smell, the same smell that hangs so pungent in the air about us. No doubt the property came to his attention on one of his trips to obtain his treasured tobacco and he managed to get access to the property through the builder's agent."

"He may have been strolling for relaxation and entered the property out of mere curiosity."

"Ah, but his beloved Marie claims that she will be very happy in America. There are also the three books on the bureau, clearly obtained from the Stone Street lending library, one of them a French-English lexicon, another a picture book of famous horses of North America, and the last a treatise on the domestication of the recently married couple by Professor Horatio Tiverton of Swansea. Finally his waste basket contains papers where he has been practicing his English letters, writing out phrases like, "My dear sir, which way are the horse stables" and "What are the most excellent children's schools in this neighborhood?" This shows me clearly that he was contemplating the rebuilding of his family with the French equestrian woman and his orphaned children right here in Fall River."

Andre clapped his hands in rhythm to a hearty laugh. "I can tell you with great confidence, Lizbeth—and may I be permitted to call you Lizbeth? It is far more suited to your dignity and grace—that your portrait of Monsieur the Russian is perfection itself, a small gem of analytical reasoning that does you very proud. But, alas, such details are useless when it comes to solving this riddle. For here we have a room where no intruder entered before the infamous deed, and no intruder exited. It is as if the Russian were attacked by *une fantome* of his own imagination."

"I don't understand," Lizzie frowned.

"Behold the testimony of the security agent." Andre went to the door and rapped three times in quick succession. A moment later, the large mustachioed man from the corridor entered awkwardly at a glacial pace, nodding respectfully at Andre and Lizzie in turn.

"Miss," he said.

"Mr. Pinkerton, I have a few questions about the evening before last," Lizzie stated. "I believe you were on duty when this deplorable theft occurred. Would you mind relating your version of the affair?"

He rubbed his chin as if trying to stir memory. "I'm not a man of very many words," he said, "but I can oblige if it will help bring about a conclusion."

"There will most certainly," Andre said defiantly, "be a conclusion, Monsieur Pinkerton. By your leave..."

"Well, it was before all this barstool nonsense. Hardly anyone was occupying this second floor but them Sporting Boys that make all the commotion a'nights with their Fancy Girls about. I was at my post at ten o'clock. I remember one of the girls yelling down the hall that her gentleman caller needed a bowl of hot water. Then all the doors were shut and everything was quiet. King Darius had turned down the lamps and you could hear all that slumbered snoring along the corridor."

"Fall River descending into twilight," Lizzie said softly.

"Yes, Miss. And that's when I do confess a profound lapse of character. I'm almost a'feared to lose my commission if I relate what I have to tell."

"You need not, I can guess. You were imbibing."

"At my post, it is true. The intent was to keep the fire going inside me, because the dark night in a hotel corridor can be mighty cold, despite the summer. I'm not a vain man, but this drinking is one act I do fear the judgment upon—especially considering its sequel."

Andre raised an assuring hand. "You need not fear prosecution since my father did determine that the whiskey was drugged."

"Drugged it was. After just a few sips, I felt myself slipping off. But I'm a stubborn man as well. I fought it all the way. On the exterior you might have just witnessed a big oaf of a man snoring in his boots. But from the interior angle I was wrestling with mighty demons. And I do declare, Miss, I won the battle. I forced myself awake."

"How long was your interval?"

"I can't rightly say, but it seemed enough for someone to have filched the key in my jacket pocket, and then slip by me into this here room to do his immoral deed. When I realized what had been done I got to my feet, roared almighty hellfire, and ripped this door nearly off its hinges, to find the Russian fellow lying on the floor with his southern exposure aiming out as bare as a babe's."

"Did you raise an alarm to the desk clerk?"

"Immediately, Miss! I figured the footpad was on his way out the front of the hotel so I bounded down the steps."

"Are there any other steps down to the lobby?"

"None, Miss. Those are the only ones from the second floor, and I blocked it with my girth the whole time. Then King Darius called the constabulary and I went upstairs to help preserve the Russian fellow's dignity."

"How long before the police came?"

"About three minutes by my reckoning. And they filled this room. They knew this was an international affair, although none of us, including myself, know the truth behind it. Something about foreign wars. I don't rightly care about those crazy tangles as long as my pay is regular, I keep my nose out of it. Leave it to the fancy politicos."

"How long were the police here?"

"About an hour, and then my brother Fred came to relieve me."

"Your brother's name is also Fred?"

"My daddy did have a hankering for that name. And when we came out twins, it seemed only right to consider us as one unit."

"I see. So Fred your brother took the second watch?"

"Right so, and we have alternated since at twelve-hour intervals. I told Fred to keep a right smart watch and to take no drink in fear it would mean the death of his ambitions."

"What about the Russian? Where was he taken?"

Andre answered, "Where no one can get at him. Needless to say he does not wish to be interrogated. You can learn nothing from him for he remembers nothing, but has a distinct soreness that may take some time to overcome."

Lizzie nodded. "I understand. Mr. Pinkerton, are you absolutely sure you saw no one leave this room?"

"None, Miss. Unless the fiend slipped out before I had awoken myself. But no one downstairs saw any man excepting myself come down those stairs. It's as if the assailant appeared from thin air and vanished into likewise."

"And the desk clerk, he saw no one go up shortly before the striking of ten?"

"No one," Andre added. "It seems as if the Russian's attacker was a passing shadow of no substance."

Pinkerton huffed. "No shadow could have taken the key from my pocket or pulled the Russian fellow off his bed to separate him from his night pants. There was flesh and blood involved, I assure you of that."

Lizzie put her two forefingers to her chin and drew in deep breath. She glanced about the room, carefully examining the walls, and then before her silent observers, walked up and down, counting her steps. After a few perambulations she turned to Pinkerton and said sternly, "I must ask you to stand guard over this room at all costs, to make sure that no one enters or leaves without your awareness."

His mustache dipped with his face in agreement. "I shall, Miss. Excepting at various times of the day or night I may be my own brother. We do take turns, and being that collectively we look like one person staring into a mirror, no one really cares if we swap out to give each other a chance to catch some snores, you understand."

"Understood," she concluded and then darted for the door, exiting into the hallway. Andre followed her out to find her walking a straight line along the corridor, pausing before each door. Then she turned about and came back, carefully putting one foot before the other.

"Curious," she said, leaning over to make sure the security guard had not followed them into the hallway. "Does he know about the pessary?"

"Not a bit."

"Does he know about the Arcady ring?"

"Even less."

"Good," Lizzie said with a nod. "Let's keep it that way. What do you know about this ring?"

"It is the signet of the Arcady Society. According to the locals that I have interrogated, it is the secret club of the Sporting Boys. Despite my father's fears that they are anarchists and assassins, I believe it merely to be a small group of rowdy youths who sample the opiates of the Orient and women of low character with equal impunity."

Lizzie furrowed her brow. "The same Sporting Boys who were present here at the time of the affair?"

"The same. Do you wish to talk to them yourself?"

"No, for now I'd like to see the desk clerk, this King Darius that everyone is talking about. He may hold an important key to this puzzle."

"I believe he is in the lobby tending to the Conclave." Andre pushed past her and led her down the steps towards the lobby.

KING DARIUS' SECRET CHAMBER

King Darius Wilbur was a man buried under burdensome mustaches that demanded far more energy and labor to keep in their pristine state than any one man could be expected to produce. Nonetheless, he wore his whiskers proudly and gave one the impression, as one talked to him, that his head was in the midst of being swallowed by them. Lizzie, facing him directly across the main desk of the Wilbur's lobby, experiencing the full impact of his face in the slanting sunlight, found herself visually lost in his whiskers' magnificence. It had been observed by many that the Wilbur hotel, a recently prospering concern, was growing in exponential proportion to King Darius' facial masterpiece and that local speculators feared that the further expansion of his business would result in the complete structural collapse of his head, which was itself already buried under the weight of his facial hair. Beyond this peculiar trait, he was jovial enough, and he seemed eager to provide Lizzie with information.

"I am quite alarmed," he confessed, "that such intrigue would go on under my roof. I did not think that the Russian would be at such risk in my own establishment, I dare say, I now do."

"And you saw no one go up those stairs at ten on the clock, or slightly before?"

His eyes hovered together near his nose. "No, Miss Borden. I was keeping watch, being mindful of that Rivers boy and his shameless carryings on with the harlot

Miss Jewett. They've been keeping company here for quite some time, and always in the same room. God's teeth, but I dare say Rivers was enraged when the Russian fellow came to town."

"Rivers? Why would he be upset about the Russian?"

"Because he took his room, he did."

Lizzie leaned forward, quite drawn in by his statement. "You are telling me that Room 209 is usually occupied by Frank Rivers and his Fancy Girl?"

The mustaches bobbed with the face. "Dare say, I do! And it was a mighty strange manner in which it transpired. I had the Russian fellow booked by order of the French Count into a right proper room, one that hadn't been darkened in spirit by these nattering nabobs. I had him in the Commonwealth Suite and was prepared to dandy him up with all sorts of linens and soaps, but at the last minute a messenger boy comes from the Commons House. Seems like there was a mix-up, a right proper one, and personages unknown have insisted that the Russian be lodged in 209. Who was I to question it? I think to myself, I did. The letter came with all sorts of city seals. I don't know this fellow's business, but I know if a French Count is involved and orders come from the Commons House, then who am I, Darius Wilbur, who possesses nothing but an humble Ordinary of quality and stupefying face brushes, to question the properly embossed seals and signatures?"

"Do you have the letter?" Lizzie asked anxiously.

King Darius poked his face about under the desk, pulling up some boxes and peering into some sliding drawers. "God's wounds but I know it's here somewhere." His eyes brightened and he brought up a folded paper. After snapping it open he handed to Lizzie, who took one quick glance at it, then handed it back.

"It's a forgery," she observed. "It's not from the Commons House. Look at the paper: tan, mere butcher paper. And the signature says Larson E. Whipsnade. Who do you know in this city with the name Whipsnade?"

King Darius's mustaches were trembling as if they had their own nervous system. "I feel the fool, I do. Like if God has a fool all His own, it would be me."

Andre took the paper from Lizzie and let out with a small chuckle. "Tchakorov was being set up for thievery. They needed him in that room."

Lizzie peered up at the ceiling, measuring with her eyes. "Mr. Wilbur," she asked, stepping back to get a cleaner view of the expansive molding. "Would you say that Room 209 is just about....there? Right near that fancy plaster cornucopia coming forth from the ceiling above?"

"Sounds about right."

"And how many feet would you say between that cornucopia and the fancy swirls by the southern face?"

"Looks to be about two or three feet, no more or less. But I can't reckon without climbing up there with a mason's rule."

"Is there another room between 209 and the southern face?"

"Not that I know of, but I do believe there's crawl spaces all over the building. That's where the Weirds reside."

"The Weirds?" Andre asked puzzled.

"Ah, pay no attention to my fired imagination. It's a folly of my besotted brain. Too much mustache wax, I presume. But there are strange noises a'nights, especially since the Russian fellow's been pinched. From my post, I hear the thumping and the cursing."

"Cursing?"

"More like the wailing of a lost spirit. I can't bring myself to go searching the corridors. Perhaps the night watch Fred would be able to tell you. Perhaps it's some suicide from long ago who's up there wandering to find his closure."

"Not being a spiritualist," Lizzie announced, "I would sooner think it was just an intruder walking about."

"But the guests are all accounted for, they are!" Darius said. "Believe you me!"

Andre produced a small calling card that had a light trace of perfume. "King Darius, you have given us valuable information."

"Right so," the bewhiskered manager beamed. "When you decipher any of its meaning, let me know what it was that I did tell you, for I'll be danged if it makes sense to me right now."

"We will. And if anything of interest comes up, here is my card."

Darius took the card just as a horde of furniture men stormed the desk, all demanding their telegrams and directions to the nearest saloons. Lizzie and Andre stepped to the side, her eyes practically glued to the ceiling. Her lips were moving silently as if she were counting.

"You think there's an extra room?" Andre said. "But you can clearly see from the corridor that 209 is at the southern end of the building."

She took her gaze from the ceiling. "Oh Andre, this is foul play indeed. For now we have to prepare ourselves for a most unpleasant encounter. Bring me to the Sporting Boys."

Andre directed her towards the dining room from where bellowed forth a loud strain of youthful, impetuous voices.

LIZZIE GETS FUZZLED

Frank Rivers and his Sporting Boys were having their mid-afternoon cigars in the attached dining hall behind the Wilbur's lobby. They sat at their usual table along the western wall before large paneled windows, Frank with his tall opera hat flanked by two bowler-hatted youths, looking like a chimney rising above two slag heaps. A flustered waiter was racing back and forth bringing them victuals while they stamped their firemen boots and howled racy ballads.

A furniture salesman at a nearby table, distracted by the boys' obnoxious hoots, boldly shouted, "Please be quiet! Decent people are trying to digest!"

"Cheese them, B'hoys!" Frank said to his crew. "They're envious of us crapulous folk who live by our own tables of morality. But I say, stockjobbers be they!"

The salesman huffed and nervously went back to his coffee just as Lizzie Borden and Andre de Camp entered the hall. As if on cue, the Sporting Boys quieted down, stifling their laughs and straightening their legs under their table.

"Frank Rivers," Andre said with a bow. "Miss Borden and I require a few moments of your time, if you would allow."

"Hi, hi!" the Sporting Boy proclaimed. "It would be our honor to host such a fine lady and her dandified beau at our table. Chas and Buster here won't mind, will you my gutterbloods?"

"Nay," Buster explained. "Ladies of quality are always welcome to take maw-wallop with us."

Rivers raised his cane and waved it delicately towards the two chairs opposite him and his gang. As Lizzie and Andre took their seats, Rivers stuffed his cigar into his mouth, removing his stovepipe hat to reveal garishly plastered soap locks running down the sides of his scalp. He spat a wad of saliva into his hand and ran his palm along the glistening locks. As he replaced his hat, Lizzie felt a displeasing stirring in her stomach.

"Have a go at us, Lizzie Borden of Second Street," Frank said. "If we're colt's tooth enough for you."

"I could judge that a bit more for myself if I knew what 'colt's tooth' was," Lizzie said smiling. "But for the moment, I'd like to bring your attention to the evening before last."

Chas let out with a rude laugh. "That's the night the Ivan sizer got bully-whacked in the renterfuge."

Frank grimaced. "Now, now, my skenchback, don't go quanking out our guests with our fuzzle talk. For in her gumbling through, she may take beastly interpretations. Miss Lizzie, renterfuge is the room I keep with my prancing pony. I got tumbled by that mustached jarkman who runs this hovel. One day I'll divorce him from his facial for that bumwush."

"He gave the Russian your room," Lizzie said plainly. "The room you frequent with your whore Sarah Jewett."

Frank jumped in his seat and glanced about. "Don't go speaking it plain-like, there's bound to be a bit of scandal-brothing by local malifuffs."

Andre leaned in close to Lizzie. "From the German words mal meaning 'speech' and pfuffen meaning 'to blow.' Literally, someone who blows speech. I suspect he fears gossip."

"My," Frank chortled. "You are indeed bent upon deciphering us, ain't you?"

"Yes, Frank Rivers, we are," Lizzie said, her patience wearing thin. "You can hide behind all your fuzzle talk, but you can't get away from suspicion. And when a crime is committed within yards of your sleeping quarters, indeed within a room to which you have a key, your account of the affair is of great interest to those trying to find the conclusion of this affair."

A shadow fell across Frank's face as a cloud interrupted the sunlight. "You want to know the unfarded truth," he said calmly, "unmistified by false beauties. Well, I'll be the first to admit I'm a scoundrel of a carpet-knight. Many a fancy girl has fallen under my glamour. But that doesn't make me a thief. One may hazard from my fuzzle talk and sporting ways that I don't have a gall of bitterness within me, that I would just as soon steal the metal from my dying grandmother's teeth for a few tankards and a romp with a tweeny maid. Yes, I have my own morality tables that I draw upon, but I do have my limits. And I don't go bully-whacking gentlemen even if they are Ivan sizers. I don't go filching and I don't play hunt-the-whistle, and I don't send any old rake juggler off to Fiddler's Green for lampoons."

"What do you know about that night?" Lizzie said ignoring his obscurity. "What did you hear and see touching this affair?"

"That Pinkerton flonker," Frank spat. "He was guzzled and fell to sonorating. We heard his guzzle moans and then the next we heard he was all in a twee over it and went stomping to the jarkman. Next we know the badgers are all about and there's talk of this Ivan sizer being glorged."

"Yeah," said Chas. "Glorged by the insensible. You ever hear such gruff?"

"So who you got testifying? Drunkard pinks and bully-whacking ghosts?" Frank said with a gentle nod to his gutterbloods. "You ever hear such mulch before?"

"So what do you think occurred that night?" Lizzie asked.

"This is my reconstruction: the big office pinks had some malifuffs trinkling on the Ivan and knew his habits. So they waited till after dragging time and all the b'hoys and g'hals be in their stables for billy winks, then they pulled a filch party on the old pink and the sizer. They got more than one maw-hole to climb in since the b'hoys like to viz their sport." He held up his left hand, the thumb and forefinger tips pressed together, poked his eye through the ring and grinned. "Who doesn't like to viz a bit of the acrobatics."

Lizzie was taken aback by his garish gesture. "But you didn't answer my question," she added. "What did you hear and see?"

Frank leaned forward, his brows pressing together. "I was strumming a'loft at the time and wasn't quite paying apple bonkers to an Ivan and a pink who was sonorating a half hallway apart from my stable. Despite what you may hazard in your think hole, my ears ain't quite that big and my eye stalks ain't that protruded. So you got a bit of a problem distance-wise."

There was a long pause while Frank Rivers and Lizzie Borden sat locked in a frozen state, their eyes pressed together over the space between them.

Then Lizzie broke the moment with a small crooked smile. "I think I've had enough information, Mr. Rivers. I take my leave knowing that the prostitute Sarah Jewett is safe in the custody of a boy who considers her a 'prancing pony' and names the hour she is taken to her 'stable' as 'dragging time' and that courtship and courtesy must take a holiday to 'billy winks.' I only hope that when I am of age to take a husband, he would use less flowery imagery to portray his affections for me."

Frank touched his cane handle to his forehead. "Pleased to have educated you, Miss Lizzie. Since we were educated at different high schools, I'm glad we can still understand each other."

Lizzie and Andre got to their feet. As they were leaving the dining hall, they could hear the snorts and sneers behind them. The flustered waiter was just entering with a full silver tray of maw-wallop.

"What did you divine from that parody of a conversation?" Andre asked Lizzie as they slowly strolled across the Wilbur's lobby.

Lizzie laughed nervously, "It is comforting to know that he draws the line at playing 'hunt-the-whistle.' I was beginning to fear for the female population of Bristol County."

Andre gave a dismissive wave. "They are mere pretenders. Just wealthy children who are too lazy to adopt their father's enterprises. They fashion their life styles after the New York City gangs who haunt Five Points and the Bowery. There is much suspicion here."

"Not necessarily," Lizzie added dramatically. "I don't suppose you noticed his left hand. When the sunlight hit at the right angle, I could clearly see the skin on his fingers."

Andre clicked his fingers. "The Arcady Ring. I did not even think to look."

Lizzie reached into her purse and brought forth the signet which she held up for Andre's perusal. "Your father let me have it. I was thinking of producing it for Mr. River's astonishment, but felt best to keep it discreet. Nonetheless there was no discoloration upon his fingers. I do not believe this to be his ring."

Andre stared at it, his jaw clenched.

"Does something strike you?" Lizzie asked.

"No," he said, rubbing his temple. "Only a headache. Shall we promenade down street? It is a striking August day, and I would very much like to know you better, Miss Lizbeth Borden."

LIZBETH OF LIGHT

As the sun sank behind the gently rolling contours of Swansea, beyond the river and the moving barges of bale, Lizzie and Andre walked along the dockside by the Troy Manufactory buildings. Already stars were beginning to appear in the firmament as the sun lowered beyond the horizon.

"I am sorry," Lizzie said humbly, "that I am so flustered. Whenever I see those youths, their futures filled with promise and possibility, their family offering them resources and capital, instead turning towards a wasteful life of mere libertinage and sensuality, I cannot feel but despair for the next generation."

"I believe," Andre said, "Frank Rivers is a nephew to Wellington Rivers, the paper mill tycoon. Needless to say, he has been disinherited. The boy is living upon the good graces of an aunt who is too old and senile to know what he is doing with her money. I still declare that he is our most likely suspect. It would explain why no one saw the thief come or go from the lobby. Rivers would have had to merely slip back into his room after the robbery, thus giving the impression that the thief had vanished into thin air."

"I cannot be fully sure, but the real thief took great care to put suspicion on Rivers and his boys. The ring was so placed to further that suspicion."

Andre shrugged indifferently. "What about the Pinkertons? Although my father puts enormous trust in them, there is no working man that cannot be bought if the price be high enough."

"No man is above perfidy," Lizzie agreed. "But my instincts tell me that the real culprit has yet to reveal his face to us. Such a pity, since your father needs a conclusion by the day after tomorrow."

Andre stopped and stared upwards into the darkening horizon. "My father," he sighed. "For him, it is all about money, I believe. Don't listen to his nonsense about the balance of power in Europe and anarchists lurking in the shadows. The man is merely concerned for his own stock portfolio."

"Is that such a crime?" Lizzie asked.

Andre was about to answer but then he pointed towards a twinkling star. "When I look upon that sky," he mused. "I realize we are but dust, mere motes of dust, compared to the vast wheels of creation. As a small boy, I would walk by twilight in the hills by Rennes-La-Chateau, past the old castles and the haunted graveyards, and watch the stars appear one by one, like celestials' candles on some vast birthday cake. Then I would lie on my back in the midst of the field and let the great spiral move about me. I would fix my gaze on one particular star and throughout the night notice how it would spin about as if on the rim of a perfect wheel. And I would feel as if I were pinned to the center, and that all of creation was whirling about me. At moments like those, my father and all his fortune would seem so inconsequential, like a forgotten dream that once had so much importance, but now was just a shard of memory."

Lizzie watched his face closely as he spoke. "You certainly have your thoughts lifted above the daily affairs," she answered. "I did not think a man of your means and title would think of anything but commerce and management of property."

"Perhaps it is the soil of my native land," he said. "There is mystery in its deep veins. It makes one yearn for something beyond the thin veil of daily sorrows. I am at heart a poet."

Lizzie sighed. "You are so very different from any man I have ever known. I have only known men like my father, and he is so very different from your own. My father never had a title, and his wealth is so small compared with your family's grand fortune. My father stands in relation to your father as we all do to the big wheel you point out in the sky. There is hierarchy indeed in this vast creation."

Andre's voice grew thin and modest. "But, Lizbeth, I see those stars reflected in your eyes. So by mirroring the light from above, you are becoming one with it. And then the modest Lizbeth who feels so unimportant is now the most exquisite being that exists."

Lizzie blushed. "I wouldn't go so far. I'm just a girl from a small family. There's nothing special about me."

"But we are all stars," Andre announced, lifting up a hand towards the heavens. "We twinkle on the great wheel of life, and we all move together in a perfect circle. I have written a poem to that effect. I call my composition, Lizbeth of Light."

A smile curled on her lips. "Why, that's my name."

He nodded in the affirmative and began his recital:

> *I call these bold words to draw your breath*
> *And to drum a beat on your warm heart*
> *I call upon life and its handmaiden death*
> *To give our child its earthborn start*
>
> *This child formed from the air betwixt us*
> *That takes a first cry from the sorrows of life*
> *From the darkness of spirit that surrounds us*
> *But mews a bold Yes in the face of the strife*
> *Against gray evening, the dawn weaves its charm*
> *And something billows on the horizon's lip*
> *'Tis the hope and the beauty and the inner calm*
> *That we have won and must never let slip*
>
> *So if verse be the beating pulse that fashions*
> *A heart that shall sing strong and bright*

Let me sing on through the daybreak that passes
Across my eternal Lizbeth of Light

A paralyzed silence fell between them. Andre stood by Lizzie's side, his shoulder barely touching her. She could feel the heat through the fabric and a chill transported along the length of her trembling body.

"When did you compose this poem?" Lizzie asked, her face turning red.

"After seeing you at your church this Saturday past."

"I did not think that you had noticed me."

"I asked my father who you may be and he answered, 'That is Andrew J. Borden's younger daughter. She is a clever, wise and commanding girl. She runs her own consulting business and has trapped several wrongdoers and corrected many harms to common people. She is indeed a flower of a girl in the midst of a rough crop.' And then I knew that I had found the one girl in Fall River in whom I could find a trustworthy soul."

"I am flattered indeed," Lizzie blushed. She was about to say more but could not find the words.

"Do you believe, Lizbeth Borden," Andre asked, "that perhaps our ancestors, on the lush fields of Carcassonne, enjoyed each other's company as we are enjoying ourselves on this most enchanted evening?"

She was stunned, standing frozen without speech, fearing to breathe.

"Perhaps they did," Andre continued. "And perhaps they partook of the dark blood of the soil, tasting together the richness of the earth into which they were born, and into which they shall pass. Perhaps a Bourdin and a Duchamps lay together under the mysterious stars and held hands as I hold yours."

And she felt a soft fluttering about her fingers, and then they were pressed together. Lizzie stiffened and found that she was no longer breathing, which embarrassed her and Andre smiled. "You have nothing to fear," he said peacefully. "I am a perfect *gentilhomme*." And he lifted her palm into the air and took a slight bow in her direction.

"There is beauty in you," she said in a bare whisper. Inwardly she blessed the darkness for hiding her blushes.

In the long distance the wail of a bale barge sang across the cloudy darkness like a leviathan of the deep calling for its home waters. Andre's face was only lightly illuminated by the hanging lamps but she could see his deep eyes sparkling with the waters below as the moonlight reflected upwards towards the pier.

There were never eyes more beautiful, she thought, nor a face so noble.

Lizzie pressed her free hand to her cheek to catch her tears.

"You are not a Sporting Boy at all, my dear Andre," she said. "You are a melancholy soul of light."

A SUDDEN REVELATION

At breakfast the next morning, Andrew Jackson Borden sat with his family at his dining room table nibbling on some leftover codfish balls, his bead-like eyes staring distantly to the wallpaper as if he were contemplating the insensible. Abby Borden, seated near him, inhaling a cup of coffee and chewing gustily on a molasses cookie, seemed afraid to draw his attention towards the present moment; while Emma stirred restlessly upon some difficult secret that was bubbling inside her, causing her to shift her posture every few moments, a gesture accompanied by uncomfortable sighs. Lizzie, like her father, sat in a grim trance, her utensil barely grazing her dish. Only the Irish maid showed signs of animation, flittering in and out of the kitchen with the various courses of their breakfast.

"What is this gloom that descends on us today," said Abby finally. "It is like being seated at a funeral viewing. My dear Andrew, where is your mind wandering?"

"What?" he said, his eyes jerking back to the present. "My apologies, Mrs. Borden. I was trying to remember Tobias Ullsworth. I cannot imagine what ill tidings he harbors towards me."

"Ullsworth?" Abby frowned. "That's the cloth doffer that you evicted for non-payment of rent. I can't imagine what *glad* tidings he would harbor towards you. I told you that being so strict with him over one month's rent was not good for your reputation."

"I was merely protecting my property rights," Andrew said with a start. "That Ullsworth was particularly unsavory." He slurped at his stew, staining his beard. "I cannot abide slackards and layabouts."

"That slackard," shouted Emma, rising to her feet, "has disappeared from the face of the earth!"

There was a harsh moment of silence broken by Lizzie coughing delicately into her hand. "It's true, Father," Emma continued. "I have heard word from my contacts down street that Tobias Ullsworth has vanished. Last Monday morning he was seen wandering down by the Durfee Mill and at noon his boots were found by the side of the Quequechan. His wife and her seven children are living in a state of despondent impecuniousness."

"They should have considered themselves fortunate when they let the place!" Andrew sputtered. "It is not my concern."

"Heartless man," Emma muttered. "You don't know their fortunes, both before they let from you, and after their cruel eviction. You don't know the vagaries that have befallen them."

"I do know," Andrew said pointing a spoon towards his elder daughter, "that I have been fined by the bank for late payment of the mortgage. Ullsworth doesn't give a fig for that, nor should I care a fig for his dilemma."

"The man is dead!" Emma howled, and then fled towards the door, her hands moving towards her face. She collided with the maid who was entering with a tray of molasses cookies. "Out of my way, Maggie," she shouted, and a moment later her feet were heard clomping up the front stairs. Flustered, the maid ran back into the kitchen.

Abby patted the table with her palms. "Well, Andrew," she said solemnly, "you have certainly topped the program this time. I have never heard such disregard for another man's plight."

"Bah. I have my rights. Landlords have rights."

"But you have no poetry," Lizzie said suddenly.

"Eh? What?" Andrew spluttered. "What kind of nonsense do you speak?"

"You see no lights in my eyes," Lizzie announced. "You see no great wheel in the sky. There is only one letter separating your name from his, but the other differences are vast and deep. His blood runs with wine, yours with sawdust!"

Andrew looked towards Abby as if trying to find an anchor of sanity. "My daughter is speaking like the inmates at the Taunton Asylum."

Abby's face went slack. "I believe I know what Lizzie is saying," she said grimly.

"Ah, you are all insane," Andrew stammered. "No one knows the humiliation I felt! Spit at me in the street he did! In front of my own people! In front of my own daughter! Told me to go be hanged in Arcady, whatever the devil that means!"

Lizzie froze, her eyes widening. "What did you say?" said Lizzie.

"He told me be hanged in Arcady. I suppose he thinks I would travel all the way to Greece to dangle myself from some fruit tree."

Lizzie bolted to her feet, her arms shaking. "Who was this man? Do you not know? Oh, Father! I must know who he was."

"Tall, mustache and beard, spectacles. I don't care one jot who he is, as long as he keeps his spittle away from my brow!"

Lizzie ran from her table, leaving behind a full bowl of codfish stew. She pushed her way violently past the Maggie, who stood in the doorway staring at the remaining Bordens sitting silently at their table along the northern wall.

"For the love of Mike," she said merrily, "did your daughters not get seized by some turned milk? You're a right queer family, I declare!"

A CLUE IN THE MIDDEN HEAP

The stable yard behind the Wilbur was filled with the whinnying and musty smells of the clientèle's beastly transports. The stable doors were wide open and the rank odors overwhelmed Andre, forcing him to hold a fine-clothed handkerchief to his nose. Lizzie's mysterious note had asked him to meet her back there at noon, and the eager anticipation that she had solved some part of the affair kept him at attention down wind of the stables' midden heap.

Lizzie appeared as if from the cabinet of a stage magician, her face bright and cheery, with a calm and ease that had not existed in her the day before. Andre greeted her with a slight kiss to the back of her hand.

"Lizbeth," he said, which made her smile.

"I have good news," she announced. "Another piece of this puzzle has fallen into place, and I am ready to test a hypothesis."

"I was hoping as much." Andre gestured towards the back door of the hotel. "Shall we?"

As they started towards the olfactory safety of the Wilbur's interior, Lizzie's eyes narrowed in on the large and distasteful midden heap upon which a dirty young girl in a patchwork dress clamored with an iron hook, digging into the tangled mass. The girl looked up with ferocity in her hungry face.

"Biddy Doren, if I am not mistaken," Lizzie exclaimed. "What are you doing far from Bishop Street? And digging in filth, no less."

The girl lowered her iron hook and stood erect. "The man said there's gold in here."

"The man? What man?"

"The man with the funny hat. He told me that I can stop my mommy being hungry if I can find her some gold." She held up an egg-shaped item that gleamed in the sunlight. "He found this and said 'Bah!' and threw it to me. He told me there's more in there if I were dog enough to scrounge for it!"

"*Bastarde*," Andre whispered. He reached forward and took the small ball that the girl was holding. It was the size of a walnut and looked like it had been forged roughly from tin. A small hinged top swung open to reveal a folded piece of paper inside. Lizzie reached in and grabbed it, eagerly unfolding the paper. In childish scrawl it read:

HANG BE YE TO ARCADY
ANDREW J. BORDEN

Without a moment's hesitation, she stepped back into the center of the horse yard and started scanning the tall back wall of the hotel, examining each and every window and small opening.

"You believe it was tossed from above?" Andre asked.

"I have been a fool! Of course! The pessary did not make it to the master criminal behind this. It is still in the hotel."

"But this is good news. That means there is a chance of finding it."

"I wonder," she said with a curious twinkle in her eye.

Lizzie unbuckled her purse and reached in, pulling out a large silver coin, and held it forth to the small girl. "Perhaps this can help with your mother's hunger." The girl stepped forward cautiously and snatched the coin, her fingers trembling as they wrapped around its circumference.

"Now run along and let your mother have the coin," Lizzie ordered. The girl sped from the courtyard, dust rising behind her.

Lizzie held the tin pessary in her hand and peered intently at the back wall of the hotel. "This is far more than I could have hoped for. Yes, I think I know what to do. Andre, I must ask you to tell your father that I have solved the case. But you must gather together the following people: the Comte de Rennes, Fred and Fred Pinkerton, King Darius Wilbur, Deputy Sheriff Wixon of the Bristol County police, and Dr. Seabury Bowen."

"A doctor?"

"Unless I am horribly mistaken, I believe we may have need of a medical man for a delicate procedure."

"I trust your instinct, Lizzie Borden, Girl Detective. Andre de Camp is at your service." And he gracefully withdrew from the courtyard, leaving Lizzie to ponder the odorous midden heap of Biddy Doren.

THE WEIRD IN THE WALL

An hour later, a small coterie gathered in the lobby of the Wilbur, clustered about their host, King Darius Wilbur, who twirled his mustaches furiously. The Comte de Rennes, clearly uncomfortable with such a public appearance, glanced about with suspicion as if he expected a bomb-hurtling anarchist to be behind every pillar and post. One of the Fred Pinkertons stood like a stone sentinel with his hanging whiskers and dusty bowler. Deputy Sheriff Wixon of Bristol County, looking very mystified, tipped his cap to Lizzie Borden and asked politely, "I don't know what this is all about, but I bet it's a pretty how-dee-do."

Lizzie laughed. "It is very simple, Deputy. The Comte de Rennes has had something stolen from him, and now we going to retrieve it. I shall want you to arrest the culprit."

"Then you have found it!" the Comte said with bated breath. "*Mon Dieu!* You must tell me where it is without delay!"

"I am waiting for one more personage in our little drama, a man whose role may turn out to be of great importance. Ah, I see Andre, your *jeune fils*, has indeed located the good Doctor Seabury Bowen."

Andre and Dr. Bowen came in through the front door, the expression on the doctor's face betraying as much confusion as the deputy's. "I have been informed you require my services," he said politely. "Is someone ill?"

"That is yet to be seen," Lizzie announced, then waved a gloved hand towards the stairway to the upper floor. "Gentlemen?"

A few moments later they had all regrouped outside of Room 209 where the other Fred Pinkerton, dressed in the same brown suit and bowler hat as his twin, stood by his wooden chair at attention. King Darius peered at him with puzzlement. "Are you you?" he asked, "Or are you your brother?"

"I'm the other one," he replied.

The entire crowd moved into the room, which was exactly as Lizzie had last seen it the previous afternoon, down to the flower bouquet on the writing desk and the French circus postcard on the dressing table.

"Gentlemen," she said, clapping her hands. "We are now in a room where four evenings ago, a robbery of great ignominy took place. A Russian inventor had a possession stolen from him as he lay unconscious, the victim of etherization. For the last twenty-four hours I have been greatly puzzled over this theft. For the thief did not seem to have entered or exited the room, or at least that was the impression of the good Fred Pinkertons and King Darius Wilbur, all three of whom I consider to be men of impeccable reputation and honesty. It vexed me greatly how the thief made his escape, and I have torturously pondered every possible solution. Then it occurred to me that perhaps the thief never made his escape at all. Perhaps—and I beg your indulgence for a moment—he is still here."

Everyone in the room shouted out with surprise, glancing suspiciously at their neighbor. Lizzie raised her hands to quiet them down. "And I am not suggesting that any one present in this room is the culprit."

"But it seems impossible," King Darius exclaimed. "Do you suspect supernatural agencies? I heard the weirds and their hideous calls in the night, I did."

"Nay, Mr. Wilbur, one need not resort to supernatural explanations. I will demonstrate the source of your nocturnal weirding calls." She reached into her purse and produced several slips of paper on which were handwritten phrases of varying lengths. She began to distribute them to her perplexed guests, keeping one for herself. Then she turned and faced the southern wall. The Poussin painting of the rustic shepherds about their tomb now seemed a bit crooked in the stark noon light. Everyone faced the wall with her.

"I may be wrong about this," she said. "But there is no other solution. Will everyone please be so kind as to read out the phrases on the paper I have given each of you? Read the phrase with a voice pursuing dramatic emotional ranges, like an actor upon a stage at a variety saloon."

The Comte de Rennes looked down at his assigned script. "But this is madness. What manner of words are these?"

"Trust me," Lizzie said.

Everyone stood staring at her, so she pumped her hand in the air and demonstrated in a loud and boisterous outburst. "It's a spouter boys! Off the bow sprits! Crank the boom lines!"

After an awkward pause, the rest of the men followed her example in loud theatrical voices as if they meant to be heard by a far-flung balcony of patrons.

"Abandon the house boys!"

"Come on, ye green-skulled dolts! Make fire-flies to the booms!"

"Ignite the blubber works! There's a goodly trough of oil to be had!"

"The winds are crossing swords, o me hearties!"

"Far to starboard the spermaceti awaits!"

"Harpooners to the boats! There she blows!"

For a few moments the men in the room raised this mighty cacophony, so much so that they began to hear feet stamping and the sound of alarm in the hallway outside. As their boisterous cries started to wind down, Lizzie egged them on. "Keep at it! Don't mind the innocents! We're almost there!"

Andre felt absurd and was the first one to stop. Just as he was about to protest and quiet the others, there was a horrific cracking noise and the entire wall before which they stood started to shake. The Poussin painting crashed to the floor, revealing more rose-flowered wallpaper, but dead in the center of the faint rectangle where the color had been faded by sunlight was a curious peephole, like a tiny eye in the middle of a rose petal. Then a thin crack appeared along the edges of a long, thin painted vine, and there was the creak of rusty hinges. Before everyone's startled eyes, a large section of the wall was pushing outwards. There was now a door where previously there had been no door, and it was swinging towards them to uncover a man-sized opening behind.

The figure that bounded from the newly exposed orifice was thin, grimy and dressed in filthy rags. His hair was wild, his eyes aglow with some feral madness. His whiskers flared out at insane angles and his cheeks puffed as he pumped against the wooden floorboards. He tried to race towards the door, but Deputy Wixon stepped forward and grabbed him.

"Lord salvage me!" the man was shouting in a creaky voice. "The spermaceti is spouting and I'm below decks! Where be my harpoon boys?! Spring, my lads! Spring!"

"How? What's this?" Wixon said incredulously, holding fast to the man's jacket tails. "Confound it, but it's our missing man!"

"May I introduce," Lizzie said, breaking out with a prideful laugh, "Mr. Tobias Ullsworth of Anawan Street. Deputy Wixon, I believe this is the man who has been missing for three days now?"

"*Mon Dieu, je ne comprend!*" The Comte de Rennes shouted, twirling his mustache. He stepped forward and peered into the wall cavity. The rest of the men stepped forward a pace to take a glance over his shoulder. Inside the wall was a tiny nest, about four feet by three feet, barely enough for a man to lie down in. Its back wall was exposed wood, through which could be heard the sounds of animals in the stable yard. On the floorboards lay a filthy pallet and a kerosene lamp, next to which rested a plate covered with insects, which had devoured what little morsels of potato and beans had been there to sustain the prisoner.

"You mean he's been in there?" Wixon said, staring at the filthy crazy man in his grasp.

King Darius let out with a howl that was both amused and offended. "Indeed he has! That's the Sporting Hole I heard slip from the skenchback Buster. Their way of spying on their Fancy Girls. I wouldn't have believed it, but there it is as evidence. And in my own ordinary, much to my chagrin."

"Frank Rivers," said Andre triumphantly. "This is proof conclusive. Shall we arrest that rogue?"

"No," Lizzie said. "We need to hear from the thief himself."

"Let go my arm so I can scratch my beard," Ullsworth shrieked. "I'm all a'crawling with critters!" Wixon released his grip, trusting that his charge wouldn't bolt for freedom, as the man savagely attacked his own facial hair like it was bursting into flames. "Oh, Flukes and Blubber! I ain't been so infested since I last went a'whaling! Damn that Rivers! Promised to send my children to school with their betters! Promised me that Tobias would never have to go to sea or work the cloth again! But he wanted me to swap the egg, he did. Give him a tin forgery, he said and let Borden take the blame! I say, let him rot in his own blubber works! Damn that Rivers!"

Lizzie nodded in silent agreement. "Wellington Rivers, the bank manager and paper merchant, is the mastermind behind this affair?" she asked directly to the hairy face before her.

Ullsworth snarled. "Aye, the ruffian! I'll savage his head, I will. He'll not suffer more in all his days!"

Andre raised an enlightened finger. "I suspected as much. Rivers must be in the employ of the British. They wish to prevent the Bulgarian expansion. Perhaps they hope to raise the siege of Plevna! Wellington Rivers is their puppet!"

King Darius snapped his fingers. "Aha!" he exclaimed. "And this Wellington Rivers was the investor behind this hotel. During the construction, he must have personally customized room 209 for his nephew Frank's lurid frolics. Dare say, that's it!"

Ullsworth focused his bloodshot eyes on the Pinkerton Brothers who stood glaring at him. "Galloping ghosts! Now he's split in two he is! I waited all these days for him to go away, now he's split in two!"

One of the Freds smirked, "That split happened a long time ago, my friend."

"But this is all getting us nowhere! Where is the pessary?" The Comte de Camp shouted. "Where are the plans for the self-acting Mule?"

Lizzie smiled and pointed a finger at Ullsworth whose face was now bloated with red swells. "Doctor Bowen," she said, "I believe if you examine Mr. Ullsworth, you will find what you are looking for." She leaned over and whispered a word into Bowen's ear, after which a strange gloom passed over the good doctor's face.

"I will do what I can do," he said resignedly, and then pulled Ullsworth across the floor and into the hole in the wall. The wallpapered doorway slammed shut and for a few uncomfortable moments the occupants of Room 209 were treated to a symphony of howls and curses, giant whoops and prayers to various North Atlantic whales and their Leviathan god. Then, after what seemed like an eternity, the doorway opened once more and Ullsworth appeared, more disheveled than before, holding up his belt-less pants so they wouldn't plummet to his heels. He stepped forward carefully with jackknifing legs giving the appearance that he was walking over gravel.

"Flukes and Blubber!" he bellowed, fleeing back to Deputy Wixon as if the policeman were some form of safe port in an otherwise hostile ocean. At that moment, the Deputy took out some metallic wristlets to bind the whale man's hands.

Dr. Bowen appeared back in the room with his jacket removed and one sleeve rolled up past the elbow. In his hand he held a shiny metallic egg about an inch in diameter. He held it aloft with delicacy.

"Careful," he said. "It must be washed."

"The pessary!" the Comte de Rennes roared and raced forward to toss both his arms about the befuddled doctor who collapsed like a boneless fish between the Frenchman's mighty timber-like arms.

Lizzie stepped before Ullsworth who quaked in his gumboots. "Aye lassie, you may think me a filthy and despicable codger," he groaned, "but I had my reasons."

"Your family is starving," she said in a whispery and sad voice. "After my father evicted you, you had no choice but to take up Rivers' offer. You have been twice betrayed."

A sparkle came into the man's desperate eyes. "Here's a girl who speaks righteous! You tell 'em!" He tugged at his shackles. "You describe how a man's beloved wife and children can be tossed into the street like so much offal! It's not a sane world, is it? Locked up in a disgusting hole for three days! I was told what would be done to my lads and lassies if I gave up the game, so I hid. For many days now, I hid and saw the sun go up and down through that accursed broken board. My life has been darkness and horse dung, I tell ye! And not even a place to empty my slops. You can imagine what I'm going to say to Rivers the next time I sees him! Yes, I'll walk right up to his fancy house and knock on the door, and when his high and mighty butler comes to toss me by the seat of his pants, I'll let loose my slops all over his European carpets! You'll see how he stands up to that! Yes, Mr. Rivers! Send me to do some bottom's up surgery on a poor defenseless Cossack! We'll see! Who'll now take care of ol' Tobias Ullsworth's poor starving lads and lassies?"

Lizzie gave a slight nod and the barest trace of a smile.

"Justice shall be done," she promised, and startled the old whaler by taking his hands in hers.

Everyone present stared in shocked silence.

A Plot Revealed

Lizzie Borden held court at the same table in the Wilbur's dining room as had been occupied the day before by Frank Rivers and his two skenchbacks. Bar keep Sam Samways, late of South Bethlehem, PA, provided some hops and spirits for the men while Lizzie drank a fresh cup of Orange Pekoe. The Comte and Vicomte de Rennes sat together, a large mountain and his smaller, thinner copy, flanked by the two Pinkerton Brothers, Fred and Fred, who resembled each other in both countenance and attire down to the last link on their watch fobs. Deputy Wixon was nursing a beer, having decided that being off duty was a much better position to be in than having to file all sorts of complicated reports, or explain to his superiors that he had solved a theft while making no arrests. Doctor Bowen was off tending to the physically ailing Ullsworth whom they promised to both morally reform and nurse back to prime health. For those present, the relief of recovering the plans for the self-acting Mule had unleashed a wave of merriment that manifested much laughter and friendly banter.

"Lizzie, you must tell us what led you to discover the whaleman Ullsworth in the wall" requested King Darius, his mustaches bristling.

"As soon as I saw the tin pessary in the midden heap," Lizzie proclaimed, "everything was absurdly simple. The message within the tin was an insult hurled at a man in the back alley from a broken plank in the outer wall of Ullsworth's hiding place. At that moment I knew that the plans had not only never left the hotel grounds, but no doubt were still in the room from whence they had been stolen. How that could be, when the entire room had been thoroughly searched, was still a mystery to me. But there was also this unnamed man, no doubt a stooge working for Wellington Rivers, who verbally and physically abused Andrew Jackson Borden on the street yesterday morning, believing my father to have been behind the betrayal. Yet his assault upon Mr. Borden provided the vital clue." Lizzie produced the folded paper from her purse and held it up for all to read. "Hang ye be to Arcady!"

"The whale ship Arcady!" Fred Pinkerton the Elder said with a start. "Sailed out of New Bedford in August of 1875, went down with all hands except for one whaler who returned in disgrace to Fall River to work as a cloth doffer to feed seven children."

"Tobias Ullsworth," Fred Pinkerton the Younger concluded. "Vanished this Monday last and not seen in physical form again until he emerged from a hotel wall this very afternoon turned into a gibbering lunatic by his long ordeal."

"The man who wailed in the night," King Darius said bemusedly. "The weird in the wall. Never again shall I ever suspect supernatural agencies when there is always a perfectly natural explanation. Indeed I won't!"

"It all does hang together," said Lizzie. "Wellington Rivers, President of the Tiverton-Rivers Paper Mill and co-chairman of the Fall River First National Bank, was suspected of sabotaging the whale ship Arcady to collect on insurance. It was his holding company that was found culpable in the sinking of the ship due to a faulty manufacturing of its hull planking, a finding that was buried under graft and corruption and never became public knowledge. The circumstances were known only to insiders like my Father who did not judge the man, and even admired him for his thrift. Tobias Ullsworth must have felt the need for vengeance against the man who destroyed his life."

"And Rivers," the Comte de Rennes said with a chuckle, "was unsuccessfully attempting to buy up stock in a certain unnamed textile mill that I was to negotiate a technological contract with, one that would seal the fate of the Crimea. Being a paper pulper, Rivers was looked down upon by those men of cloth who run the looms and spindles of Fall River. He would have the perfect motive to steal the plans. He would have been able to open his own textile mill and triple his wealth with his exclusive use of a revolutionary new type of Mule."

"Not to mention," Andre said triumphantly, "he wanted to cast the shadow of suspicion on his nephew Frank who had taken to the Sporting Boy life, and so disgraced the family name."

Deputy Wixon breathed a deep sigh. "I am hearing all that you folks are saying, but I have a pretty predicament here. I can't just march into Rivers' Paper Mill and arrest him, don't you know? What crime has the man committed that we can prove? Ullsworth can only be charged with breaking and entering and his ramblings about Rivers will be dismissed by folk who would sooner believe a man of wealth than a common cloth doffer."

"I'm afraid Wellington Rivers is untouchable," Lizzie mused. "His only punishment shall be his failure to procure the pessary."

"And what about Frank Rivers?" King Darius said with an evil twitch in his eye. "I can ban him and his likes and their libertine ways from under my roof, but they shall continue to roam the streets of Fall River, spreading their sensualist ways, and provoking our finest women into lives of wanton decline."

The Comte de Rennes stood to his feet. "The Rivers boy and his scurrilous gang shall be dealt with accordingly. Perhaps I can persuade some local men of substance to form a committee to abolish this social issue of Sporting Boys and their Fancy Girls once and for all. Why Lizzie, I shall even recommend that your father be appointed as a committee member since he has confessed to me in confidence his outrage at these acts of youthful folly."

"I thank you on behalf of Mr. Borden," Lizzie said. "I'm sure he would be most eager to join your committee."

"More appropriately," the Comte said, getting to his feet and bowing politely in Lizzie's direction. "I must thank you, Lizzie Andrew Borden, on behalf of the French government, as well as the Royal Czar of Russia, for the recovery of our most valuable industrial asset. I will apply to my superiors for a special rate of compensation for you and your entire family, which will come from the sale of the self-acting Mule technology."

"*Merci*," Lizzie said, winking at Andre who smiled back at her.

Fred Pinkerton the Younger shrugged. "If you fancy folk would only have told us simple folk about all these Russian intrigues, foreign wars, and golden eggs from the very beginning, perhaps the Pinkerton Brothers would have been of more use. Perhaps we could have shared in the glorious wealth of this Mule, whatever the blazes it be!"

Lizzie laughed. "Have no fear, Fred and Fred. Payment for your services shall be paid liberally from my family's profits. And young Biddy Doren, the poor girl with the consumptive mother on Bishop Street, shall have a trust set up for her from the Lizzie Andrew Borden Fund for Destitute Children, as shall all seven sons and daughters of the lamentable Tobias Ullsworth. Nor shall I forget the orphaned children of Tchakorov, the poor Russian inventor, or his lovely new equestrian bride, who yet needs the funds to travel to America. I shall donate my entire share of the Mule plans to that effect."

"Hear, hear!" King Darius said, snapping his fingers in the direction of the corpulent Samways, motioning for a round of rice beer. "Let us all congratulate Fall River's most excellent Girl Detective!"

When the drinks had been brought, all cheered and raised their tankards to Lizzie Borden. "Hooray for Lizzie!" they shouted as one.

Lizzie sat smiling against the white wash of the tall dining hall windows, her hands cupped around her warm mug of coffee, since she was of the temperance and did not drink spirits.

The bellhop from the front desk appeared holding a letter stick which he extended across the table to Lizzie. She jumped in fright at its appearance before her nose, snatching the note while the bellhop receded into the lobby. She read the hastily written words and then turned to her assembled friends.

"You must forgive me, but a Mr. Butterworth of the Saloon Furnishing Corporation of Keene, New Hampshire is requiring my presence in the horse yard. I suspect he wants to engage me as a liaison between him and my father's business. Excuse me."

Everyone continued to banter and drink as Lizzie stepped from the room and disappeared into the lobby. Andre, his instincts inclined toward her protection, eyed her through the dining hall windows as she turned the corner of the building, her hat bobbing, and disappeared behind the building.

A moment later, King Darius twirled his mustaches, a sign that he was perplexed. "Strange," he muttered. "Mr. Butterworth was representing a furnishing concern in Boston. I think that he did leave early this morning."

"Butterworth?" Andre said, lifting himself from his seat.

"Exactly," Fred Pinkerton the Elder added. The man's face leapt into animated life. "By Jupiter, he did leave this morning! I carried his baggage to the waiting coach!"

"Zounds!" Andre howled, and reached behind his chair for his slender walking stick. Before anyone could comment, Andre had bounded away from the table and was sprinting towards the door of the dining hall, his cane swirling before him.

KIDNAPPED!

Upon entering the stable yard, Lizzie immediately sensed an unusual quiet; only the sounds of traffic and pedestrians from the other side of the tall hotel broke the stillness, but within the yard itself there was a strange vacancy of sound. Her instincts told her to run, that a horse yard was no place for a furniture salesman to meet with a lady of quality. She had encountered fake notes before. Why had her instincts failed her on this occasion?

"Butterworth!" she shouted, hoping that her voice would reach her friends through the dining hall window.

"I'll give you your worth of butter," came a familiar sneer. Out from behind a lumber shack came a swaggering figure balanced under a stovepipe hat, walking carefully in stocky fireman boots. "Don't be all in a twee, my dear. This ain't no dragging time; I have arranged for safe transport to a place where you can fuzzle with a man of great import."

Frank Rivers raised his arms above his stovepipe and upon this cue the yard's stillness was broken by the roar of a thumping horse. Before Lizzie could form any estimation of her predicament, a large barouche had entered the yard from the street, but unlike any barouche that she had seen before. It was an imposing four-wheeled high flyer pulled by a feverish white quarter horse, its nostrils blazing with wind. The bellowed hood formed a self-enclosed space over the carriage seats and draped black curtains hung down from exposed protruding dowels to conceal those who sat within. A pair of hands holding leather reins emerged from the curtain that draped over the outside box seat to drive the quarter horse that thundered before it. The barouche very quickly overtook Lizzie as she spun to make her escape.

Frank Rivers had raced forward to grab her, and the flailing arms of Sporting Boys emerged from the hidden recesses of the concealed cabin to pull her up towards the gaping curtains.

"Mercy!" Lizzie cried, her body flush with panic. Before she knew it, she was inside the shaky cabin surrounded by Chas and Buster, their faces convulsed in vulgar leers. The barouche was bouncing up and down with ridiculous exaggeration as she struggled. Surely, she reasoned, anyone witnessing this from outside would think it peculiar and raise an alarm. All she had to do was to keep her limbs flailing.

Frank Rivers popped through the curtain like he had been swinging on a vine, his hat missing from his head and his soap lock grease dripping down his cheeks. "Quiet, my lamb," he said. "I am playing mere stumpet usher this afternoon. There's a man on the Hill. Yea, he's got reason to maw-wallop with you. Snaggle her to me, he said. And so we snaggle you."

"I'm going to scream," Lizzie said. She could feel the barouche starting to move into the traffic of North Main. Knowing that her chances to salvage her situation were rapidly diminishing, she broke one arm free from Buster's grip and lashed out at Frank Rivers, her finger nails which had been grown to a fashionable length, tore across his cheek, slipping off his sweat and soap lock. "Gaaaah!" he cried, raising a palm to his slashed flesh which had started to ooze blood. "You boggled dolly! You monster!"

"You're the monster," she said defiantly, and feeling the barouche gallop into full speed down North Main Street, she spat in his face.

"For that," he said, wiping at his nose, "you will know a grand rib roasting."

Lizzie closed her eyes, expecting the worst, but was immediately surprised to feel the entire balance of the carriage lean backwards, as if it were tumbling over. Sunlight splashed her face, and she opened her eyes to see the vast expanse of the afternoon sky flanked by the moving tops of buildings. Some one, or some thing, was pulling back the collapsible half-hood above her, ripping it aside as if it were made of tissue paper, and the draped curtains to her left and right were falling to the street. All the grips holding her were loosened. She fell back as the barouche tipped and for a brief moment, she saw Andre de Camp, stripped to his shirt sleeves, locked in a tangle with Frank Rivers against the clouds, then all was a spiral towards the ground and she felt the hard road beneath slamming her knees and elbows.

Rolling over to prevent her face from hitting the dirt, she saw the broken pieces of the barouche and a sad image of the collapsed quarter horse lifting its whinnying head upwards. It took but a moment for her to realize that Andre de Camp had chased the vehicle of her abduction and had overrun it on foot. Somehow he had managed to get on board and rip apart, seemingly with his bare hands, the collapsible hood, at the same time knocking the

Sporting Boys off the vehicle. She caught a brief glimpse of Chas and Buster racing down the street, limping and screaming, until they crashed into a solid wall of Pinkerton Brothers.

"Apple bonkers!" Chas cried.

"Fancy some friendly fuzzle!" Buster said in a panic.

"Let bygones be made," Chas pleaded. "No rib roasting for us, my skenchbacks!"

Within second, the Freds had chosen their targets and the two Sporting Boys were air bound, hurled and twirled under. They fell like lifeless lumps to the ground, where they were assaulted by heavy workman boots. There was a gathering crowd on both sides of the street full of respectable men and women in their fine dresses and suits, all of whom were cheering on the melee.

Then Lizzie saw Andre and Frank Rivers standing arm's length apart from one another in front of the phaeton's shattered carriage, their feet in angry boxing stances, their hands up and curling into fists.

The startled crowd was now frozen in suspense as the two boys circled about an invisible center between them. A woman screamed, another fainted, dogs were barking, a gentleman cried out that someone should call the police. Far in the distance came the screeching of birds as they flew their indifferent path against the clouds. The entire scene was suspended in space as if it were part of some famous painting, as if Andre and Frank were two titans wrestling in some mythical moment that existed outside of time.

"You think you know this stockjobber!" Frank Rivers snarled, and Lizzie realized to her horror that he was talking to her. "Not in a sloven's year! Let him tell you the truth! Hang ye be to Arcady!" Then he lashed forward violently, his arms swinging in graceful and powerful arcs.

Andre stepped into the punches and reached for Frank's soap locks. At first his grip slipped right off them, but in that instant he managed to disorient the Sporting Boy. Lashing out again, he seized the locks like they were horns on a rampaging bull and pulled with all the full force of his physical being.

"Yoiks!" Frank Rivers cried, then sped forward, pulled by his own hair. Andre brought a knee up into the boy's abdomen, which brought another exclamation, one that could not be represented by any word, and then Frank Rivers was limp and defenseless. Andre spun him about and kicked him full in the seat of his trousers, sending him in a comical arc over the stunned quarter horse. Frank Rivers hit the ground with a graceless thud, his face landing in some equine feces that his own animal had treasured the street with, and then lay disturbingly still, the only sounds being a very thin and listless muttering of some random fuzzle talk: "Glorged I be…gored to the bumwush…all in a twee, my skenchback…" And then he was silent.

Lizzie forced herself to her feet, which turned out to be the easy part. Staying upright was a task she started feeling was beyond her capacity. Her pulled muscles dragged her downward as a frightful state of shock began to pass over her startled body. Andre stood before her, his face covered in dirt, his shirt torn, his body still braced for action, not exhausted or weakened but strong and virile.

Warm waves spread downward from her head into her limbs, a delayed reaction to the fear, the anxiety, the deathly grip that had taken hold of her body ever since her ordeal had begun. But she was held together by the sight of her brave soldier, her beautiful Vicomte, drenched in sweat, heaving with fear for her safety. Her feelings were very shameful, but in Andre's presence she couldn't but surrender to them.

She ran forward and into his arms, her face trembling, her tears staining her cheeks, her arms grabbing desperately at him, begging to be embraced.

For a moment there was warm comfort, like she was falling through soft down in a summer's breeze with no physical pain, no fear, no danger. Her reverie was broken only by a startled yelp that dispelled the waking dream. "Lizzie Andrew!" She lifted her eyes from Andre's shoulder to see her sister Emma in an afternoon dress at the periphery of the startled crowd, her face aghast, her hands raised to her ovaled mouth.

"It is all correct, Emma," Lizzie said, not even loud enough for her sister to hear, "Andre is my skenchback."

Then she fell into blackness, her last impression being Andre's arms catching her as she plummeted.

JUSTICE AND LOST LOVE

The conclusion to the affair held little comfort for Lizzie's shattered heart. Despite the justice that had been executed and the financial reward reaped by the suffering innocents who had been involved directly and indirectly in the affair, there was still the small matter of the signet ring with the scarlet A embossed upon it.

All else was neatly concluded. The pessary with its enclosed textile technology was returned to the Comte de Rennes. A few months later, a new textile mill owned and operated by a Russian industrialist became operational along the banks of the Quequechan, to much ballyhoo and a titanic flood of profits due to the introduction of a new self-acting Mule that increased production and the pick of the yarn. All who held stock in the venture, including Lizzie Andrew Borden and her father Andrew Jackson Borden, had more money flow into their accounts than they previously could have dreamed. Lizzie, in turn, donated all her proceeds to a charitable fund for destitute children. The Doren woman in Bishop Street was able to find a proper home for her small child Biddy, who Lizzie saw every Saturday afternoon thereafter for ice cream down street, and who eventually matured into a fine young woman, the first in her family to study at a university. In later years, Lizzie heard that Biddy Doren wrote serialized novels about social issues that gave Upton Sinclair a run for his money in the literary market place.

Tobias Ullsworth was set up in a proper apartment and, much to her father's disconcerted grumbles, given a job as a clerk at Borden and Almy's furniture concern, where he had responsibilities ranging from taking warehouse inventory to swaying customers' buying instincts towards certain preferred items. The more difficult concession that Andrew had to make was to allow Ullsworth to hang the copy of Poussin's *The Shepherds of Arcady* that had been salvaged from room 209, the most enduring symbol of his long ordeal, on the store's back wall over a field of rose-colored wallpaper.

Frank Rivers and the Sporting Boys were arrested and brought up on charges of kidnapping and assault, plus the theft of a barouche from a carriage yard in Tiverton. Wellington Rivers attempted to persuade anyone who would listen that his nephew Frank had been under the spell of a charlatan mesmerist named MacAlister Mundi, and so, Rivers contended, could not be held accountable for his deeds. However, Lizzie came round to Rivers office one afternoon, spending no more than one half-hour sequestered privately with the paper tycoon, after which all claims of his nephew's innocence were inexplicably dropped. Rivers produced one statement to the local newspaper in which he said, "Frank is indeed of bastard stock from a degraded branch of the family. My sister found him on the steps of a local saloon wrapped in fish paper. I cannot with clear conscience defend his kind."

After serving a spell in prison, Frank Rivers, along with his Bedford Street B'hoys, effectively disappeared from New England altogether. It was rumored that years later Chas and Buster were hanged at the Tombs, the large police dungeon in New York near Paradise Square, where they had been charged with "crimes of innumerable unpalatabilities." It was believed that Frank Rivers became the notorious Bowery Boy Strangler who terrorized Mulberry Street in the late 1880s, writing taunting letters to the police with phrases like, "I am only at my lick-for-leather for the last was for colt's tooth. The next one shall be a grand rib roasting!" But that could have been mere coincidence. The Strangler was ultimately caught and strangled to death by a vigilante mob, but the photographs then taken by the New York Herald of his corpse in an upright coffin are no longer extant.

As for Andre de Camp, Lizzie saw him on a Tuesday afternoon one week after the affair at the Wilbur. For several days, her father had prevented the two from meeting, for he was seized with a sudden suspicion of the boy's intentions towards his daughter, and also embarrassed by the publicity that the public beatings had drawn to the Bordens and the de Camps. Disregarding the fact that Andre had quite possibly saved his daughter's life, Andrew bolted shut his home and stayed indoors during his normal business hours, just to make sure that Lizzie sat in her room all day, alone and despondent. He was hoping that some sense could be driven into the French boy who still, despite the father's precautions, insisted on calling at the Borden home every day at noon.

By the seventh day, Lizzie had howled at her father to let him in, and Andrew reluctantly consented. "Ten minutes," he said. "I give you ten minutes with the boy and then you are to forget you ever knew him."

She found Andre in the sitting room, standing near the piano. He looked as dashing and well-kept as always, his facial scuffs a mere phantom of the past. His eyes brightened when he saw Lizzie cross the floor. He moved forward to embrace her but she held her body back. She was giving the impression that there was an invisible line on the floor between them beyond which he was not allowed to cross.

"It is madness that we are kept apart so," he said, tears forming in his eyes.

"No," she said, her face cold and blank. "It is best."

"*Mais mon Dieu*, what can you mean."

"I know you have the best of intentions, and I do believe, Andre de Camp, that you love me. I have never doubted it. And I have committed your poem Lizbeth of Light to precious memory. But I can never let you any closer than you are now. Perhaps not even this. We shall see each other in church, we shall see each other at the board meetings for the textile concern, but outside of indifferent and necessary encounters, we shall never talk again. Never, do you understand?"

A dark shadow passed over his face. "*Pourquoi?*" he asked.

"Because you lied to me. You deceived me. In your attempt to save your father's reputation, you tampered with the truth. That was your ring that was found in the poor whaleman. The A on the signet stood for Andre, not Arcady. It was you upon which Wellington Rivers was attempting to cast suspicion. In your clever machinations, you conceived of this Arcady society, an anarchist cabal targeting Fall River, to divert suspicion from your own guilt in the affair."

He was horrified. His mouth trembled as he struggled to find the words. "I was only trying to retrieve the pessary. I didn't think that my father's obsession with this Arcady Society was of any consequence. In France he saw them lurking everywhere, and here in the wild land of America he is even more fearful."

"I do not believe that this society even exists." Lizzie's face went dark as she contemplated something even more unthinkable. "Or perhaps you are the Arcady Society. Perhaps you have attempted to bring this French breed of political unrest to our ordered community. Perhaps Rivers was trying to wipe out this pestilent breed of revolutionary activity before it could get a foothold in our town." She paused, trying to read the shifting shadows on his face. "Or perhaps I shall never know the truth. Andre de Camp holds many secrets, and this secret society that bears his initial is his best kept."

"I wish I could tell you the truth," he said, puffing up his chest. "But I am bound by oaths. If you only knew, Lizzie Borden. If you only knew."

"It is best," she replied, "that I never know. For the past seven days I have tormented myself over this decision, and I must now reveal that I choose not to have anything to do with you. I care not if the Arcady Society is a mere figment of everyone's suspicions and you are blameless. But after your painful lie, I can never trust you again."

He lowered his eyes towards his feet. Somewhere in the distance a fruit peddler was hawking his wares, and a bale barge blew its horn across the deep waters of the Taunton.

"I am sorry," he said solemnly, "that you feel that way."

"But I shall never forget your kindness," she said assuredly. "And I shall never forget your poem. And I shall never forget the melancholy boy who once upon a time did indeed have love for me."

Andre nodded, forcing back his anguish. He stared at her for a moment and then spoke very lyrically: "'Tis the hope and the beauty and the inner calm/That we have won and must never let slip.'"

She moved slightly towards him, as if she were ready to embrace, but then stopped. "Yes," she said. " 'Never let slip.' And I never shall."

"I cannot live without you," he said languidly.

Her eyes widened as red came across her face.

"Oh, yes you can!" she replied angrily, and left the room as quick as a whirling tornado.

On her way to the staircase she met with her father who stood broad-shouldered, his chin jutting forward, a look of triumph on his countenance. "What did I tell you," he said smugly. "The boy is obviously a liar and a..."

"Say nothing more Father," she cautioned him. "Do not talk to me for three weeks or I shall twist off your head!"

Andre-Lude

It was not the last time that she would meet with Andre de Camp, le Victome de Rennes. Their paths were to cross again in several more of her cases, most notably the Adventure of the Phantom Thespian and the Strange Affair of the Hottentot Venus. And it was only a matter of time before she had cracked the code of the dreaded Arcady Society and discovered Andre's true role. In a strange tender way he was eventually redeemed, but she would never again open up her heart to him as she had done the night that she first heard the words to Lizbeth of Light.

Indeed, for all these long and sad years, Lizbeth Andrew Borden kept the words to the poem in a locket about her neck. It stayed with her throughout many an adventure, kept her company at night in the cruel days of her incarceration, provided inner strength when all around was darkness. And occasionally, when pressed by the rare Fall River resident who was old enough to remember the Comte de Rennes and his daring son and the summer of 1877, she found herself transported back again to that time indelibly marked upon her inner soul by Andre's lyricism. As the sun descended over French Street and the sloping shadows amidst the elms reminded her of the faded evenings of yesterday, all she could do was to sigh and stare into empty space, perhaps inwardly numbering the years to see if it were even indeed possible that he could still be alive and upon the earth, and remark with confident melancholy:

"This coming summer I shall be sixty-seven, which means I do have a chance of perhaps talking to him again, of walking by the river and remembering. To see that Great Wheel in the sky and wonder…and wonder… for we are but passing shadows and shall soon be gone. To see him once more, before no more. Yes.

"The Poet really did find a hope and beauty that he wanted to share with me. I turned my back upon it, and perhaps that was the gravest mistake of my life. But I have never let it slip. I have held it right here, in this locket, for all these lonely years.

"Perhaps it would be nice to see him again. Very nice indeed. Yes.

"For I was very fond of him when I was a Girl Detective.